Manuel Vázquez Montalbán lives in Barcelona where he was born in 1939. He is a journalist, novelist and creator of Pepe Carvalho, a fast-living, gourmet private detective. Montalbán has won both the Spanish Planeta Prize and French Grand Prix of Detective Fiction for his thrillers, which are translated into all major languages.

Also by Manuel Vázquez Montalbán and published by Serpent's Tail

Murder in the Central Committee
The Angst-Ridden Executive
Off Side
An Olympic Death

Manuel Vázquez Montalbán

Southern Seas

Translated by Patrick Camiller

Library of Congress Catalog Card Number: 99–65166

A complete catalogue record for this book can be obtained from the British Library on request

First published in 1979 as *Los Mares del Sur*
by Editorial Planeta, S.A., Barcelona

First published in this 5-Star edition by Serpent's Tail in 1999
4 Blackstock Mews, London N4 2BT
website: www.serpentstail.com

Printed in Great Britain by Mackays of Chatham plc,
Chatham, Kent

10 9 8 7 6 5 4 3 2 1

*

'Let's go.'

'I ain't got the strength to move.'

'I can think of something that'll move you.'

Loli gathered her fat cheeks into a smile and gave a little snort, tossing her fringe à la Olivia Newton-John.

'You're feeling horny.'

'Today's the day, baby.'

Darkie stood up on his bandy legs. The galactic dome of the building formed a fluorescent arch above his head. He hitched up his trousers and his crazy legs carried him towards the bar. The bar staff seemed miraculously capable of working in near total darkness. Piles of flesh heaped at the bar resolved into a tangle of arms and tongues belonging to a myriad of courting couples. Darkie prodded one of the shapes with his fist.

'Move yourself, Roebuck. Me and your sister are off.'

'Go away! You're always interrupting.'

Freckles had withdrawn her roughened tongue, and was now using it to protest at Darkie's interference.

'OK. If you two don't fancy a ride, that's too bad for you.'

'A ride? Count me out this time, Darkie. I want a quiet night.'

'I had my eyes on a tasty blue Jag . . .'

'A Jaguar! Well, that's different. I've never been in a Jag.'

'A Jaguar!' exclaimed Freckles, her eyes fixed on some vague horizon.

'I think it's even got a phone. It looks more like a travelling lounge than a car, man! All four of us can screw in it, and the wheels will still hold up.'

'I like it, I like it,' Roebuck laughed. 'I'll call my old lady: "Hi, baby. I'm fucking in a Jag".'

'Go out with Loli and wait on the corner by the paper factory.'

Darkie crossed the dance floor in the glow of the flashing lights, and the white surface seemed to send bursts of electricity rippling through his legs and up to his black, twisting hair.

'You still here, old 'un?' he said, as he passed the doorman. 'You look like part of the furniture.'

'You take my place, and I'll be jiving around in there with the best of them. OK? So piss off!'

'All right, all right, no need to get all worked up.'

Darkie felt protected by the darkness as he moved away from the rotating flicker in the hall. He put his hand in his right trouser pocket and fondled the picklock resting against his prick. He stroked his balls thoughtfully. Then he extracted the picklock and tried flexing it, as if to test its solidity. Casually, he walked up to the Jaguar and inserted the pick. The door sprang open with a little click, solid, like the steel door of a safe. It smells like a rich woman's cunt, thought Darkie. Jesus . . . cigars! And a whisky flask! He opened the car bonnet and, with a caressing movement, brought the wires into contact. This done, he settled into the driving seat with the imagined assurance and grace of its owner. He reached for the whisky bottle. He lit up a cigar. Then he moved smoothly into gear and gave a wrench on the wheel so that the tyres squealed as he pulled away. Picking his way through piles of old bricks and parked cars, he came to the corner, where Loli, Roebuck and Freckles were waiting. Loli sank into the seat behind him, and the three passenger doors shut with a polite thud.

'I want advance warning next time. Taking this kind of car isn't our scene. Too much aggravation.'

'Maybe not your scene. It's mine, though. I feel like a lord.'

'You sure are, Darkie,' Freckles laughed from the back seat.

'But I'm the one who'll have to go street-walking while he's behind bars.'

'The only reason you go on the game is because you like it.'

'Like hell! What a motor! We'll fuck in Vallvidrera tonight.'

'I'd rather fuck in bed.'

'It's brilliant with the smell of pines around you,' said Darkie. He took one hand off the wheel, reached down Loli's low-cut dress and kneaded a hard, ample breast.

'Don't go through the centre of San Andrès. It's crawling with cops.'

'Take it easy. You guys are too nervous. With cars like this, you've got to act like you're born to it.'

'What's that you're smoking, Darkie? You're gonna wet the bed tonight. You're not old enough for cigars like that.'

Darkie took Loli's hand and placed it on his bulging prick.

'What d'you think of this cigar, then?'

'Dirty pig!'

Loli smiled, but she took her hand away as if she'd had an electric shock. Roebuck leaned forward and worked out the route that Darkie was taking.

'Don't go to the centre, I said! It's crawling with police.'

'Cool, man, keep cool.'

'Cool's got nothing to do with it. This is just bloody daft.'

'Roey's right,' Freckles cut in. But Darkie was already heading for the Rambla de San Andrès, and came out onto the Plaza del Ayuntamiento.

'You stupid FUCKER . . .'

Roebuck's impotent cry made Darkie smile.

'Nothing's going to happen, man. Cool, man, keep cool.'

'Watch out! Over there!'

Loli had seen a patrol car parked on one corner of the Ayuntamiento.

'Relax . . .'

Darkie arched one eyebrow, to look unconcerned, and drew level with the patrol car. A peaked cap made a movement. A face looked up, profiled against a yellow street light whose beam was interrupted by an election banner drawn high across the street: 'City Hall Could Be Ours!' The arched eyebrows registered sharply on the yellow face. The dark eyes seemed to grow smaller.

'He's looking at you.'

'They always look like that, like they're forgiving you for being alive. Give them a badge and they think the world belongs to them.'

'They're coming after us!' shouted Freckles, her eyes on the rear window.

Darkie's left eye flicked to the wing mirror. He saw the yellow headlamps and rotating rooflight of the patrol car.

'I warned you, shithead. What an arsehole you are!'

'Shut up, Roebuck, or I'll smash your face. See if they can catch me now!'

Loli screamed and gripped Darkie's arm. He elbowed her aside, and she burst into tears against the side window.

'That's great! Now the stupid fucker's going to race them. I suppose you think they'll just give up? Stop the car, cunt, and we'll make a run for it!'

The flashing lights were joined by the wail of a siren. Waves of sound and light from the patrol car signalled to the Jaguar to stop.

'I'm going to shake them off.'

Darkie put his foot down, and the world shot up dangerously close, as if the nose of the car was swelling and going out to meet it. He turned a corner and ran out of space, caught between parked cars on his right and a mini with its back end jutting out into the street. The Jaguar crashed, and Loli's head hit the windscreen. Darkie reversed. The rear of the car hit something with a crunching metallic groan. Darkie barely heard it over the noise of the approaching siren. He managed to get the car up the side-street, but his arms were shaking so violently that he couldn't steer, and the Jag began bouncing off cars left and right. Finally, the steering wheel jammed and his limp hands could get no more action out of it. The rear doors opened. Roebuck and Freckles dived out.

'Don't move. One step and you're dead!'

Darkie heard feet running up. Loli was still in the front seat, crying hysterically, her nose and mouth pouring blood. Darkie got out with his hands raised, and barely had time to straighten up before uniformed hands shoved him against the car.

'You won't forget this little jaunt in a hurry. Get your hands on the roof.'

As they gave him a thorough body-search, Darkie recovered enough to register that Roebuck was getting the same treatment a few yards away, and that another cop was searching Freckles's handbag.

'She'd badly hurt,' said Darkie, pointing to Loli. She had got out, and was still crying tears and blood as she leaned back against the patrol car. The policeman looked aside for a moment, and Darkie gave him a solid right-hander. A path opened for him in the night, and he ran into it as fast as his legs would carry him. His arms worked like pistons. Police whistles screeched. More whistles. Curses, muffled in the distance. He cut round several corners, but still heard the sound of running feet behind him. He breathed in damp, coarse air which came in great gulps and scorched his lungs. Sidestreet followed sidestreet without yielding a suitable bolt-hole. High walls built of lifeless brick or wrapped in sandy, dusky cement. Suddenly he came out onto the Rambla de San Andrès, and all the lights in the world revealed him poised on one leg and braking with the other. A few yards away, the sentry in his hut outside the barracks looked on in amazement. Darkie sprinted across the brightly lit avenue in search of the open ground he could make out, up by Holy Trinity. He needed to stop. He was suffocating. He had a stitch in his side. He was on the verge of vomiting from the burning in his lungs. An old, much-painted, weathered wooden door promised access to an area of waste ground. Using the unevenness of the eroded wood to get a grip, Darkie got a toehold and began pulling himself up by a sheer effort of will. But his arms lacked the strength for the weight of his body, and he fell back onto his haunches. He took a few paces back, gathered fresh momentum and hurled himself at the door again, struggling to raise himself against the wobbling resistance of the wood. He felt the top of the door in his groin as he gave a final thrust and then found himself falling down a clay slope and slithering over rubble. He sank to his knees. He was in the concrete foundations of a house under construction. The door over which he had jumped was like a crown at the top of the slope. It stared down at the intruder.

His eyes scanned the dark, weatherbeaten patch of ground. He reckoned that the building work had been abandoned for a fair while. The battering he had blindly inflicted on himself was now becoming identifiable sources of pain. His muscle joints were strained and aching, and a cold sweat was soaking him. He looked for somewhere to hide, in case they tried to follow him onto the site. It was then that he saw him – a man, with his head resting against a pile of bricks, his eyes staring back, and his hands palms-upwards to the sky.

'Jesus! Damn!' said Darkie, panting. He went up to take a closer look, but maintained a respectful distance. The man was not looking at him. His eyes seemed to be fixed on the old door at the top of the slope, as if it had been his last hope before he died. On the other side, the whistles were getting closer, and the sounds of pursuit became more distinct. The dead man and Darkie seemed to share a mutual moment of hope in the door. Suddenly, someone began pushing against it, and Darkie collapsed in a flood of tears and a hysterical 'Aaaaaah' that came all the way from his stomach. He looked for a pile of rubble, to sit down and await the inevitable. The look that he gave the dead man was full of reproach: 'You bastard! You're all I needed tonight. Now I'm fucked!'

*

'Do you realize, Biscuter – we private eyes are the barometers of established morality. I tell you, this society is rotten. It doesn't believe in anything.'

'Yes, boss.'

Biscuter backed Carvalho up, not only because he guessed that the boss was drunk, but also because he could recognize a catastrophe when he saw one.

'Three months without an assignment. Not a single husband chasing his wife. Not a single father looking for a runaway daughter. Not even the occasional pathetic wretch wanting proof of his wife's adultery. Don't women run away from home any more? Of course they do, Biscuter. More than ever. But nowadays their husbands and their fathers don't give a shit if they do. The basic values have been lost. You people wanted democracy, didn't you?'

'It was all the same to me, boss.'

But Pepe Carvalho wasn't talking to Biscuter. He was questioning the green walls of his office, or an imaginary person seated on the other side of his desk – a forties-style desk with a smooth French polish that had faded over thirty years, as if it had slowly absorbed the gloom of the detective's office on the Ramblas. He swallowed another glass of ice-cold orujo, and puckered his face at the shiver that ran down his spine. Hardly had he put the glass on the table than Biscuter returned to fill it again.

'That's enough, Biscuter. I'm popping out for a breather.'

He went out onto the landing, where the sounds and smells of the building assailed him. The foot-tapping and castanets of the ballet school; the meticulous tap-tapping of the old sculptor; the mustiness emanating from thirty years' worth of sedimented garbage, combined with the smell of faded polish and the impacted dust that had found refuge in the window frames and the opaque, rhomboid skylights poised above the stairwell. Carvalho took the stairs two at a time, helped or driven by an alcoholic energy, and went out to savour the brisk, chill air of the Ramblas. Spring had gone mad. It was cold and overcast on that early evening in March. A short walk and a few deep breaths helped Carvalho clear his dulled brain and intoxicated liver.

He had one million two hundred thousand pesetas in the savings bank, which brought in five per cent at fixed intervals. At this rate, he would not have enough capital to retire at fifty or fifty-five and live on the interest. The crisis, the crisis of values, he mused, with the dogged persistence of the alcoholic. He had read in the papers that labour lawyers were also in crisis, because workers were now turning to the unions' legal advisors. Both were victims of democracy. Doctors and notaries were also victims of democracy. They had to pay their taxes now, and they were beginning to think that perhaps it was preferable to have been professionals living under fascism while practising a degree of liberal resistance.

'We private detectives are about as useful as rag and bone men. We retrieve from the garbage can that which doesn't yet belong with the garbage, or that which, on closer inspection, was never garbage in the first place.'

No one was listening to him. Threatening drops of rain sent him running towards Calle Fernando, in search of the canopied shop windows of Beristain. There he found himself in the company of three prostitutes, who were swapping advice on the best way to make packet soup. A very small boy left the shop with a very large hockey stick. His father was asking again and again: 'Are you sure that this one's right for you?' 'Yes, yes, of course,' replied the boy, obviously peeved by this paternal lack of confidence. Carvalho left his shelter and began to walk faster in the direction of a delicatessen where he often bought cheese and sausage. He stopped again, this time attracted by the sight of a litter of puppies wriggling on a pile of wood shavings behind a pane of glass that separated them from the street. With one of his fingers he made as if to play with the pert nose of a little German shepherd dog, whose hind paws were being nibbled by two spaniel puppies. He spread his hand flat on the window, as if to communicate warmth or some message to the little creature. The dog licked the glass in a vain attempt to reach Carvalho's hand. Pepe moved away abruptly and completed the short distance to the deli.

'The usual.'

'The tins of pork loin and butifarras in sauce have arrived.'

'I'll take two of each.'

The assistant went through the rest of the order with routine precision.

'This Salamanca ham isn't what it used to be.'

'They call everything Salamanca ham these days. If ham isn't Jabugo or Trevélez, then it's Salamanca. You've got to be so careful. But even then you can't be sure whether the ham you're eating is Salamanca or Totana.'

'Yes you can.'

'*You* can tell, because you know about these things. But I've seen people selling Granollers as if it were Jabugo. You see what I mean?'

Carvalho left with a bag containing Casar, Cabrales and Ideazábal cheeses, Jabugo chorizos, Salamanca ham for everyday eating, and a small portion of the Jabugo for when he was feeling fed up.

He was in a better mood by the time he reached the pet shop again. The owner was just shutting for the day.

'That dog . . .'

'What dog?'

'The one that was in the window.'

'It was full of dogs.'

'The little wolf one.'

'It was a bitch. I've got them all inside. I put them in cages for the night, so that no one comes smashing the window and taking them off to torture them. There's a lot of sick minds around these days.'

'I'd like to buy her.'

'What, now?'

'Now.'

'It'll cost you eight thousand pesetas,' answered the owner, without reopening the door.

'Can't be much of a shepherd dog at a price like that . . .'

'She's got no pedigree. But she's a very healthy dog. You'll see for yourself. Very brave. I know the father, and the mother belongs to one of my brothers-in-law.'

'I'm not worried about pedigree.'

'Fine.'

The dog wriggled as Carvalho tucked her under his arm. In his other hand, he was holding a bag full of cheese, sausage, tins of dogfood, rubber bones, insecticide, disinfectant and a brush – everything a man and a dog could need to be happy. Biscuter was surprised at the dignity of the little dog. It planted itself solidly on its hind paws, sticking out half a yard of tongue. Its huge ears looked like the swept-back wings of a plane going into a nosedive.

'Looks like a rabbit, boss. Shall I keep her here?'

'I'll take her up to Vallvidrera. She'll shit over everything here.'

'By the way – there was a call for you. I jotted his name down in the office book.'

Jaime Viladecans Riutorts. Lawyer. As Carvalho dialled the number, he called for Biscuter to heat up some food. He heard him moving around in the kitchenette that he had built next to the toilet. Biscuter was humming a tune, happy in his work, and the little dog was chewing the telephone wire. Two secretaries testified to the importance of the man he was calling. Finally the voice of an English lord, speaking with the accent of a Catalan dandy, came onto the line.

'It's a very delicate matter. We'll need to speak in private.'

Carvalho noted the details of a rendezvous, hung up, and leaned back in his swivel armchair with a certain air of satisfaction. Biscuter laid before him a steaming portion of wild rabbit with vegetable stew. The dog was trying to get a share of his meat, so Carvalho gently put her on the ground and tossed her a little piece of the rabbit.

'It's true what they say. Children do sometimes arrive with a loaf of bread under their arms.'

*

Viladecans was wearing a gold tiepin and platinum cufflinks. He was impeccable from head to foot, starting from his balding pate which shone like a dry riverbed confined between two banks of white hair. Judging by the care with which the lawyer periodically brushed his hand back over the surviving undergrowth, it had recently been trimmed by the best hairdresser in the city. At the same time, a diminutive tongue moved with relish across a pair of almost closed lips.

'Does the name Stuart Pedrell mean anything to you?'

'Rings a bell.'

'It may ring several. It's a remarkable family. The mother was a distinguished concert pianist, although she retired when she married and subsequently only performed for charity. The father was of Scottish origin, and was an important industrialist before the war. Each of the sons is a public figure in his own right. You may have heard of the journalist, the biochemist, the educationalist, or the building contractor.'

'Probably.'

'I want to tell you about the building contractor.'

He placed before Carvalho a set of local press cuttings mounted on file cards: 'The body of an unidentified male has been found on a building site in Holy Trinity.' 'The body has subsequently been identified as that of Carlos Stuart Pedrell.' 'Pedrell had parted from his family a year ago on the pretext of a trip to Polynesia.'

'Why "on the pretext"? Did he need a pretext?'

'You know the language journalists use. The embodiment of impropriety.'

Carvalho tried to embody impropriety in his mind, but failed. Viladecans launched into a resumé of the situation, peering over folded hands that had been cared for by the finest manicurist.

'This is how things happened. I've known my friend – and he was, I must tell you, a really close friend – since we were at a Jesuit school together. Recently he was going through a sort of crisis. Some men, especially men as sensitive as Carlos, find it hard to adjust as they pass forty and see fifty looming up. That's the only reason that I can find, why he should spend months and months on a plan to abandon everything and head off to some island in the South Pacific. Suddenly the project picked up speed. He let the business side of things drop and disappeared without trace. We all assumed that he'd taken off for Bali or Tahiti or Hawaii, or some such, and that he would soon be back. But the months passed, and everyone had to face up to the fact that he was apparently gone for good. So much so that Señora Stuart Pedrell moved to take charge of the business.

'Then, in January, came the report that Stuart Pedrell had been found dead, here in Barcelona, stabbed, on a building site in Holy Trinity. We now know that he never reached Polynesia. But we've no idea where he was and what he was doing for all that time. That's what we want you to find out.'

'I remember the case. The murderer was never caught. Do you also want to know who killed him?'

'Well, if the murderer comes to light, well and good. But our real concern is to find out what he did during that last year of his life. You must understand, there are a lot of interests at stake.'

The office intercom announced that Señora Stuart Pedrell had arrived. The door opened almost at once on a forty-five-year-old woman who gave Carvalho an ache deep in his chest. She entered without so much as looking at him, and imposed her slim, mature figure as the only presence worthy of attention. Her face had dark, striking features that were showing the first painful signs of age. Viladecans's introductions merely allowed her to accentuate the distance between herself and Carvalho by means of a curt 'How d'you do'. As Carvalho replied, he was staring so intently at her breasts that she felt obliged to check with her hands to make sure there was nothing wrong with her dress.

'I was just filling in Señor Carvalho on the background.'

'I'm glad to hear it. Viladecans will have told you that I require discretion at all costs.'

'The same discretion with which the case has been reported in the press. I see that none of these stories carries a photo of your husband.'

'That is correct.'

'Why is that?'

'My husband went off at the height of a personal crisis. He wasn't in his right mind. On those rare occasions when he calmed down a bit, he would grab anyone who cared to listen and tell them the life story of Gauguin. He wanted to be a Gauguin too. Leave everything and go off to the South Seas. Leave me, his children, his business and his social world – everything. A man in that state of mind becomes easy prey, and if too much had been said about the case, all kinds of unscrupulous characters could have come out of the woodwork.'

'Did you come to some understanding with the police?'

'They did all they could. So did the Ministry of External Affairs.'

'External Affairs?'

'There was a possibility that he had actually set off for the South Seas.'

'But he hadn't?'

'No,' she replied, with a certain satisfaction.

'And you're pleased about that?'

'Yes I am, a little. I got fed up with the whole business. More than once I told him: "Stop talking about it. If you're going to go, then go!" He was suffocated by his money, you know.'

'Mima . . .'

Viladecans tried to cut her short.

'Everyone round here feels suffocated. Everyone except me. When he went, I was finally able to breathe properly. I've worked hard. I've done his work as well as he ever did it. Better, in fact. Because I've done it without complaining all the time.'

'May I remind you, Mima, that we're here for a very special purpose.'

But Carvalho and the widow were looking each other up and down, as if to gauge each other's capacity for aggression.

'In other words, you have a certain attachment to the job.'

'Laugh if you like. A certain attachment, yes. But not a very great attachment. This business has shown me that no one is indispensable. But then we are all usurpers in the positions we hold.'

Carvalho was troubled by the dark passion emanating from those black eyes, from the two lines that curved round a mature and knowing mouth.

'What exactly do you want to know?'

'What exactly did my husband do during that year? A year when we all thought that he was in the South Seas, but when he was God knows where, doing God knows what. I have an eldest son who's turned out like his father – and, what is worse, who is going to inherit even more money. Another two are probably at this minute doing motorbike trials on one of the hills around here. I have a daughter whose nerves have never recovered since her father's body was found. And a young son whom the Jesuits have expelled from school. I have a great many things that I need to keep an eye on.'

'What do you know so far?'

Viladecans and the widow looked at each other. It was the lawyer who replied:

'The same as you.'

'Wasn't there anything on the dead man that might give us a lead?'

'They'd emptied his pockets.'

'This is all they found.'

The widow took from her bag a crumpled page from a diary. Someone had written on it with a felt-tip pen: *più nessuno mi porterà nel sud*.

*

'I don't even know you.'

He had short hair and was wearing a brown suit and no tie. A pair of very dark sunglasses threw into even sharper relief the gleaming pallor of an adolescent face. Despite the lightness of his figure, there was something oily in his manner, as if his joints had been greased.

'If they find out that I'm giving you this information, they'll run me out of the force.'

'Señor Viladecans is a very influential person.'

'All his influence wouldn't save me. Besides, they've got their eye on me. For political reasons. This place is full of hypocrites. Everyone talks about how terrible things are, but they won't do anything. They're all too worried about promotion and not losing their cushy jobs.'

'Are you a socialist?'

'No way! I'm a patriotic policeman.'

'I see. Were you involved on the Stuart Pedrell case? Tell me everything you know.'

'There's not much to tell. At first we thought it had something to do with queers. It's not very often that a rich guy disappears and turns up stabbed, a year later. It looked like a clear case of buggery. But then the forensic people told us that he had a virgin arse, and none of the male prostitutes had heard of him. Then there were the clothes. They weren't his own. He'd been dressed in a set of shabby old clothes, second or third hand. Obviously they didn't want to leave any clues.'

'But why did they leave that note?'

'To keep us chasing around, I guess. Do you understand it?'

'No more will anyone carry me south.'

'Yes. We found that much out. But what was he trying to say?'

'He'd been planning a trip to the South Seas, to some place in the Pacific.'

'But look at the note carefully. No more . . . will anyone . . . carry me . . . me . . . me . . . south. It refers to someone who might have taken him, but didn't. That's where we got stuck. And why in Italian?'

'Was it his handwriting?'

'Yes, it was.'

'Conclusion . . . ?'

'He must have been suffering from amnesia or something. He got caught up with the underworld, and they stuck a knife in him. Unless he was kidnapped and the family kept very quiet about it. Maybe they didn't want to hand over the bread and left him to croak. Another idea is that it was something to do with business, but that's been more or less discarded. The roughest business he was involved in was construction, and there he always used front men. Anyway, here's a list of all the people we've been chasing: partners, friends, associates and rivals. I've already told Viladecans that we're not taking it any further.'

'The police have dropped it?'

'Yes. The family did everything they could to stop us continuing. They waited a reasonable time and then moved in to close down the inquiries. For the good of the family, and all that . . .'

The young policeman made a strange sound with his tongue

against the inside wall of his cheek, which Carvalho took to be a sign of departure. He stood up to walk to the door, but the dog waylaid him and started snapping at his heels.

'Down, boy!'

'It's a she.'

'That means trouble! You having her neutered?'

Carvalho frowned, and the policeman departed. Feeling hurt by the snub, the dog bent her head to left and to right, as if to work out which way lay good and evil in the world.

'You're very soft.'

'A *bleda*.' Biscuter used the Catalan word as he appeared from behind the curtain.

'That's right. We'll call you Bleda because you're a real softy.'

'And she shits wherever it takes her fancy,' added Biscuter. Reproachfully.

The difference between Biscuter and Bleda was that, more or less, and for better or worse, Bleda had a certain breeding, and Biscuter did not. In Carvalho's old prison companion nature had produced the miracle of an innocent ugliness: a fair-haired and nervous ugly duckling condemned to premature baldness.

He heard Charo's footsteps on the staircase. The landing door opened.

'So you're still in the land of the living! Don't tell me you were just about to ring.'

'All right, I won't.'

Carvalho took a bottle of wine from a metal bucket, dried it with a napkin, and filled the three glasses that Biscuter had laid on the table.

'Try it, Charo. The Catalans are learning to make wine. It's a *blanc de blancs*. Excellent. Particularly at this time of day.'

'Which time?'

'This time. Between lunchtime dessert and the first course of dinner.'

Charo fell into the trap. Sitting with her knees together and her feet apart, she drank the wine, taking her rhythm from Carvalho. Biscuter tried to do the same.

'Ugh! What's that?'

'A dog. Or rather, a bitch.'

Charo rose to her feet, alarmed by Bleda's insistent sniffing.

'Is this your new girlfriend?'

'Brand new. I bought her yesterday.'

'Bit scruffy, isn't she? What's her name?'

'Bleda.'

'Sleepy?'

'In Catalan, *bleda* doesn't just mean sleepy. It also means softy.'

'Having contributed his expert knowledge, Biscuter disappeared into the kitchen. As the dog sat on her lap and tried to lick her face, Charo directed a string of accusations at Carvalho. His mind was on something else, but he refilled the glasses, and they drank with thirsty boredom. The fresh, acidic flavour of the wine caused a tingling sensation behind his ears, and the whole of his mouth worked to counteract it. He felt somehow authenticated, as if he had recovered a little corner of his homeland within himself.

'I'm sorry, Charo, but I've been very tired. I still am. How's business?'

'Bad. The competition is getting out of hand. The economic crisis has got even nuns screwing for money.'

'Don't be so vulgar, Charo. Anyway, I thought your clients were pretty select.'

'Why don't we talk about something else, darling?'

Pepe had forgotten that she didn't like discussing her work with him. Or maybe he hadn't forgotten? He wanted Charo to leave, but didn't want to offend her. He looked at her as she raised the glass to her lips. Sitting there with her legs apart, she had the awkwardness of a visitor. Carvalho gave an enigmatic smile that puzzled her. He had suddenly realized that, for all his efforts not to get involved, he was now morally and emotionally responsible for three people and a dog: himself, Charo, Biscuter and Bleda.

'Come on, Charo, let's go out for a meal.'

He went over to where Biscuter was bustling about behind the door.

'You too, Biscuter. It's on the firm.'

*

They ate at the Túnel restaurant. Biscuter was surprised at the dish of haricot beans and shellfish that Carvalho decided to order.

'What will they think of next, boss?'

'The recipe's as old as the hills. Before the potato reached Europe, people had to find something to eat with their meat and fish.'

'You're a mine of information, boss.'

Charo decided on a vegetable casserole and grilled tuna. Carvalho was still obsessively absorbed with his wine, as if performing a transfusion of chilled white blood.

'What are you working on at the moment?'

'A missing corpse.'

'Someone's stolen a corpse?'

'No. A man disappeared and showed up dead a year later. He wanted to find a new life, a new country, a new continent, a new world . . . and he ended up dead on a pile of old cans and rubble. Stabbed. A stiff. A rich stiff.'

'He was rich?'

'Rolling in it.'

Carvalho took out his notebook, and started to recite:

'Tablex Incorporated, specialists in the manufacture of plywood; Argumosa Dairy Industries; Iberia Construction Inc.; advisor to the Banco Atlantico; member of the Chamber of Commerce and Industry; consultant to Privasa Construction and Demolition. Plus fifteen other companies. The most surprising thing is that two of them are pretty low-key publishing outfits. One brings out volumes of poetry, and the other a left-wing cultural magazine. Looks like he used to dabble in charity.'

'You mean flinging his money around. Just look at the number of magazines there are nowadays, boss. And books. If you go to a bookstall, there's nothing worth reading.'

'It's all rubbish,' Charo commented, as she lifted a forkful of tuna with garlic and parsley.

'Full of women and blokes with no clothes on.'

Biscuter left as soon as he had finished eating. He was sleepy, and he had to get up early to tidy the office and go to the market. Carvalho pictured him a few minutes later sleeping alone on the office's folding bed.

'Or wanking.'

'Who are you talking about?'

'Biscuter.'

'Why does he have to be wanking?'

Carvalho waved his hand as if to erase what he had said, and gave Charo a look that suggested she finish her meal quickly. He had the feeling that she would want to go back with him to his house in Vallvidrera, and he didn't see how he could stop her. She polished off the ice cream in three or four mouthfuls and attached her arm to Carvalho's. She got into the detective's car, whereupon Bleda began barking loudly and licking every bit of flesh within reach. The drive was silent, as was the ritual of checking the mailbox, climbing the stairs to the front door and turning on the lights. The garden vegetation absorbed some of the lamplight and cast patches of darkness onto the gravel. Carvalho breathed in the air, looking at Vallés far off in the distance and listening indifferently to Charo's chatter from inside.

'My house is nice and warm. While yours . . . I presume you're going to light the fire today. You're so crazy that you only light it in summer.'

Carvalho went into the bedroom, took off his shoes and sat on the bed. His hands were clamped between his legs, and his eyes were fixed on an empty, twisted sock.

'What's the matter with you? Are you ill?'

Carvalho stirred himself and played for time by wandering around the bed a few times. Then he left the room, brushing past Charo, who was trying to light the fire with all the copies of *Vanguardia* she could find in the house. He went to the kitchen and took from the refrigerator one of the ten bottles of *blanc de blancs* that had been waiting for him. Maybe it's not as good as I think, Carvalho said to himself, but one small obsession never did anybody any harm.

'More wine? You'll ruin your liver like that.'

Charo also drank, while Carvalho stopped his aimless meandering and lit a blazing fire with the help of one of the books from his tatty library: Forster's *Maurice*.

'Is it bad?'

'It's quite extraordinary.'

'So why are you burning it?'

'Because it's garbage, like all books.'

Charo reddened slightly in the glow of the flames. She said she was going to make herself comfortable, and returned wearing the loose-fitting Chinese dress that Carvalho had brought her from Amsterdam. He remained sitting on the floor, his back propped against the corner of the sofa and a glass of white wine in his hand.

'When you give in, you certainly do it in style.'

Charo stroked his hair, and Carvalho took her hand, meaning to push it away. But he kept hold of it instead, and gripped it with a certain fervour.

'What's come over you?'

Carvalho shrugged his shoulders. Suddenly he jerked to his feet and hurried across to open the door. Bleda entered like a whirlwind.

'Poor thing. I'd forgotten all about her.'

Charo sank resignedly into the sofa, and all but bit into her wine glass. Carvalho resumed his former position and busied himself stroking the animal's neck and Charo's leg.

'You'll have to choose. Either the dog or me.'

Charo was laughing. Carvalho hauled himself up onto the sofa, opened her Chinese dress and fondled two breasts browned by ultra-violet sunlamps and sunbathing on balconies. Charo's hand slipped under the blue of his shirt, pinched his nipples and opened wide paths through the hair on his chest. But Carvalho stood up, poked the fire, and then turned round, as if surprised that Charo was still sitting there.

'What are you doing there? Let's go.'

'Where to?'

'Bed.'

'I fancy doing it here.'

Charo's hand fitted like a shell over Carvalho's flies. As if responding to government propaganda on the need for growth, the bulge of his penis swelled to fit the mould. Carvalho stooped to pick up Bleda, took her next door and deposited her on the bed. When he returned to the fire, Charo was already naked. The half-light created by the fire outlined the features of a woman out of bloom.

*

He was ushered in by a secretary who had the air of an ex-convent girl about to marry her fiancé after a twelve-year courtship.

'Señora Stuart Pedrell told me that you were coming . . .'

They were in the dead man's sanctuary, the private office to which he retired for meditation – and the one he preferred above fifteen others maintained for him at his various other business addresses. The smooth Scandinavian style so fashionable in the mid-sixties was tempered by roughcast stonework set against a dark beige hessian wallcovering. Paper lampshades of vaguely oriental origins, a beige carpet, and, above the far office door, a curiously out-of-place traffic light. Its lamps extinguished, it was like a dead body, fixed to the wall like a gigantic butterfly in someone's collection. Noticing Carvalho's look of puzzlement, the secretary explained: 'Señor Stuart Pedrell used it to signal whether people were or were not to be admitted to the main office – both us, and visitors.'

Carvalho moved towards the signal, half expecting it to flicker miraculously. He even stopped for a moment before pushing the sanctuary door. But man and signal looked at each other without prompting a reaction. Finally, he pushed the door and went into the main office, while the secretary opened the venetian blinds.

'You'll have to excuse the state of the office. It's shut nowadays, and it gets very dusty. It's only cleaned once a month.'

'Were you Señor Stuart Pedrell's secretary?'

'Yes. At least, I was here.'

'What did he use this office for?'

'For listening to music. Reading. And receiving intellectual or artistic friends.'

Carvalho prepared to check through the books meticulously arranged on meticulous bookshelves, the signed paintings decorating the walls, the cocktail cabinet with its built-in refrigerator, and the Charles Eames reclining sofa, the *nec plus ultra* of reclining sofas in contemporary patriarchal society.

'I'd like to be left alone.'

The secretary left the room, pleased to have been ordered out so decisively. Carvalho looked through the books. Many of them were in English. American publishers. Kuhn's *The Structure of Scientific Revolutions*, Eliot's *The Waste Land*, Melville, various German theologians, Rilke, American counter-cultural theorists, Huxley's complete works in English, Maritain, Emmanuel Mounier, and *For Marx*. A number of yellowing news clippings were stuck to the bookcase with drawing pins. Some were reviews of new books from the *Times Literary Supplement*. Others seemed rather strange, at least for a man like Stuart Pedrell. For instance, Carrillo's statements on the Spanish CP's renunciation of Leninism . . . or an item on the Duchess of Alba's marriage to Jesús Aguirre, editor-in-chief of *Música*.

Pinned here and there to the shelves were postcard reproductions of Gauguin paintings. On the wall, sandwiched between them, was a series of ocean maps: a huge Pacific dotted with little flag-pins marking somebody's idea of a sea cruise. On the rosewood table, an embossed ivory vase full of pencils, ball-points and felt-tip pens. On an antique bronze desk, a jumble of schoolboy paraphernalia: erasers in various colours, pens, nibs, penholders, razor blades, blue-and-red Hispania pencils, a Faber paint-box, and even pens for italic and round-hand script, as if Stuart Pedrell had been spending his time on calligraphy and handwriting exercises.

In the drawers, there were more cuttings from articles, and a poem from a poetry magazine: *Gauguin*. In free verse, it followed Gauguin's path from the time he gave up his bourgeois life as a bank employee until his death in the Marquesas Islands, surrounded by the world of the senses that he depicts in his paintings:

Exiled to the Marquesas
he saw the inside of prison
under suspicion of not arousing suspicion
in Paris
he was taken for an arrant snob
only a few natives knew of his passing impotence
and that the *or de ses corps*
was a pretext
for forgetting the black choir stalls
the cuckoo of a Copenhagen dining room
a trip to Lima with a sorrowful mother
the pedantic chatter of the Café Voltaire
and above all
the incomprehensible verse of Stéphane Mallarmé.

So ended the poem, by a writer unknown to Carvalho. He

opened a desk diary bound in a fine leather adorned with acanthus leaves. Handwritten notes dealing with domestic economic matters. Receipts for personal effects ranging from books to shaving cream. A phrase in English caught Carvalho's attention:

> I read, much of the night, and go south in the winter.

and underneath:

> Ma quando gli dico
> ch'egli è tra i fortunati che han visto l'aurora
> sulle isole più belle della terra
> al ricordo sorride e risponde che il sole
> si levava che il giorno era vecchio per loro.

Finally:

> Più nessuno mi porterà nel sud.

Carvalho made a quick mental translation:

> But when I tell him
> that he is among the fortunate ones who have seen day break
> over the most beautiful islands on earth
> he smiles at the memory and replies that when the sun
> rose the day was already old for them.

and:

> No more will anyone carry me south.

He racked his brains for a possible cabalistic meaning that might lie concealed in the three pieces of verse. He opened the cocktail cabinet and poured himself a glass of ten-year-old Fonseca port. He didn't have bad taste, this Stuart Pedrell. Carvalho turned the lines over in his mind. Maybe they were indicative of the man's frustrations or maybe they were the key to a project that had expired with his death. He put the paper in his pocket and searched every corner of the room, even behind the cushions of the three-piece suite. Then he turned to the wall displaying the map of the Pacific Ocean. He followed the route traced by the flags: Abu Dhabi, Ceylon, Bangkok, Sumatra, Java, Bali, the Marquesas

. . . An imaginary voyage? A real voyage?

Next he examined the audio-visual equipment in a corner of the office and on a desk to the left of where Stuart Pedrell would have sat. Ultra-high fidelity. A compact television incorporated in an American radiocassette player. He tried all the tape recorders, in case something had been left on them. Blank. He looked over the cassettes of classical music and modern rock. Nothing you could call a clue. He called the ex-convent girl, who approached with tiny steps as if not to disturb the sanctity of the place.

'Did Señor Stuart Pedrell book a trip in the days before he disappeared?'

'Yes. To Tahiti.'

'Did he book it direct?'

'No. Through Aerojet. It's a travel agency.'

'Had he already paid a deposit?'

'Yes. He also ordered a very large sum in traveller's cheques.'

'How much?'

'I don't know. But it would have been enough for a year or more abroad.'

Carvalho looked at the canvases on the wall. Thoroughly modern painters. The oldest, Tàpies, was still no more than fifty years old, and the youngest, Viladecans, was around thirty. One signature was particularly familiar to him: Artimbau. He had known him during the years of the anti-Franco struggle, before he himself had fled to the United States.

'These painters used to come here?'

'A lot of important people used to come.'

'Do you know them by name?'

'Some of them.'

'What about this one, Artimbau?'

'He was the nicest one. He used to come often. Señor Stuart Pedrell wanted to commission him to do a big mural on his estate at Lliteras. A huge wall was spoiling his view, and Señor Stuart Pedrell wanted Señor Artimbau to paint it for him.'

*

Artimbau's studio was on Calle Baja de San Pedro. As usual, Carvalho felt a flicker of nervousness as he passed the police headquarters in Vía Layetana. He had only bad memories of the barracks-like building. However much they tried to give it a democratic face-lift, for him it would always be a grim fortress of repression. Vía Layetana itself, though, struck him differently – a first, hesitant step towards a Barcelona Manhattan that was never going to be completed. A pre-war street with the harbour at one end and the small industry of Gracia at the other, it had been extended through Barcelona to provide the city with a commercial nerve-centre. Over time, it had come to house trade unions and employers' organizations, as well as policemen and their victims. It also housed a large branch of the National Savings Bank. In the forefront of an expansive, sub-Gothic public park stood a monument to one of the weightier members of the Catalonian aristocracy. Carvalho walked along Calle Baja de San Pedro until he came to a large doorway giving onto a courtyard. He picked his way across the yard and began to climb a narrow, time-worn staircase that gave access to a number of rickety landings. Opening onto these were the kind of small studios favoured by architects just embarking on their careers and craftsmen on the verge of retirement. Others merely provided storage space in which leather pelts, cardboard boxes and other bits and pieces were piled high. Stopping in front of a door painted with optimistic patterns of foliage coloured in green and lilac, Carvalho rang the bell and waited for an answer. A little old man, his apron covered with marble dust, opened the door wide with slow, silent gestures and nodded for the detective to enter.

'Do you know who I'm looking for?'

'It'll be Francesc. No one ever comes to see me.'

The old man disappeared into a little cubby-hole carved out of the vastness of the artist's atelier. Carvalho advanced a couple of steps, and found Artimbau engaged in painting a girl in the act of removing her jumper. The painter turned round, surprised, and took time to read the past in Carvalho's face.

'You! Well I'll be damned!'

The dark, babyish face, circled by a black beard and a receding hairline, seemed to emerge from the tunnel of time. The model had lowered her jumper to conceal her white, waxen breasts: two firm, solid hemispheres.

'That's all for today, Remei.'

The painter touched Carvalho for a moment, and then clapped him on the back, as if he had just rediscovered a part of himself.

'You'll stay and eat. If you like my cooking, that is.'

He pointed to a covered earthenware casserole simmering on a butane cooker. Carvalho lifted the lid and was assailed by the aroma of a strange, potato-less stew in which vegetables vied with meat.

'I have to watch my weight, so I don't put in potatoes. And hardly any fat either. But it tastes OK.'

Artimbau patted his paunch, which jutted out from his relatively slender body. The model murmured a goodbye and cast a long, slow look at Carvalho.

'I wish I knew how to paint that look,' laughed Artimbau when the model had left. 'Nowadays I busy myself painting gestures. Body movements. Women dressing and undressing. I've gone back to the human body after spending a lot of time on society, social things . . . Spending time as a painter, I mean. I'm still in the Party. I go out and paint murals before elections. The other day I did one at the Clot. What about you?'

'I don't paint.'

'I know. I meant are you still involved in politics?'

'No. I don't have a Party. I don't even have a cat.'

It was a stock reply which once upon a time might have been true. But not any more, Carvalho thought to himself. To start with, I've got a dog now. Am I going to end up with as many things as other people? Artimbau had things. He was married, with two children. Maybe the wife would come and eat with them, and then again maybe she wouldn't. Artimbau showed him his paintings, and a book of drawings on the death agonies of General Franco. No. He knew that the climate still wasn't right for it to be published. He tried to get Carvalho to reciprocate with some news about his own life. Carvalho summed up his last twenty years in one short sentence. He'd been in the United States, and was working as a private detective.

'That's the last thing I'd have expected. A private eye!'

'In fact I've come to see you about a case. A client of yours.'

'Somebody complaining that I've plagiarized a painting?'

'No. He's dead. Murdered.'

'Stuart Pedrell.'

Carvalho sat down and prepared to listen. But the usually talkative Artimbau became rather reticent. He laid plates and cutlery on a little marble table and produced a bottle of Berberana Gran Reserva. As always, Carvalho was happy to discover a new example of gastronomic corruption. The painter carefully removed the casserole from the stove. Then he phoned his wife. She wouldn't be coming. He filled the plates with the low-calorie stew and was plainly delighted at Carvalho's favourable comments.

'It's excellent.'

'The green vegetables – artichokes, peas and so on – give off their own moisture, so you don't need so much oil. The only dietetic heresy is the glass of cognac I added. But the doctors can get stuffed.'

'Yeah, stuff the doctors.'

Carvalho did not press his business. He hoped that Artimbau would return to the subject of Stuart Pedrell. The painter chewed slowly, and advised Carvalho to do the same. That way, you digest your food better, you eat less, and you lose weight.

'It's always tricky talking about a client.'

'He's a dead client.'

'The wife still buys some of my work. And she pays better than her husband used to.'

'Tell me about her.'

'That's even trickier. She's a living client.'

The bottle was already finished, and the painter opened another. In no time at all, this too was half empty. Their thirst was well served by large glasses designed for mineral water.

'The wife is quite a woman.'

'So I've seen.'

'I offered to paint her in the nude, but she wouldn't have it. She's certainly got class. More than him, I'd say. Both of them were made of money. Both had an impressive education, and their different connections gave them a very varied life. I was his court painter, I suppose. One day they could be sitting where you are now, eating one of my concoctions with me and my wife. And the next day, they might have López Bravo or López Rodo round to dinner – or some minister from the Opus Dei. You see what I mean? That should give you an idea. One day they'd be skiing with the king, and the next they'd be smoking joints with left-wing poets at Lliteras.'

'Did you paint the mural in the end?'

'Ah, you've heard about that. No. We were still discussing terms when he disappeared. We never agreed anything concrete. He wanted me to paint something very primitive. The faux-naif style of Gauguin's Canaques period, but transposed to the native life of Lliteras. I did a few sketches, but he didn't like them. I was still into realism, and maybe something a bit too militant slipped in. The peasantry and suchlike . . . To be honest, I wasn't really all that interested in the idea. Between you and me, he was a bit of a loudmouth.'

By now, the two of them had disposed of the second bottle.

'A loudmouth?'

'Yes. A loudmouth,' Artimbau repeated, as he went in search of a third bottle.

★

'Well, maybe I went a bit far, writing him off as a loudmouth. Like anyone else, he both was and wasn't what he was.'

Artimbau's eyes, half buried in a forest of hair, gleamed with satisfaction. Carvalho provided the perfect audience, as if he were a blank canvas on which the artist could paint his image of Stuart Pedrell.

'Like any rich man with angst, Stuart Pedrell was pretty careful. Every year he would get dozens of proposals asking him to help finance cultural ventures of one sort or another. Someone even suggested the idea of a university. Or maybe he was the one who suggested it . . . I can't remember. There were publishing houses, magazines, libraries, foundations, all kinds of projects . . . You can imagine what it was like, as soon as people smelt that there was money around attached to cultural angst. After all, there's not a lot of money round here, and not much cultural angst among the rich either. That's why Stuart Pedrell always took a long time before coming to a decision. But he was also a bit of a dabbler. He would get interested in all sorts of projects and give them money – then he'd suddenly come down to earth and leave them in the lurch.'

'How was he thought of among the artists and intellectuals?'

'They all thought he was pretty weird, really. Artists and intellectuals didn't value him too highly – because they don't value anyone highly. If that ever changes, it'll mean that our egos have collapsed and we're no longer artists and intellectuals.'

'The same thing happens with butchers.'

'Yes, if they own their own shops. But not if they're just employees.'

Carvalho attributed Artimbau's social-Freudian demagogy to the third bottle of wine.

'Rich people had respect for him, because in this country they respect anyone who's made a lot of money without too much effort. And Stuart Pedrell has certainly done that. He once told me the story of how he got rich, and it was enough to make you wet yourself laughing.

'It was in the early 1950s, when there was that sudden block on imports. Raw materials were coming here only in a trickle, or via the black market. By then, Stuart Pedrell had finished studying to be a commercial lawyer. His father had already marked him down to take over the business, because his brothers had struck out on their own. He was still unsure of himself. He investigated the raw materials market and found out that there was a shortage of casein in Spain. Fine. So, where was casein to be got? In Uruguay and Argentina. Who wanted to buy it? He drew up a list of potential customers and visited them one by one. They were willing to buy from him if the ministry gave import permission. Easy as pie. Stuart Pedrell mobilized his contacts, who included government ministers, and they opened doors at the Ministry of Trade. The trade minister himself thought the whole project was very patriotic, because that was how Stuart Pedrell presented it to him. What would Spain do without casein? What would become of us without casein?'

'I hate to think.'

'Stuart Pedrell flew to Uruguay and Argentina. He talked with manufacturers. He went to meetings. He danced the tango. He even got into the habit of telling jokes with an Argentinian accent. He used to do that when he was on a high, or feeling down, or when he was playing the piano.'

'In other words, all the time.'

'No, no, I exaggerate. He got the casein at a reasonable price, a third or a quarter of the price that had been agreed in Spain. Everything went according to plan, and he used his first millions to make more. That's not the best way to put it, of course, because he was clever enough to associate himself with businessmen who could make up for his personal aloofness. You could say that he was a Brechtian entrepreneur – the kind with the best prospects for the here and now. An alienated capitalist won't have much chance in the social-democratic future that faces us.'

'Who were his partners?'

'There were two main ones: Planas and the Marquess of Munt.'

'Sounds like big money.'

'Big money and very good connections. For some time it was said that the mayor was also in on the act. Not just the mayor, but various banks and religious and semi-religious sects as well. Stuart Pedrell would put up the money and then take a back seat. In a way, I suppose, he was schizophrenic. The world of business was one thing, and his intellectual circles quite another. When he'd made enough money to assure the future of four generations, he went back to university and studied philosophy and politics in Madrid. Later on, he enrolled at Harvard and the London School of Economics. I know for sure that he wrote poems which he never published.'

'Did he ever publish anything?'

'Never. He used to say that he was too much of a perfectionist. But I think it was because he couldn't find a style. That happens to a lot of people. They have everything that they think they need in order to create, and then they find that they haven't got a style. So they bring literature into their lives, or painting into their wardrobes. Some rich people decide to buy up magazines or publishing houses instead. Stuart Pedrell was involved in financing a couple of small publishers, but he never gave them a lot – just enough to cover their annual losses. The money was a pittance for him.'

'What about his wife? Why is she called Mima?'

'From Miriam. It's quite normal. All my clients are called Popo, Puli, Peni, Chocho, Fifi or somesuch. These days it's chic to be "tired", and nothing tires you more than having to say someone's full name. But Mima was rather different. She seemed to be just an appendage of Stuart Pedrell at first, the typically cultured and affected wife of a rich and cultured man. She never dropped her social airs, even when she was sitting here. But she never gabbled. She's been a different woman since her husband disappeared. She's brought so much energy into the business that the partners are even getting a bit concerned. Stuart Pedrell was easier to work with.'

'And Viladecans?'

'I only see him when he has to pay me. He's the typical smart-arsed lawyer who helps the boss keep his hands clean.'

'Girlfriends?'

'That's a very delicate area. What are you interested in? Past, present, or more wine?'

'Wine and the present.'

Artimbau brought another bottle.

'It's my last one of this vintage.' He spilt a little as he filled Carvalho's glass. 'The most recent one is called Adela Vilardell. She was more or less permanent. But there were also plenty of short-term relationships – younger than most people would think acceptable. Stuart Pedrell had passed the fifty mark, and he favoured the classical style of erotic vampirism. I can set you on the trail of Adela Vilardell, but not of the one-nighters.'

'Did you know him well?'

'Yes and no. A painter can get to know these types quite well, especially if they're clients. They bare their souls . . . and their pockets. It's a revealing dual operation.'

'The South Seas?'

'His obsession. I think he'd been reading a poem about Gauguin, and he started to pursue the myth. He even bought a copy of the George Sanders film – *The Moon and Sixpence* I think it's called – and screened it at home.'

Carvalho handed him the sheet of verse that he had found among Stuart Pedrell's papers. He translated the line from *The Waste Land*.

'Do you know where these lines in Italian could come from? Can you see any hidden meaning? Maybe something Stuart Pedrell said to you?'

'I often heard him say: "I read, much of the night, and go south in the winter." It was his pet phrase. The Italian doesn't remind me of anything special, though.'

*

Stuart Pedrell had lived in a house on the Puxtet, one of the hills which used to overlook Barcelona, in the same way that the Roman hills used to dominate Rome. Now it is carpeted with flats for the middle bourgeoisie, interspersed with the occasional penthouse occupied by an upper bourgeoisie that has some sort of relation to the older inhabitants of Puxtet's surviving mansions. It had become the custom among the owners of the surviving mansions to provide their offspring with a duplex apartment close to home, a pattern repeated on the fringes of Pedralbes and Sarriá, the last bastion of an upper bourgeoisie clinging to its dignified towers. They too preferred to have their little ones close to hand.

Stuart Pedrell had inherited the turn-of-the-century house from a childless great aunt. It was the work of an architect influenced by the ironwork styles current in Britain at the time. Even the gates were a statement of principle, and an ornamental iron crest like the mane of some glazed dragon ran along the ridge of the tiled roof. Neo-Gothic windows; an ivy-covered façade; white-wood furniture with blue upholstery in a trim and disciplined garden. The elegance of a tall hedge of cypress framed the controlled freedom of a cluster of pine trees and the precise geometry of a little maze made of rhododendrons. Underfoot, turf and gravel.

A polite sort of gravel, that crunched discreetly under your feet. Turf that must have been nearly a hundred years old: well-fed, brushed and trimmed, a green, springy velvet on which the house seemed to float, as on a magic carpet. Black and white table trimmings, in silk and pique. A gardener dressed in the clothes of a Catalan peasant; a butler with symmetrical sideburns and a striped waistcoat. Carvalho noted that the chauffeur who got into the Alfa Romeo to collect Señora Stuart Pedrell was not wearing gaiters. But he appreciated the stylish grey uniform with velvet lapels and the hands dressed in a pair of fine, whitish-grey leather gloves that contrasted elegantly with the black steering wheel.

Carvalho had asked if he might move freely around the house, and the butler ushered him in with a movement of the head that hinted at an invitation to dance. And Carvalho, taking his cue, glided his way through the house with the Emperor Waltz humming in his head. He mounted a garnet-marble staircase, with a wrought-iron handrail on one side and a banister on the other. The stairs were bathed in the refracted light of a stained-glass window depicting St George and the Dragon.

'Is the gentleman looking for anything in particular?'

'Señor Stuart Pedrell's rooms.'

'If the gentleman would be so kind as to follow me . . .'

He followed the butler up the staircase onto a kind of open balcony. A perfect film setting. The heroine leans over and sees her favourite guest arriving; she calls out: 'Richard!'; a flurry of long, blonde curls; she lifts her long skirts and hurries trippingly down the stairs into a long embrace. The butler, however, seemed oblivious to the cinematic potential of the scene. He asked Carvalho to follow him down a carpeted corridor, at the end of which he pushed open a high door of carved teak.

'Some door!'

'Señor Stuart Pedrell's great uncle had it made. He had copra holdings in Indonesia,' the butler explained, for all the world like a museum guide.

Carvalho entered the library. The desk had the imperious presence of a royal throne. He imagined some sixteenth-century cleric poised over it, writing with a quill pen. The bedroom lay through a door on the right, but Carvalho took a long, slow look around the library, noting the dimensions of the room, the patterned stucco of the ceiling, the solid wooden wall-panelling which provided a backdrop for hefty bookcases full of leather-bound volumes, and several eighteenth- or nineteenth-century paintings by disciples of Bayeu or Goya, and a historical-romantic work by Martí Alsina. It was inconceivable that anybody could actually work there, except perhaps on the compiling of an Aramaic-Persian comparative dictionary.

'Did Señor Stuart Pedrell use this study often?'

'Almost never. In winter, he would sometimes light the fire and sit and read by firelight. The reason he kept the room like this was because of the value of what is in it. The library contains only books that are old and precious. The most recent is from 1912.'

'You're very well informed.'

'Thank you. The gentleman is very kind.'

'Do you have any other functions in the house, apart from being the butler?'

'That's the least of my responsibilities. In fact, I am responsible for the general upkeep of the house, and I also do the household accounts.'

'Are you an accountant?'

'No. By training, I am a teacher of commerce. In the evenings, I study philosophy and literature. Medieval history.'

Carvalho caught the look of pride in the butler's eyes, the obvious delight that he felt at having caused confusion in the detective's brain.

'I was already living in the house when the Stuart Pedrells arrived as a young married couple. My parents had been in the service of the Misses Stuart for forty years.'

The bedroom had nothing of particular note in it, other than a first-rate reproduction of Gauguin's painting *What Are We? Where Are We Going? Where Do We Come From?*

'This is a new painting.'

'That is correct.'

There was a noticeable lack of enthusiasm in the butler's voice.

'Señor Stuart Pedrell had it hung over the head of his bed when he decided to come and live alone in this wing of the house.'

'When was that?'

'Three years ago.'

The butler turned a blind eye as Carvalho rifled through every drawer in the room, pushed back the bed so as to look behind it, and examined every item of clothing in the wardrobe.

'Did you have a particularly close relationship with Señor Stuart Pedrell?'

'Nothing out of the ordinary.'

'Did you ever discuss personal things, apart from the daily routine of work?'

'Sometimes.'

'What sort of things?'

'The usual.'

'What do you mean by "usual"?'

'Politics. Or a film, perhaps.'

'How did he vote in the June 1977 elections?

'He didn't tell me.'

'UCD?'

'I don't think so. Something more radical, I would imagine.'

'And you?'

'I don't see why that should be of any interest to you.'

'I'm sorry.'

'I voted for the Republican Left of Catalonia, if you really want to know.'

They left Stuart Pedrell's crypt, and through the real world of the house there wafted the distant chords of a well-tuned piano.

Hands that moved with discipline, but not much feeling.

'Who's playing?'

'Señorita Yes,' the butler replied, struggling to keep up as Carvalho strode rapidly towards the source of the music.

'Yes? What, like in the English?'

'It's Yésica.'

'Ah, Jésica.'

Carvalho opened the door. A red belt accentuated the narrowness of the girl's waist. Jean-clad buttocks rested their tense and rounded youth on the piano stool. Her back was arched with a studied delicacy. A blonde ponytail hung from a head thrown back as if to accompany the notes on their journey through the house. The butler cleared his throat. Without turning round or interrupting her playing, the girl asked:

'What is it, Joanet?'

'Excuse me, Señorita Yes, but this gentleman would like to have a word with you.'

She swung round on the stool. She had grey eyes, a skier's complexion, a large soft mouth, cheeks that were a picture of health, and the arms of a fully-formed woman. Her eyebrows were perhaps a little too thick, but they underlined the basic features of a girl who would not have looked out of place in an American TV commercial. Carvalho felt himself also coming under scrutiny, but it was a general scrutiny, rather than the detailed examination to which he had subjected her. Get a Gary Cooper in your life, girl, thought Carvalho, as he shook the hand that she offered with a seeming reluctance.

'Pepe Carvalho. I'm a private investigator.'

'Oh. I suppose it's about Daddy. Can't you people let him rest in peace?'

The glamour-girl façade crumbled. Her voice quivered, and her eyes flashed at him, full of tears.

'It was Mummy and that dreadful Viladecans who started all this.'

The sound of the door closing suggested that the butler had heard as much as he wanted to hear.

'Dead people don't need to rest, because they don't get tired.'

'How would you know?'

'Do you know otherwise?'

'My father is alive – here in this house. I can feel him around me. I talk to him. Come here. Look what I found.'

She took Carvalho's hand and led him to a lectern in a corner of the room. A large photo album was lying open on it. The girl slowly turned the pages, one after another, as if they were fragile between her fingers. She placed a grey-framed photograph in front of Carvalho. It showed Stuart Pedrell as a dark-skinned young man in shirt-sleeves, flexing Mr Universe muscles.

'He's handsome, isn't he.'

The room smelt of marijuana, and so did she. With her eyes closed, she smiled ecstatically at the vision in her mind's eye.

'Did you have a close relationship with your father?'

'Not before he died. When he left home, I'd been studying in England for about two years. We used to see each other in the summer, but not for long. I only got to know my father after he'd died. It was a beautiful escape. The South Seas.'

'He never reached the South Seas.'

'How would you know? Where are the South Seas?'

There was a will to fight in her wild eyes, her pursed lips and her whole body that seemed turned in on itself.

'OK, let's agree that he went to the South Seas. Did he ever try to get in touch with you or any of your brothers?'

'Not with me. I don't know about the others, but I don't think so. Nene has been in Bali for months. The twins were almost strangers to him, and the little one is only eight.'

'But the Jesuits are throwing him out.'

'So much the worse for them. It's crazy to send a kid to the Jesuits in this day and age. Tito is too imaginative for that kind of education.'

'When your father appears to you, does he say where he was, all that time?'

'There's no need. I know where he was. In the South Seas. In a wonderful place where he could make a fresh start. The same young man who went to make his fortune in Uruguay.'

The girl's account was a bit wide of the mark, but Carvalho had a soft spot for emotional myths.

'Jésica . . .'

'Jésica . . . No one ever calls me that. Nearly everybody calls me Yes. Some say Yésica, but no one says Jésica. It sounds nice. Look. My father, skiing in Saint-Moritz. Here he's giving someone a prize. You know, he looks like you.'

Carvalho had tired of the sentimental journey through the album. He waved aside the possibility of any resemblance, and half sank back into a black leather sofa. This position of forced relaxation allowed him to contemplate the girl as she bent over the album. Her jeans were unable to conceal the strong, upright legs of a sportswoman, just as her short-sleeved woollen jumper failed to hide two firm breasts with immature nipples. Her neck served as a long, flexible column for the continual leftward and rightward movement of her head. The ponytail trickled down slowly like honey from some wonderful pot. Sensing that Carvalho was looking at her, she took the swinging ponytail in one hand and turned to face him. He met her gaze. They stared into each other's eyes until suddenly she ran towards the sofa and sat on Carvalho's knee. She put her arms around him and buried her blonde head in his chest. The detective reacted without haste. He allowed the girl to let herself go, and slipped in an embrace that went a little beyond calming a young girl's secret terrors.

'Let him sleep. He's gone to sleep. He went looking for purification, and now he's asleep. The only reason they keep chasing him is because they're jealous.'

The Ophelia type, thought Carvalho, and he was unsure whether to shake her or sympathize with her. In the end, he gently stroked her head, suppressing an urge to embark on an artful exploration of her neck. Irritated by his own indecision, he moved her away with a gesture that was sudden but controlled.

'When you get the marijuana out of your system, I'd like to come back and talk with you.'

She smiled, with her eyes closed. Her hands were loosely clenched between her legs.

'I'm fine now. If only you could see what I see!'

Carvalho went towards the door, and turned to say goodbye. She sat there, still in ecstasy. Once before in his life he had slept with a girl like that – twenty years previously in San Francisco. She was a paediatrician whom he had been trailing in connection with Soviet infiltration of the early American counter-cultural movements. There was something missing from Señorita Stuart, though: the kind of imperial presence which only a North American body could express. Instead, she had that measure of frailty which, however small, clings to every southerner in the world, whatever their social class. Without thinking, he jotted down his name, address and phone number on a piece of paper, and walked back to hand it to the girl.

'Here.'

'Why? What for? What's the point?'

'In case you remember anything else when your head has cleared.'

He virtually ran from the room. Large steps that faked a sense of purpose.

*

Planas had agreed to meet him at one of his companies, the Central Beer plant where he had to attend a board meeting. He would be able to spare twenty minutes at the most. Then he had to leave in order to prepare his speech as the incoming vice chairman of the Employers' Federation.

'The elections are this evening, and I'm bound to win.'

Carvalho had not been expecting this outpouring of self-confidence, but he accepted the appointment and prepared to meet Stuart Pedrell's partner with the same enthusiasm that one might go to play tennis with someone determined to win in straight six-love sets. Carvalho's prompt arrival deprived Planas of the pleasure of an irritated consultation of his watch.

'A punctual man. A miracle!'

He took a notebook from his back trouser pocket and wrote in it.

'Whenever I meet someone who is punctual, I note it in my little book. You see? I'm writing your name and the date. It makes a lot of sense. If ever I need a private detective, my first consideration is whether I know him, and the second is whether he's punctual. The rest looks after itself. Do you mind if we walk as we chat? It gives me a bit of exercise between meetings. Afterwards I have to give an interview about my garden city on the Melmató Heights.'

The lines of his body were Roman. Classical. Not an ounce of surplus fat. His head had been shaved almost clean, as if in a pre-emptive strike against inevitable baldness. Planas walked beside Carvalho, with his hands behind his back. He looked hard at the ground as he gave carefully considered answers. No particular problems in Stuart Pedrell's business life. All the projects were going splendidly. He stressed that they had never gone in for dramatic speculative ventures. Everything had full cover and very sound backing. Most of the initial capital belonged neither to him nor to Stuart Pedrell, but to their other partner, the Marquess of Munt.

'Have you not met him yet? Alfredo's a rare type, a truly great man.'

Their largest operation was in San Magín – the creation of a completely new neighbourhood, new down to the last lamp post.

There had been times when the appropriate authorities had been willing to provide facilities, but not any more. It's as if capitalism were a sin, and capitalists were Public Enemy Number One.

Why had Stuart Pedrell gone off like that? 'He couldn't face the trauma of reaching fifty. He found it hard enough passing forty, and then forty-five. But he cracked when he came to fifty. He'd made too big a thing of it. And he'd turned his work into a parody. He'd distanced himself from the business side of things. He was like two people, one who worked, and one who was a thinker. A certain amount of distancing is all right, but not if you pull right out of things. In the end, he was becoming a nihilist, and nihilists can't run companies. A good businessman has to have a pretty thick skin. He's got to be able to soak up punishment. Otherwise he'll never get anywhere – or get other people anywhere.'

'But Stuart Pedrell was a rich man.'

'Very rich. Rich from birth. Not quite as rich as Alfredo Munt, but rich all the same. My case is very different. My family was not badly off but, at the age of forty, my father went under. The bankruptcy was a big scandal. He had tried to set up a bank with the Busquets, and they went bust. My father had to pay over seventy million pesetas to the creditors. Seventy million pesetas. In the 1940s, that was a very large amount of money. He was left without a cent. I was at university at the time, but I was fully aware of everything that was happening. What was your youth like, Señor Carvalho?'

The detective shrugged his shoulders.

'Mine was sad, very sad,' Planas continued, his eyes fixed on the uneven tarmac of the yard through which they were walking.

'Stuart relied on us, on the security of Munt's financial backing, and on my capacity for hard work. He contributed "the general perspective", as he called it. I never quite knew what he meant, but he maintained that it was absolutely fundamental. He spent too much time contemplating his navel and chasing after women, here, there and everywhere. I haven't had a proper holiday since 1948. Seriously. Just the occasional trip, to please my wife. Oh, and every May I go to a German clinic in Marbella. It's designed to clear the toxins from your body. They start you with a day on a diet of fruit, and then a litre of some revolting purgative. That's when the torture really begins: a fortnight of almost total fasting! Every other day, they give me an enema, which seems to go on forever. But, my friend, just when you think you're going to collapse – pow! Your body starts to flow with new energy. You play tennis, you climb mountains. You think you're Superman. I've been going for five years now, and I always come out feeling as if I could float on air.'

He drew closer to Carvalho, and lightly touched the rings under his eyes.

'Those rings. You must have a tired liver.'

He walked ahead of Carvalho to an office on high ground overlooking the warehouse. He asked a secretary for the address of the Buchinger Clinic in Marbella, and gave it to Carvalho. With a brisk glance at his watch he invited the detective to follow him back into the yard.

'One must try to grow old with dignity. You're younger than I am, but not much. I can see that you don't look after yourself. I thought private detectives did gymnastics or ju jitsu. Every morning, I go jogging near my house in Pedralbes. I choose a path, and off I go, up the hill to Vallvidrera.'

'At what time?'

'Seven in the morning.'

'I'm just getting up then. Frying up a couple of eggs with chorizo.'

'I don't want to hear that! Anyway, as I was saying, I run up the hill, and then I run back down again. And then there's the water massage twice a week. Have you ever tried it? Fantastic. It's as if some water pressurizer were pounding your whole body. A jet of water, at full pressure. You stand like you were going to be shot. Try standing like that yourself.'

Planas moved three metres away from Carvalho and aimed an imaginary hose at him.

'From this distance, they shoot a stream of lukewarm water at you, concentrating on the parts of your body you want to slim down. Then they do the same with cold water. By the end, your blood is circulating incredibly well. And that helps to break down the fat. You have a splendid figure, but I can see pockets of fat that you ought to get rid of. Around your kidneys and your stomach. Here. Yes, this is where it hurts. A good jet of water – whoosh . . . Discipline, that's the key. And don't overdo it with the drinking. Hell! It's two o'clock . . . The publicity people are waiting . . . Was there anything else?'

'During the period when he dropped out of sight, did Stuart Pedrell ever make contact with you?'

'Never. It wasn't necessary for the business. And he had given authority to Viladecans for any decisions that had to be made on his behalf. Also, Mima started to work herself, and she proved much better than her husband.'

'What about the personal side of things?'

'We never had much to say to each other. Probably our only long conversation was the first one, twenty-five years ago when we decided to become partners. We must have seen each other thousands of times since then – but never to talk, never just for a chat. Munt had a different kind of relationship with him, though. You should ask Munt.'

He held out his hand as if he were shooting and offering his condolences at the same time.

'Don't forget what I said about the clinic. There's nothing so healthy as a good enema.'

'Bye-bye, Planas,' thought Carvalho. 'I hope you have a healthy death.'

*

'I'm afraid we're out of that one.'

'What else do you have by way of chilled whites?'

'Viña Paceta.'

'That'll do.'

He ordered some sea snails as an appetizer. For his next course, the proprietor offered a choice: a mixed seafood platter that would include more snails or a dish of baked dorado fish. Carvalho chose the dorado, both because he wanted to stay on the white wine, and because the fish would help him reduce the swelling under his eyes and improve the state of his liver. He liked to eat at Leopoldo's from time to time. It was a restaurant he had retrieved from the mythology of his adolescence.

One summer, when his mother was in Galicia, his father had invited him out to a restaurant. This was a rare event in itself, because his father was the kind of man who believed that all restaurants fleeced their customers and served up garbage. But someone had told him about a restaurant in the Barrio Chino which offered huge portions at reasonable prices. It was there that he took Carvalho. The young man stuffed himself on squid alla Romana – the most sophisticated dish he knew – while his father stayed with more familiar dishes.

'It's certainly good. And there's lots of it. Now let's see what it's going to cost us!'

A long time passed before he set foot in a restaurant again. But he always remembered Leopoldo's as the place where he had been initiated into a ritual that was to become a passion. He returned many years later, when the restaurant was no longer run by the attentive man who had taken their order and treated them with all the courtesy due to regular and discriminating customers.

Now it was merely a good-quality fish restaurant, where a local petit-bourgeoisie mingled with people from the north of the city who had heard of the restaurant by repute.

Carvalho had chosen a diet of fish and chilled white wine. Whereas once he used to fight off anxiety attacks by diving into snack bars and restaurants and ordering with a combination of greed and good taste, he now tried to overcome them by consuming the country's reserves of white wine.

The proprietor was surprised at the modesty of his choice for dessert, and his omission of a liqueur after coffee. 'I'm in a hurry,' Carvalho said, by way of excuse. But on reaching the door, he decided that he had acted against nature, against his nature. He sat down again, called over the proprietor and asked for a double measure of ice-cold brandy. After the first sip, he knew he was returning to his normal self. My liver? To hell with it! It's mine, after all. It'll do what I tell it. He ordered another double brandy and decided that the transfusion that he had needed for several days was now complete.

He left the restaurant and walked down Calle Aurora in search of the lost scenery of his adolescence. He passed a building whose modern appearance was surprising in a street that dated from the assassination of Noi del Sucre. He saw a group of people hovering around a doorway, and noticed a poster advertising a series of discussions on the *roman noir*. With alcoholic self-assurance, Carvalho joined the people waiting for one of the sessions to begin. He knew these types. They had that look of hard-boiled eggs which was common to intellectuals everywhere, although among Spaniards it had a particular inflection: the hard-boiled eggs seemed less solid than in other latitudes. They had an awareness, born of underdevelopment, that the egg was in danger. They were divided into tribes, according to background and affinity. There was one tribe that enjoyed a higher intellectual status than the others. This could be seen in the way they were regarded in the eyes of others. Seemingly casually, people went out of their way to cross their paths, and felt a need to greet them and be recognized in return.

The session finally got under way, and Carvalho found himself in a blue auditorium, together with a hundred or so people who were eager to demonstrate that they knew more about the *roman noir* than the seven or eight experts on the platform.

The platform contribution began with a 'confidence-boosting' operation in which the several brains limbered up by identifying the function, the place and the precise identity of the object under discussion. The process was then repeated according to post-Vatican Council rites. Two round-table participants, having appointed themselves senior members, proceeded to play a private game of intellectual ping-pong over whether or not Dostoyevsky had written *romans noirs*. Then they moved on to Henry James, via an obligatory allusion to Poe, and finally announced their discovery that the *roman noir* was invented by a French book-jacket designer who used the colour black for Gallimard's series of detective novels. Someone else on the platform tried to break into the monopolistic duologue being conducted by the bearded contributor and the short-sighted Latin American. But he was invisibly, metaphysically elbowed aside by the senior members.

'The point is . . .'

'In my opinion . . .'

'If you will allow me to . . .'

They didn't allow anything. For a few moments, he tried to squeeze in the sentence: 'The *roman noir* was born with the Great Depression . . .' But his voice only reached the first row and part of the second, where Pepe Carvalho was seated. The particular way in which the two soloists moved their Adam's apples suggested that they were about to pronounce a final conclusion or enunciate some synthesizing formula.

'We could say . . .'

Silence. Expectant faces.

'I don't know if my dear Juan Carlos will agree . . .'

'How could I not agree with you, Carlos?'

Carvalho deduced that their ascendancy was due to a degree of onomastic complicity.

'The *roman noir* is a sub-genre, to which only a few great novelists were committed. Chandler, Hammett, McDonald . . .'

'What about Chester Himes?'

The voice which tried to make itself heard had a high-pitched tone – the result, perhaps, of having been bottled up for so long. But this initial defect proved to be an advantage, because it impinged on the duologue, and they turned to trace the origin of that thin sound.

'You were saying?' said the short-sighted man, with a tired affability.

'I was saying that those three names should be supplemented by Chester Himes, with his great descriptions of life in Harlem. Himes's work was on a par with that of Balzac.' The two leading actors seemed temporarily tired from their exertions, and left the intruder to explain himself. Now everything was wheeled into play, from Chrétien de Troyes' *La Matière de Bretagne* to the death of the novel following on the epistemological excesses of Proust and Joyce; not to mention McCarthyism, the crisis of capitalist society, and the social marginalization inevitably induced by capitalism, which provides the suitable cultural milieu for the *roman noir*. The audience was impatient to intervene. As soon as he had the opportunity, one of them got up to denounce Ross McDonald as a fascist. Someone else added that the *roman noir* writers always tended to be on the brink of adopting fascist positions. Hammett was excused on the grounds that he had been a member of the American Communist Party at a time when the communists were above suspicion and had not yet been decaffeinated. Every *roman noir* has a single hero, and that in itself is dangerous. It's simply neo-Romanticism, retorted another contributor, intent on rescuing the *roman noir* from the inferno of history.

'I'd prefer to say that there exists a certain neo-Romanticism which is the driving force of the *roman noir*, and which makes it necessary in the times we live in.'

Moral ambiguity. Moral ambiguity. That's the key to the *roman noir*. Marlowe, Archer, the Continental Op – they're all awash in this moral ambiguity.

The two stars were not pleased to have lost their leading role. They now tried to reassert themselves within the rising flood of words: closed universe . . . lack of motivation . . . linguistic conventions . . . the new rhetoric . . . it's the opposite of the *Tel Quel* school in that it affirms the personal specificity of the author and the central hero . . . the viewpoint of *The Murder of Roger Ackroyd* . . .

*

Carvalho left at this point, with a thick head and a dry throat. He went to order a beer at the bar, and found himself next to a brunette with huge green eyes, whose body was enveloped in a poncho that first saw life on some arid plain of the Andes.

'Hello!'

'Hello! I know you . . . You're . . .'

'Dashiell Hammett.'

She laughed, and then insisted that he give his real name.

'Horacio introduced us at the signing of Juan's book, isn't that right? It's boring in there. That's why I left. I'm not to keen on all this *roman noir* business. I agree with Varese: when the bourgeoisie can't keep control of the novel, it starts to lay on the colours. I've read what you write. I like it a lot.'

Carvalho was bemused. Had Biscuter or Charo published something under his name? He would ask them for an explanation as soon as he returned home.

'Well, my heart hasn't really been in it recently.'

'Yes. One can see that. But it happens to all of us. I agree with Cañedo Marras: great tiredness presages great enthusiasm.'

Carvalho felt like saying: Take off your poncho, *mi amor*, and let's go to bed. I don't care whether the bed's black or white, or round or square, because when the bourgeoisie can't keep control of bed, it starts to lay on the adjectives.

'Are you going to stay here? Or would you fancy coming and drinking six bottles of absolutely sensational white wine?'

'You're quick on the draw, stranger. What are you getting at?'

'That we go to bed.'

'Obviously. Do you know Juanito Marsé? That's his technique too. He says he's had a lot of slaps in the face, but also quite a few lays.'

'What do I get? A slap in the face?'

'No. But not a lay either. I'm waiting for my girlfriend. She's still stuck in there. You see, ours is an impossible love!'

'It never got beyond birth.'

'That's the best sort.'

Carvalho made a slight bow and left. Outside, he mused on the theme of budding affairs. He went back to his days as an adolescent, falling for girls in the street, following them, taking their bus or tram, saying nothing, but hoping for an encounter charged with a sense of the aesthetic. Any minute now, she'll turn round, take my hand, and carry me to the end of the rainbow, where I shall live forever, in contemplation of the one I love. When he actually fell in love with someone, he found himself expecting that she would be waiting for him at some precise point in the city, probably by the harbour. He would turn up there, impatiently glancing at his watch, and convinced that the appointment would be kept.

Maybe I needed to be in love, maybe I needed a degree of self-deception. You can't survive stripped of everything, without the possibility even of entering some church. You can't live without prayer. Nowadays, you can't even believe in the liturgy of wine, ever since the experts decreed that red wine should be chilled and not served at room temperature. Who ever heard of such a thing! The race is degenerating. Civilizations go under when they start to question the unquestionable. The Franco regime began to collapse on the day when Franco first said: 'It's not that I . . .' A dictator must never start a speech by placing a negation before himself.

You can't escape by getting drunk every day. Nor suddenly surprise yourself with gritted teeth, as if you'd been making some superhuman effort. What superhuman effort were you making? I suppose you think it's nothing? To wake up. Day after day. In a city where the restaurants are all mediocre, uninspired and expensive. Two weeks ago, he had taken his car and set off south in search of a Murcian restaurant. He had a nap en route, to give himself an excuse for a large lunch. And as soon as he arrived at Murcia, he transferred himself from the car seat to the restaurant seat and bewildered the head waiter by ordering a dish of local sausages, prawns and aubergines in a cream sauce, Tía Josefa partridges, and a milk pudding. He drank four carafes of the Jumilla house wine, asked to be given the partridge recipe, and thought once again that if the Thirty Years' War had not sealed France's hegemony in Europe, it might just be possible that French cuisine was currently passing under the hegemony of the Spanish. His only patriotism was gastronomic.

Without realizing it, he had walked all the way to the Rondas. He gazed at their decomposed geography, feeling hurt, as always, by the violation of his childhood landscape. Just as he was about to plumb the depths of self-pity, he went into a telephone booth and called Enric Fuster, his friend, accountant and neighbour in Vallvidrera.

'You know the literary types at the university. Find me someone who can unravel the meaning of some Italian poetry. No. If I knew who it was by, I wouldn't be needing to ring you.'

Fuster seized the opportunity to arrange a meal.

'I'll get in touch with Sergio, my fellow-countryman from Morella. He'll make us a fine old meal. He doesn't cook very well, but he's always got good, fresh ingredients.'

Like the Chaldeans who thought that the world ended with the mountains that encircled them, Enric Fuster, along with everyone else from the Maestrazgo, thought that anything beyond his own horizon was intergalactic. Carvalho sat down to restore his strength for the evening. The white, acidic after-effects of drunkenness were wearing off. He was thirsty. He looked at girls in blossom and imagined what they would be like twenty years hence, when they too would have passed the forty-year meridian. He looked at forty- and fifty-year-old women, and imagined them as young girls playing at princesses. He remembered a poem by Gabriela Mistral.

And now to reconstruct a year in the life of a dead man. It seems grotesque. Every murder reveals that humanism has no existence in the real world. Society is interested in the dead man only in order to find the murderer and inflict an 'exemplary' punishment. If there is no chance of finding the murderer, neither the dead man nor the murderer has any further interest. Except to someone who has a good cry on your shoulder. Like children cry when they've lost their parents in a crowd. He started walking faster towards his parked car, but then he thought of the effort of driving off, finding the Marquess of Munt's house, parking the car again, and then driving it home. He got into a taxi and began examining the driver's ideological credentials. A medallion of the Virgin of Montserrat. Photos of a rather plain-looking family. A warning sticker: 'Drive Carefully, Dad'. A little ribbon with the colours of the Barcelona football team. The taxi man was speaking Andalucian, and after two minutes' conversation had already confided that he voted PSUC at the last general election.

'What does the Virgin say about the fact that you voted communist?'

'It's my wife who's into all that.'

'Is she religious?'

'Like hell! My wife, religious?! No. But she likes Montserrat, you know. Every year, I go to rent some cells at the monastery. Well, they call them cells, but they're really hotel rooms. Simple, but very clean. There's everything you need. So I have to rent them every May and go up there with my wife and children for three days. You probably think it's a bit crazy given that neither of us pisses holy water. But she likes the mountain.'

They read Marx much of the night, and go to the holy mountain in spring.

'I tell you, I'm the one who gets most out of it now. There's a kind of peace up there. I get the urge to become a monk. And it's incredibly beautiful, the mountain. Almost magical. How those stones stand up! For centuries, you know, for centuries. Before my grandfather was born, or his grandfather.'

'Or your great-great-great-grandfather's grandfather.'

'Nature teaches us everything. On the one hand, just look around you here. Shit. Nothing but shit. If we knew what we were breathing! Sometimes I have to drive up to Tibidabo. And from Vallvidrera – Jesus! – you can see all the shit floating over the city.'

'I live in Vallvidrera.'

'Lucky you.'

The taxi dropped him on a street in Tres Torres, an old residential district whose family houses had been pulled down to make way for bright, low-rise blocks, nicely set back from the pavement to allow a growth of dwarf cypresses, myrtles, a well-protected banana tree, palms and oleanders. An entrance hall, which would not have disgraced the New York Sheraton, served as a vast backdrop for the bustling of a musical-comedy porter, who registered the name Marquess of Munt with more respect than Carvalho had shown in uttering it. He opened the door to the lift and got in with Carvalho. As they were going up, he murmured nothing more than: 'The Marquess is expecting you.' The lift passed the doors of all four tenants of the four-storey building. Carvalho was shown into a reception room, thirty metres square, decorated in a Japanese style that predated *Madame Butterfly*.

A mulatto servant dressed in white and pink took charge of the detective and led him into a bizarre stage-setting. A vast space of eighty square metres, carpeted white throughout. The only furniture was a piano and, at the far end, designer seating fastened to floor and wall. On the white carpet, the only foreign body was a metal cone which tapered up from the floor to an ultra-fine point, in an apparently vain attempt to reach the ceiling. The Marquess of Munt was relaxing on a sofa, with a perfectly composed air of gravity. Seventy years of snobbish living were condensed in the thin frame of a fair-skinned, smartly dressed old man, with eyes like shining slots in which a pair of malignant pupils danced and darted. The lilac veins in his lightly made-up face had been raised like scratch marks by the wine that was keeping cool in the ice bucket. He held a glass in his right hand, and a copy of Michel Guérard's *Cuisine Minceur* in the left. The book beckoned to Carvalho to sit down on any of the lumps that emerged from the milky landscape.

'Will you eat with me, Señor Carvalho? My partner, Señor Planas, tells me that you breakfast on fried eggs and chorizo.'

'I said that to beat off his dietary assaults.'

'Planas has never learnt the pleasure of eating. It has to be learnt around the age of thirty. That's when human beings cease to be imbeciles – and in return, they have to pay the price of growing old. This afternoon, I've decided to have some morteruelo and chablis. Do you know what morteruelo is?'

'It's a kind of pâté from Castille.'

'From Cuenca, to be precise. A most striking pâté. Made of hare, pork shoulder, chicken, pig's liver, walnuts, cloves, cinnamon and caraway. Caraway! A fine word for an excellent flavour!'

The mulatto had the scent of a homosexual stud – a solid,

fragrant, woodish kind of smell. He placed before Carvalho a tray with a tall, clear, shapely quartz crystal glass on it.

'You will doubtless agree with me that it is quite unspeakably bad taste to drink white wine from green glasses. I'm against the death penalty except in cases of nauseating bad taste. How can people deny wine the right to be seen? Wine must be seen and smelt before it can be tasted. It requires transparent crystal, as transparent as possible. It was some vulgar French *maître* who started the fad for green glass. Then the more vulgar elements of the aristocracy took it up, and since then, it's moved down to department-store windows and the caterers who do weddings for social nonentities. There's nothing so infuriating as a lack of culture when people have the means to avoid it.'

It seemed to Carvalho that the purple veins had grown a shade darker beneath the thin layer of face powder. The Marquess of Munt had a graceful sort of voice, like that of a Catalan radio actor who is continually trying to conceal his accent and ends up with a weird Castilian pronunciation. The mulatto brought two dishes full of morteruelo, two sets of cutlery, and two baskets containing small rolls.

'Drink, Señor Carvalho, before the wine comes to an end, before the world comes to an end. Remember what Stendhal said: you do not know what it means to live unless you have lived before the revolution.'

'Are we living before the revolution?'

'Without a shadow of a doubt. A revolution will come soon. Its shape still has to be decided. But it will come. I know, because I have devoted a lot of time to political science. And then I have Richard, my Jamaican servant. He's a great expert in drawing up astrological charts. A great revolution is approaching. Is something disturbing you? The Carbero sculpture?'

The menacing needle was a sculpture. Carvalho felt more secure.

'I've spent years and years trying to educate my class by force of example. They've defended themselves by accusing me of being an exhibitionist. While I was racing hot-rods, my classmates were begging in Madrid for permission to import an Opel or a Buick. When I separated from my wife and went to live with some gypsies in Sacromonte, word went out to all the high-class homes in Barcelona that I was never to be received again.'

'Where did you live in Sacromonte?'

A shadow of vexation passed across the marquess's eyes, as if Carvalho had tried to cast obscure doubts on something as clear as crystal.

'In my cave.'

He drank some more wine, and contentedly watched Carvalho do the same.

'The aristocracy and high bourgeoisie of Barcelona are scouting for servants in Almunecar or Dos Hermanas. I look for mine in Jamaica. Rich people have to display what they're made of. Here everyone's afraid of displaying it. During the civil war, some FAI people came looking for me here, and I received them in my best silk dressing-gown. Their leader asked me: "Don't you feel ashamed to be living a life like this, with everything that's happening in the country?" I answered that I'd feel ashamed to be going round dressed up as a worker without being one. He was so impressed that he allowed me twenty-four hours to pack and leave. I went over to the *nacionales* and was unlucky enough to get involved with the Catalan group in Burgos. A bunch of upstarts who changed sides in order to remain ambassadors. As soon as I entered Barcelona with the *nacionales*, I lost interest in their whole operation and took advantage of World War Two to do some spying for the Allies. I have the Légion d'Honneur, and every 14th July I go to Paris for the Champs d'Elysée parade. My style of life ought to merit some attention from this fat ruling class in Catalonia. But not a bit of it. Now they've discovered bottled wine and goose with pears. They're a million miles from their grandparents. The ones who made Barcelona a modernist city, big tuna fish in a land of sardines. They too were rather uncouth, but their blood pounded in rhythms that were Wagnerian. Nowadays it pounds to the rhythm of some TV jingle. You are a plebeian who drinks chablis in fine style. I have been watching you.'

'Did you pay a low rent for your cave in Sacromonte?'

'It was the biggest one I could find with no one in it. I went to a luxury shop in Granada and bought a turn-of-the-century English iron bed at three times the price that I paid for the cave. I put the bed in the cave, and spent some very happy years trying to promote gypsy singers and dancers. Once I collected a folk group and took them to London in their performing clothes. Imagine: flowing dresses, thick country boots, Cordoban sombreros, false beauty marks, carnations blossoming from their hair. At London Airport, they wouldn't let us through immigration. "You're not coming into the country looking like that." I asked to be shown the laws which banned people from coming into Britain in their work clothes. There was no such law, but they still wouldn't let us through. Finally I rang Miguel Primo de Rivera, who was then ambassador in London, and explained what was happening. They sent us some embassy cars and escorted us into the country under the protection of the diplomatic corps.'

'Have you been as imaginative in your business life?'

'It hasn't been necessary. While my father was alive, it was all plain sailing. He respected my personality. He knew that I was creative and that I needed to change my life and other people's. When he died, I was nearly fifty years old, and came into an absolutely staggering inheritance. I put a lot of it into fixed-interest securities, so that I could live like a prince for the rest of my life. I used some more to compensate my wife for bearing me five children, and I made them my heirs. With the remainder, I set myself up in business, always using fellows like Planas or Stuart Pedrell. Fellows with drive, with a fierce ambition for power, but with the possibility of gaining only economic power. Planas is an impressive and dangerous operator: in four years he can triple any sum of money you care to give him. Eat and drink, Señor Carvalho, before the revolution comes.'

*

He gave no opportunity for the conversation to take a different track. His observations were entirely self-centred, and he went on to talk of his travels.

'Yes, Señor Carvalho, I stand guilty of having travelled three times around the world – by ship, by plane and by land. I know all the worlds there are to know on this earth. I don't have time today – Caballé is singing *Norma* at the Liceo and I don't want to miss it. But another day, I'll take you round my private museum. It's in my ancestral home at Munt de Montornés.

'It alarms me that the possibility of enjoying life seems to be disappearing. It's not just a question of money, although that's not unimportant. When I was a child, I discovered what happiness was, what pleasure was – in a piece of pumpkin and a slice of salami. Have you read *Cuore* by D'Amicis? Nowadays, the educational experts rule it out of court, but it was part of the sentimental education of my generation, and probably yours too. I remember one scene where Enrico, the young hero, goes on a trip to the country with some of his school friends, including Procusa, the son of a bricklayer. In fact it's Procusa's father who organizes the trip, and at one point he gives them a slice of pumpkin with salami on top. How does that strike you? I find it truly marvellous. A simple joy in nature and in spontaneous eating. You have to wait for Hemingway before there's an eating scene that even compares. In *Beyond the River and Into the Trees*, he describes in simple language a scene with a fisherman eating a plate of beans and bacon that he has cooked over a fire by the river. None of the great banquets of baroque literature come anywhere near the meals in *Cuore* and Hemingway's short story. But such possibilities of enjoyment are coming to an end. The stars don't lie. Everything is carrying us towards death and extinction.'

'But you're still making money . . .'

'It's my duty.'

'You'd be ready to defend your heritage by every available means. Even war.'

'I don't know. It depends. Not if it was a very dirty war. Although I suppose that any war can be made to look attractive. But no, I don't think that I'd come round to supporting violence.'

'So? What are you afraid of?'

'That an era in which necessity rules over imagination will deprive me of this house, this servant, this chablis and this morteruelo – although the morteruelo may just survive, because the left has recently promised to preserve the "hallmarks of popular identity", and cooking is one of those.'

'Stuart Pedrell tried to escape from his condition. You take yours on, and try to turn it into an aesthetic. Planas is the only one who works.'

'He's the only one who's alienated, although he doesn't recognize it himself. I've tried to help him. But he has the balance of an unbalanced mind. The day he looks in the mirror and says "I'm mad", he'll fall apart.'

'I imagine that your pessimism stems from a fear that the forces of evil – the communists, for instance – will become masters of the things that you love and possess.'

'Not just the communists. The Marxist horde is more diverse nowadays. It even contains bishops and flamenco dancers. They're fighting to change the world, to change man. If the struggle between communism and capitalism keeps to the road of peaceful competition, communism is bound to win. The only escape open to capitalism is war, so long as it's a conventional war without nuclear weapons. But that's going to be very difficult to achieve by agreement. So, there's no solution. Sooner or later there will be a full-scale war. The survivors will be very happy. They will live in a sparsely populated world and enjoy the technological legacy of millennia. Automation plus a low population. Perfect! Just keep the demographic pressure under control, and happiness will become a real possibility.

'You may ask what kind of political regime will prevail in this heavenly future. Well, I'll tell you. A very liberal social democracy. If there's no war, and we continue along the path of co-existence, we'll reach a blockage of growth in the capitalist system, and maybe in the socialist system too. Have you read Wolfgang Harich's *Communism Without Growth*? It's just been published in Spain, but I'd already read it in German. Harich is a German communist, and he predicts: "If the present rhythm of world growth continues unchanged, mankind will disappear in two or three generations." He advocates a communism of austerity – a model for economic survival that is opposed both to the capitalist programme of continual growth and to the Eurocommunist idea of an alternative controlled development, financed by taxation of the masses and designed to secure the rule of the working class. I'm already an old man and I won't live to see it.

'I'm not particularly worried about what will become of my family. What does sadden me, though, is the thought that Barcelona and my beloved landscapes will disappear. Have you ever seen the sun go down over Mykonos? I have a house on Mykonos, built on rocks which face the setting sun and the island of Delos. I love beautiful views. But there are very few people that interest me – in an emotional sense, I mean. Stuart Pedrell and Planas are like children to me. I could almost be their father. But they have too many ties to this century and the one to come. They believe in the rising curve of history, that humanity is progressing. Of course, they see it from a capitalist perspective, but they still believe in it. Planas is standing in the elections to the CEOE – the "Employers' Union", as the press calls it. I'd never have done anything like that.'

'Of your alternatives for the future, which would you lay your money on?'

'I'm too old for betting. Everything will happen after I'm dead. I haven't got long to go.'

He poured Carvalho some more wine and filled his own glass to the brim.

'It was a Goytisolo, *Distinguishing Marks*, which taught me to drink white wine between meals. White wine was also used to sensational effect in the Resnais film *Providence*. Until then, I'd always stuck to strong-bodied ports and sherries. But this is a real blessing. It's also the alcoholic drink with the fewest calories – if one excludes beer. Which white wine do you drink?'

'*Blanc de blancs*, Marqués de Monistrol.'

'I don't know it. I'm a fanatic for chablis. This one in particular. And if it can't be chablis, then let it be an Albariño Fefiñanes. It's an impressive hybrid, with roots in Alsace or Galicia. One of the best things they brought us along the road from Santiago de Compostela.'

'Did you have anything in common with Stuart Pedrell?'

'Nothing. He was a man who never knew how to get the best out of life. A narcissistic sufferer. He suffered for himself. He had a Jewish anxiety. But he was a high-flier in the business world. I knew him as an adolescent, almost as a child. I was a good friend of his father's. The Stuarts set up in Catalonia in the early nineteenth century. They were involved in the hazelnut trade between Reus and London.'

'Where could a man like him have disappeared to, for a whole year, without leaving a single trace?'

'Maybe he enrolled at some foreign university. He'd been getting interested in ecology – he was always getting carried away with some new idea. I once told him: your great advantage over ninety-nine per cent of the population of this country is that you read the *New York Times* every day. If Planas had had the same curiosity, by now he'd be planning some deal to import water purification plant. What do you think of this morteruelo? Excellent, isn't it. I sent my cook to Cuenca for a month to learn how to make it. It's the best pâté I have ever tasted. Have you ever thought that if you exclude stews, Spain hasn't created a single major hot soup. But it is a world leader in the field of cold soups. There are as many different gazpachos as there are rice dishes. Morteruelo is wonderful at this time of day, especially with the bread – which I have sent from Palafrugell. Other people drink tea at this time of day, but how can you compare tea to this chilled white wine and morteruelo? Pity grapes aren't in season. It would be perfection to round off this little snack with a few muscatel.'

'Do you have any actual evidence that Stuart enrolled at a foreign university?'

'None at all.'

'So?'

'Maybe he went on a trip, but not to the South Seas. Border controls aren't infallible, you know. In fact, I'd say the opposite. A man with an urge to disappear will disappear. Do you know what people were claiming when I went off to the Sacromonte caves? That I had gone to Antarctica with an expedition that I financed. There was even a report in the Movimiento press commenting on the mettle of the Spanish race – that would not be intimidated by the most inaccessible secrets of the world. I remember one sentence in particular: "Our holy ones explored the heavens with their aesthetics; our heroes are able to explore even in hell." That appeared in the press, Señor Carvalho. I do believe it did.'

*

He called Biscuter to find out what was new at the office.

'A girl called Yes phoned.'

'What did she want?'

'To speak with you.'

'She'll have to wait . . .'

Carvalho picked up his car and drove up Tibidabo to his house in Vallvidrera. He threw in the rubbish bin a pile of unsolicited mail that he found in his letter box, and lit the fire with Eugenio Trias's *Philosophy and Its Shadow*. He calculated that he would have to slow down with burning his library. He still had some two thousand books to go: at one a day, they would last six years or so. Intervals between books would have to be introduced, or he would have to go out and buy more – an option that was not attractive. Maybe he could play for time by splitting the various volumes of Brahier's *Philosophy* and the Pléiade classics collection. It hurt him to burn the Pléiade classics, because they had such a good feel to them. Sometimes he would take down a volume or two, just to feel them, before returning them to the jumble of the bookshelves and erasing the memory of how, once, he had thought it enriching to read them.

He did a little tidying up, so that the cleaning lady would not complain too much. He took a long, slow shower. Then he made himself a long sandwich of French bread with tomatoes and swallowed down the Jabugo ham. He was still wavering over whether to open a bottle of wine when someone rang the bell on the garden door. He looked out of the window and saw through the heavy bars the silhouette of a girl. As he went down the stairs to the door, the silhouette took on the shape of Jésica.

He opened the wrought-iron gate. She walked towards the house and turned at the front doorstep.

'May I come in?'

Carvalho invited her in with a sweep of his hand. Bleda came out to meet her and cleaned one of her shoes with a couple of hefty, well-aimed licks.

'Does it bite?'

'She doesn't know the meaning of the word.'

'I adore dogs,' she said, not altogether convincingly. 'But I was bitten by one when I was a kid, and now I'm afraid of them.

What a lovely house you've got. Wow, what a beautiful fireplace!'

She marvelled at everything, with that polite insincerity which well-bred people adopt to show that they still have a capacity for envy and surprise. The air of a class fugitive, thought Carvalho, as he adjusted his dressing-gown to avoid some sudden display of his private parts, but still a product of her class.

'You look like you've settled down for the night. Were you in bed?'

'No. I'd just finished eating. Would you like something?'

'No. Food makes me feel sick.'

She spread her perfectly shaped hips on the sofa.

'I behaved like an idiot this morning, and didn't help you at all. I wanted to apologize. I'd like to help you as much as possible.'

'This is out of working hours. I'm not on piecework, you know.'

'Forgive me.'

'Shall we have a glass of something?'

'I don't drink. I'm macrobiotic.'

Carvalho had to do something with his hands. He looked for his cigar box and took out a Filipino Flor de Isabela. It was smooth and substantial.

'I've been suffering remorse ever since my father's body was found. I could have prevented it. If I'd been here at the time, it would never have happened. My father went away because he was lonely. My eldest brother is an egotist. And so is my mother. My other brothers are lumps of meat who happen to have been baptized. I'm the only one he got on with. I'd grown up enough to talk with him, to look after him. I'd always admired him from a distance. He was so handsome, so intelligent and sure of himself, so elegant. Yes, he was an elegant man: I don't mean in the way he dressed, but in the way he was. Warm.'

'And your mother?'

'A brute.'

'Did your father have anything important to say when he wrote to you in England?'

'No. Just a few postcards. One or two lines, usually. Maybe something he'd read, that he found interesting. He came to London twice, on business, and it was marvellous. At least, it seems marvellous now. At the time, I have to admit, he got on my nerves a bit – I felt he was taking up my time. If only we could turn the clock back. Here. Read this.'

She took a folded sheet of paper from her straw basket:

> You will return from the world of shadow
> On an ash-coloured horse
> You will pick me up by the waist
> And carry me over the horizon;
> I will beg your forgiveness
> For not having known
> How to stop you dying of desire.

'Not bad.'

'I'm not asking for your literary opinion. I know it's awful. I'm trying to show you how this is getting to be an obsession with me. I can't go on like this.'

'I'm a private detective, not a psychiatrist.'

'Do you want me to go?'

Their eyes met. Despite the distance between them, Carvalho could smell the life in her body. It hadn't been a defiant question – more a complaint. Carvalho let himself relax. He sat on the sofa opposite Jésica, presenting an easy target for Bleda, who started worrying at his slipper.

'Put some music on,' she said.

Carvalho stood up. As he picked Mahler's Fourth Symphony, he saw out of the corner of his eye that Yes was settling back and relaxing. She moved her legs apart, spread her arms, and rested her neck on the back of the sofa.

'It's nice here. If you had to live in that mausoleum . . .'

'Not bad, for a mausoleum . . .'

'Appearances can be deceptive. It's so cold and constricting.

It's mother's style. Of course, she doesn't care two hoots about protocol and all that. But since she had to go through so much to get herself established, now she gets her own back by making everyone else suffer.'

She opened her eyes, and turned to Carvalho, as if preparing to say something momentous.

'I want to leave home.'

'I didn't think people said things like that nowadays. I thought they just did them. I sounds kind of old-fashioned.'

'Very old-fashioned. That's the way I am.'

'I still don't see what all this has to do with me. I'm working for your mother. A temp job. But a job all the same. I'm investigating your father's death. That's all.'

'You've got kind, human eyes. The same as him. You won't let me down.'

'You're well-proportioned yourself . . . I mean, you've got all kinds of resources to pull you through. Anyway, it's not my field. I don't see how I can help.'

The girl moved from her seat and knelt in front of Carvalho. She rested her head on his lap.

'Let me stay here.'

'No.'

'Just tonight.'

Carvalho's fingers began to stroke her mane of hair. Then they moved down the secret paths leading to the nape of her neck.

*

She stood naked, as if emerging from the night sea. With slow, hesitant gestures, she nervously tucked a strand of hair behind each ear, and then hunted in her bag and brought out a mirror and a crumpled piece of tissue. She held out her hand, as if to give or ask for something, but she wasn't even looking at him. She left the room with jerky steps, and returned with a knife in her hand. Carvalho drew up the sheets to cover himself, and the girl sat at the bedroom table. She cleared a space among the jumble of papers and objects, put down the mirror in the way that a priest might handle the sacred host, gently opened the tissue and removed something resembling a tiny piece of chalk. She scraped the cocaine with a knife until it was a pile of dust on the mirror.

'Have you got a straw?'

'No.'

'Or a biro?'

Not waiting for an answer, she returned to her bag, and took out a cheap biro made of transparent plastic. She removed the refill and placed the crystalline tube next to the mirror. Then she ran over to the bed, took Carvalho's hand and smilingly pulled him out from under the sheet. He found himself sitting naked beside the girl, under a metal lamp which highlighted the little pile of cocaine on the table. Closing one nostril with her finger, she took the biro tube into the other and snorted up the cocaine. Then she offered the tube to Carvalho. She met his refusal with a slow smile and snorted up some more. Carvalho went off to find a bottle of wine and a glass. He sat down and started to drink, while the girl dealt with the white dust with the concentration of an expert.

'Do you use it often?'

'No. It's very expensive. Do you want some? There's still a little left.'

'I've got my own drugs.'

'Give me a drop of wine.'

'It'll be bad for you.'

She shut her eyes and smiled, as if she were living a beautiful dream. She took Carvalho's hands and pulled him up. She glued her body to his startled skin, and rubbed her cheek against his shoulder, his chest, his head, and then his whole body, while her hands explored his back. Carvalho had to force up feelings of desire, and she responded with drugged obedience to his erotic advances. She lavished reflex kisses on his mouth, then moved her lips down the trail of his chest, abdomen and penis as Carvalho bent his head slightly back. She changed position at his merest gesture, all her resistance and passion overcome. Her skin and will became his instruments. They made love in two different orbits, and only when the ceiling came back into sight did she frantically grip Carvalho's hand and murmur that she loved him, that she didn't want to leave. Carvalho felt as if he owed her something. He was upset with himself.

'Do you always take drugs whenever you go to bed with someone?'

'I feel fine with you. You don't scare me. It usually scares me, but I don't feel scared with you.'

Carvalho turned her over, put her on all fours and made ready to sodomize her. Not a sound of protest came from the submissive head hidden by its soft hair. Linking his arms around her slim waist, he felt the dark lust ebbing away from him.

'Do it if you like. I don't mind.'

Carvalho jumped up and reached for the box of Condal Number Six. He lit a cigar, sitting on the edge of the bed and watching the spectacle of his slowly drooping penis. *Adios, muchacho, compañero di mi vida . . .*

The girl's silence made him turn. She was asleep. He covered her with the sheet and a blanket, then found his pyjamas and put them on. In the next room, he replayed the Mahler record, stoked the fire and sprawled on the sofa with his cigar in one hand and the wine within reach of the other. Bleda was sleeping beside the fire, the most contented animal in the world, and Yes was sleeping in a room shaped for the taciturn solitude of a man who burned away days and years as if they were bad habits to be got rid of. He jumped from the sofa, disturbing Bleda in her sleep. With eyes wide open and her ears straining, the dog seemed to be back in the uncertainty of the wilds as she watched Carvalho move towards the kitchen.

His hands delved simultaneously into cupboards and drawers as he laid out ingredients on the marble top. He cut three aubergines into one-centimetre rounds, and sprinkled them with salt. Then he put oil in the frying pan and fried a clove of garlic until it was burnt almost black. He tossed some prawn heads in the same oil. He shelled the prawns and diced some pieces of ham. He removed some of the prawns' heads and put them to boil in a pan. Having rinsed the salt from the aubergine slices, he dried them individually with a tea towel. Next he fried all the aubergines in the garlic-and-prawn oil, and left them to drain in a colander. Still in the same oil, he sautéed grated onion with a spoonful of flour, and added the bechamel and prawn-head stock. Having arranged the aubergines in layers in an oven-proof casserole, he strewed them with shelled prawns and diced ham, and bathed everything in the bechamel. He grated cheese all over the crisp whiteness of the bechamel, placed the casserole in the oven, and waited for the cheese to melt. He cleared everything from the kitchen table with a sweep of his elbows, laid two sets of cutlery on the white tablecloth, and brought a bottle of Jumilla claret from the cupboard outside the kitchen. When everything was ready, he returned to the bedroom.

Yes was sleeping on her side, with her face to the wall. Carvalho shook her awake, helping her to stand up, and virtually carried her into the kitchen. He sat her down in front of a plate, and served. *Aubergines au gratin*, with prawns and ham.

'I admit it's not very orthodox. Normally it's made with chemically pure bechamel and much less of a prawn flavour. I have rather a primitive palate.'

Yes looked at the plate, and at Carvalho, and made no comment. She was not yet fully awake. She dipped her fork into the delicate crispness, put it in her mouth, and chewed thoughtfully.

'It's very good. Is it out of a packet?'

*

Carvalho was in luck. Teresa Marsé was up early, and he found her busy at her cash register. The boutique had a smell of strawberries to it. A customer dressed like a peasant designed by Yves St Laurent picked up her change and left Carvalho and Teresa standing amid third-worldist designer garments made for those who shun the made-to-measure market.

'You're up early. It's twelve o'clock.'

'I got here a quarter of an hour ago.'

'Did you know this guy?'

Teresa took the photograph of Stuart Pedrell without taking her eyes off Carvalho.

'I know you from somewhere, stranger, but I don't know where. Two years ago, or maybe it was three, you came asking me about a corpse. How come you're always asking me about corpses? You invite me to dinner, and then you start on about corpses. Is this another one?'

'Yes.'

'Looks like Stuart Pedrell. He was much better looking in real life.'

'The reason I'm asking you is because he was part of your world.'

'Maybe. But he had much more money than most of us. When I was married, I used to see quite a lot of the Stuart Pedrells. My husband was in the building racket too. Where are you taking me to eat today?'

'I can't today.'

'I don't work for nothing, and especially not for the likes of you.'

She hung her arms around Carvalho's neck and tickled the front of his palate with her tongue.

'Teresa, I haven't had breakfast yet . . .'

The woman passed her hand through her red afro and drew away from him.

'Come after breakfast next time.'

She took him into the back room of the shop. Carvalho sat on a piano stool, while she enthroned herself in a wicker chair from the Philippines.

'What do you want to know?'

'Everything you know about Señor Stuart Pedrell's sex life.'

'Obviously I come into your story-line as the cultured whore. At least you haven't been slapping me about lately. You hit me that first time. And worse. As far as sex goes, Señor Stuart Pedrell was not on my books. When I knew him, I was the virtuous wife of an upright industrialist. We used to go to sessions for Catholic couples organized by Jordi Pujol. Have you heard of him?'

'The politician?'

'Yes. Once a week, young married couples from Barcelona high society would meet together with Jordi Pujol, to discuss morality and the Christian way of life. The Stuart Pedrells came along from time to time. They were older than us, about the same age as Jordi. But they listened, and joined in the discussions.'

'Were the Stuart Pedrells very reactionary?'

'No. I don't think so. But the sessions set the tone. We were young bourgeois, with a controlled degree of anxiety. Moderate anxieties. We used to talk about Marxism and the civil war too. Against them, of course. Against Marxism and against the civil war. I remember it well. On Tuesdays, we would meet at the Liceo. And on Wednesdays, at my house, or whoever's turn it was, to talk about morality.'

'Is that all you know about Stuart Pedrell?'

'No. Once he chased me round the room, sitting on a chair. I was on a chair too.'

'Don't tell me – you were playing musical chairs!'

'No. He would start moving his chair closer to me. And his

hands. Then I'd move my chair away. And then it would start over again.'

'Was this in front of Jordi Pujol?'

'No. In another room.'

'And?'

'My husband arrived. He chose not to see what was going on. But that was the first and last time. Stuart Pedrell led a double life, or rather a multiple life. He didn't just stick to chasing young married women on chairs. I see you're beginning to get interested.'

'Are there any interesting stories?'

'Nothing out of the ordinary. A string of married women. Problems with husbands incapable of expressing themselves. Stuart Pedrell had the advantage of knowing how to talk. The biggest scandal was probably the business with Cuca Muixons. But even that was nothing much: a few slaps in the face.'

'The husband?'

'No. Stuart Pedrell's wife decided to start hitting Cuca Muixons at a polo match. Then everyone got more civilized about it, and went on their way. Particularly after Stuart Pedrell began an affair with Lita Vilardell. That was different, though. An intense passion, just like in a novel. Stuart suddenly arranged to meet her in a London park, and he turned up in a bowler hat, dressed as an English City gent. He took a lot of care over the way he dressed. Another time, he met her in Cape Town. I don't know what he was dressed as, but I do know that he arrived on time.'

'Didn't they travel out together?'

'No. That way, it was more romantic.'

'Could she afford the trips?'

'The Vilardells have as much money as the Stuart Pedrells, if not more. Lita got married very young to an ultra-rich merchant shipowner, and had two or three daughters by him. Then one day, her husband found her in bed with the Sabadell centre-forward. He took the daughters, and Lita took off for Cordoba with a flamenco guitarist. There was also a wild affair with a

Marseilles gangster who marked her with a flick knife. When she gets drunk, she swears she's even had it off with Giscard d'Estaing. But no one takes her seriously. She's a pathological liar. The affair with Stuart Pedrell lasted for ages. It was a very stable relationship, almost as if Stuart had married for a second time. You men are disgusting: you always want to marry the women you sleep with. So that you can own them for life. Anyway, no point in my getting all worked up . . .'

'What are people round here saying about his death?'

'I'm a bit out of touch with that crowd, really. I hardly see them at all. Maybe a customer now and then. They say it was another case of womanizing. He'd started going off the deep end a bit. Age spares no man, particularly those who discover their flies at forty. My father's generation was very different. In those days, they'd get married, and while they were doing up the family apartment, they'd set one up on the side for their wife's hairdresser, or her manicurist. That's what my father did for Paquita, my mother's dressmaker. A really cute woman. Sometimes I go to see her in Pamplona. I managed to pull some strings and get her into an old people's home. She's had a bad stroke . . . As for Stuart Pedrell, he was a victim of Francoite puritanism, the same as Jordi Pujol.'

'How was he getting on with Lita Vilardell before he disappeared?'

'Normal enough. They'd have dinner together once a week, and both enrolled on a course about Tantra art. I know that, because we met there once.'

'Has she observed a period of mourning?'

'Who? Vilardell?'

Teresa Marsé laughed so hard that the wicker chair groaned under her.

'Sure. She probably set her coil at half-mast.'

*

'The señorita is out at a music lesson, but she said that you should wait. She won't be long.'

The cleaning woman carried on hoovering the carpet. Carvalho walked to a balcony that looked out over Sarriá and beyond Vía Augusta, to the hazy landscape of a city drowning in a sea of carbon monoxide. Sub-tropical plants in glazed tile window boxes. A pair of beach chairs, with blue canvas and white-painted wooden frames. One was badly worn; the other was the exclusive domain of a dachshund bitch who lifted her head, to cast a wary glance at Carvalho, and then barked and jumped down, trailing her teats, and came over to sniff his trousers. She wrinkled her nose, unpleasantly surprised at the smell of another bitch. She started yapping at Carvalho. He tried to make friends, bringing to bear all his recently acquired authority as a dog owner. But the dog shot under its deck chair, from where it continued to express its radical incompatibility with the intruder.

'She's very spoilt,' the cleaning woman shouted over the din of the vacuum cleaner. 'But she doesn't bite.'

Carvalho stroked a banana palm that was obviously blighted by urban pollution – condemned to the fate of a botanical orang-utan in the zoo of this classy penthouse suite. He leaned over the balcony and looked down the smart Sarriá thoroughfare, where a few towers still survived in their garden settings.

'The señorita!' called the herald, and at that moment Adela Vilardell appeared before Carvalho, clutching Béla Bártok's *Microcosms* and a book of sheet music under one arm.

'What a morning! I feel as if I've been in the wars.'

Thirty-year-old grey-blue eyes were gazing at Carvalho – eyes inherited by every Vilardell since the founding of the dynasty.

The first of the line had been a slave trader, at a time when most people no longer trafficked in slaves. He had returned to his home town with enough money to make himself a Count and pass the title on to his children. She had her grandfather's grey-blue eyes, the body of a flat-chested Romanian gymnast, the face of the sensitive wife of a sensitive violinist, and hands that must have stroked his penis as if it were Mozart's magic flute.

'Do you like the view?'

'I'm very demanding.'

Without removing her coat, Adela Vilardell sat on the deck-chair and immediately had the grub-like hound on her lap. Carvalho tried not to look at her, so as to avoid yet another defensive conversation. He leaned again on the balcony rail, and looked sideways at the woman. She in turn was studying him, as if to calculate his weight and the effort that would be required to push him over the edge.

'How are your studies going?'

'Which studies?'

'Music. Your cleaning woman tells me you're taking music lessons.'

'Yes. I started them again, just like that. When I was young, I got as far as the fourth grade, but then I dropped it. It was a torture that my mother inflicted on me. But now it's sheer delight – the best hours of the week. I'm not the only one who goes. It's at the Centre for Musical Studies, a new place that's full of people like me.'

'What does "people like you" mean?'

'Adults who want to learn something they've never been able to do before, for lack of time, or money, or interest.'

'With you, of course, it was lack of interest.'

Adela Vilardell nodded and waited for the interrogation to continue.

'When was the last time you saw Stuart Pedrell?'

'I don't remember the exact date. It was towards the end of

1977. He was preparing for his trip, and we talked briefly.'

'You weren't planning to go with him?'

'No.'

'Was it that he didn't want, or you didn't want?'

'There was never any question of it. Our relationship had been cooling off for some time.'

'For anything – or anyone – in particular?'

'It was a question of time, really. Our relationship lasted nearly ten years, and there were periods of great intensity. We'd spent whole summer months together, when his family was away on holiday. By then, we were a long-established couple. We were very used to each other.'

'Besides, Señor Stuart Pedrell was spending time on other women.'

'Everyone that came along. I was the first to realize it. Or rather, the second, because I suppose his wife Mima was one step ahead of me. I didn't care. The only thing that bothered me was the way he went round picking up infants.'

'Infants?'

'Up to the age of twenty, every man and every woman ought to be in infant school.'

'Did you benefit financially from your relationship with Stuart Pedrell?'

'No. He didn't support me. It's true that he paid for me sometimes. When we ate out together, for instance, he would pay the bill for both of us. Maybe that strikes you as excessive.'

'Didn't you ever offer to pay?'

'I am, or used to be, a young lady. And I was brought up on the principle that women don't pay in restaurants.'

'It would seem that you live on investment income. A lot of it.'

'Yes. I have my great-grandfather to thank for that. He was a shepherd from Ampurdán who got together enough money to send my grandfather off to what remained of our American colonies.'

'I know your family history. I read it a short while ago in the *Correo Catalan*. It was a bit toned down, though.'

'Daddy had shares in the *Correo*.'

'During the time that Stuart Pedrell was missing, did he ever make contact with you?'

The grey-blue eyes opened wide, as if to reveal the absolute transparency of Adela Vilardell's body and soul as she answered:

'No.'

The 'no' had faltered slightly as the air rose from her flat chest.

'You see how it was. Years and years of a relationship, and then nothing.'

She waited for Carvalho to make some observation. But when he remained silent, she added:

'Absolutely nothing. Sometimes I thought: "What can this man be doing . . . ? Why doesn't he get in touch with me?" '

'Why did you think that? Didn't you think he was in the South Seas?'

'I was in that part of the world myself, once, and I know that they have postboxes! I've posted cards there myself.'

'It didn't take you long to find a replacement for Stuart Pedrell . . .'

'Are you asking me or telling me?'

Carvalho shrugged.

'Why does my private life interest you so much?'

'Normally, it wouldn't. Not at all. But now it may have some bearing on my work. You were seen recently in black motorcycle gear, riding a powerful Harley Davidson. You were with a male lookalike on an equally powerful Harley Davidson.'

'So, I like motorbikes . . .'

'Who's the rider you go with?'

'How did you find out about all this?'

'It may seem hard to believe, but you people don't have private lives. Everything about you is common knowledge.'

'What do you mean by "you people"?'

'You know very well. All I have to do is knock on the door of someone who has even a half-acquaintance with you, and they know all there is to know. For instance, is the bowler-hat story true?'

'Which story?'

'Is it true that Stuart Pedrell arranged to meet you some years ago in a London park? And that he turned up as a City gent, bowler hat and all?'

'That's correct.'

'So, will you tell me the name of the rider?'

'You must know already.'

'I do.'

'Well then.'

*

Biscuter was sitting in the corner, on the edge of a chair. As soon as he saw Carvalho arrive, he jumped up.

'There's this girl waiting to see you, boss.'

'So I see.'

Carvalho slipped a glance at Yes and ignored her movement towards him. His mission accomplished, Biscuter disappeared behind the curtain. Carvalho sat in his revolving chair and contemplated Yes's frozen gesture in the middle of the room.

'Are you annoyed that I've come here?'

'Annoyed isn't the word.'

'After you left, I started thinking. I don't want to go back home.'

'That's your business.'

'Can I stay at your place?'

'No.'

'Just for two or three days.'

'No.'

'Why not?'

'My duties as your mother's employee and your companion in bed go only so far.'

'Why do you always have to talk like a private detective? Why can't you say normal things, give normal excuses? That you're expecting relatives, or that you don't have room?'

'Take it or leave it. I'm sorry. Anyway, it's bad to see each other so often. I'm planning to have a quiet meal here, by myself. I wasn't thinking of inviting you.'

'I'm lonely.'

'Me too. Please, Jésica. Don't use me up all at once. Keep me for when you really need me. I've got work to do. Go away.'

She didn't know how to go. She gesticulated with sadness, whilst looking for the door.

'I'll kill myself.'

'That would be a pity. But I don't prevent suicides. I only investigate them.'

Carvalho busied himself opening and closing drawers, putting his desk in order, and making a phone call. Yes closed the door gently behind her. Her exit coincided with Biscuter's reappearance, ladle in hand.

'You were too hard on her, boss. She's a decent kid, even if she is a bit loopy. Do you know what she asked me? If I've killed anyone. And then she asked whether you have.'

'What did you say?'

'What do you think? But she went on asking questions. She never stopped. Don't worry. I kept mum. Is she dangerous?'

'Only to herself.'

So saying, Carvalho slammed down the phone and raced towards the door.

'You're not going, are you, boss? Aren't you staying to eat?'

'I don't know.'

'I've made you some potatoes and chorizo à la Rioja.'

Carvalho stopped, with one foot outside the door. Potatoes and chorizo à la Rioja.

'They're hot,' Biscuter insisted, when he saw him waver.

'Later.'

He took the stairs two by two, and emerged onto the Ramblas. Straining his neck, he glanced from one distant head to the next in search of Yes's honey-coloured hair. He thought he saw her, and ran towards the arches of the Plaza Real. It wasn't her. Perhaps she'd gone north to where she lived, or maybe south, to sink her thoughts in the harbour waters and the bustle of the *golondrinas* that carry trippers out to the breakwater. Carvalho strode off southwards, his arms accentuating the physical effort and his eyes scouring the street. He kept telling himself he was a fool. He darted across the big intersection at the Christopher Columbus monument, and became the instant target for malevolent stares and occasional insults from passing cars. The Puerta de la Paz seemed drained of people, although the sun was warming a few old folk on the benches, and street photographers were pursuing the occasional passing tourist.

By the hut that sold tickets for the *golondrinas*, a dirty, ragged girl lay breast-feeding a half-sleeping baby. A piece of cardboard told how her husband had cancer, and that she had no money. Beggars. The unemployed. Followers of the Infant Jesus and the most sacred Mother who bore him. The city seemed inundated with fugitives from everything and everywhere. A boat passed by slowly, casting a heavy wash in the greasy waters. Carvalho was struck by the sight of a dignified pensioner, who was wearing an outsize jacket, an undersized pair of trousers, and a felt hat as tall as any worn by the Canadian mounties. One of those careful old men who move with terrifying resolve towards a grave that has been bought in instalments over the past forty years, with payments on the first Sunday of every month.

Who's calling? Tell me, is an innocent person being strangled in this house? No, this is just a straightforward strangling. Where had he read that? Who's that? Funeral insurance. Who's that? The dead. Anyway, what's the point of my looking for Jésica? She's not my responsibility. She'll screw fifteen guys in a month, and then she'll be back to normal.

He retraced his steps to the office, but he still took an occasional look up the Ramblas, in case Yes suddenly appeared. He went into a bar near Amaya, where they only serve wine from the south. He downed three glasses of manzanilla. He gave five pesetas to one of the five little gypsy girls who swept in and held their hands under the noses of the customers as they sipped their drinks and discussed football, bullfighting, homosexuals, women, politics, and strange little deals involving scrap lead or a truckload of cloth bought cut-price from a bankrupt store on Calle Trafalgar. The cloth shops down there seemed permanently on the edge of bankruptcy, to the chagrin of proprietors, salesmen and old bachelors who measured old pieces of cloth with old rulers dating from when the metric system was first introduced. They had survived for decade after decade, since Carvalho's childhood years, but now they had to face up to the realities of old age and death.

What about those chestnut-coloured rulers. Will they be sold off too? Pliant animals wrapped in yellow oilcloth; rigid, lignified serpents; coiled, cracking metal whips; folding rulers aware of their concentrated power to measure the world. Children play with rulers until they kill them. Rulers in the hands of children are measuring-animals which struggle in the clutches of their tormentors, gradually becoming aware that they will never again measure anything. With a folding-rule, one could measure a pentagon or the near side of the moon.

He went into the street. The girl was wearing a flimsy blue cardigan, a skirt more like a pair of trousers, but without enough style to make its shape clear, and a pair of shoes which raised her twenty centimetres above sea level. She seemed at once ugly and beautiful as she said: 'Excuse me, do you fancy going to bed with me? A thousand pesetas plus the price of the room.' Carvalho noticed her bruised eye and a little scratch on the thin, veinous skin of her forehead. She walked further down the pavement and repeated her proposition to another passer-by, who passed her by with a swift semi-circular movement, as if drawing a ring of suspicion round her. She practises her prostitution as if she was asking the time, Carvalho thought. Maybe it's a new whore-marketing technique. I'll have to ask Bromuro and Charo.

He couldn't make up his mind whether to go back to the chorizo and potatoes, or pay a call on Charo. She would just have got up. She would be irritated at his continued thoughtlessness and failure to contact her, and would be preparing her body for the afternoon's telephone punters. They were mostly regular clients, who asked her advice on family problems and even on the best way to fix an abortion for a precocious daughter or a wife made pregnant after a five-glass binge on Aixartell champagne. Or maybe she'd be preparing reproaches for the increasingly absent Carvalho.

'It won't take a moment to heat it up, boss. Looks like mash. The potatoes should crumble a little, but not that much. The chorizo has completely disintegrated, but it's very good. I managed not to overdo the chilli this time.'

Carvalho began to shovel down the potatoes and chorizo. But his palate gradually made him aware that he ought to pay more attention to the food.

'It's wonderful, Biscuter.'

'One does what one can, boss. Some days things go right, and others . . . You know how it is.'

Biscuter's self-satisfied explanation sounded like rain on sheets of glass, and he looked for the splashes produced by the words. It was raining. It was raining hard on the Rambla de Santa Mónica, and Carvalho felt a sudden shiver down his spine that made him nostalgic for sheets and blankets, for gentle bouts of flu and the muffled sounds of domestic bustle. Pepe, Pepe, shall I make you a lemonade? *Treasure Island* in his hands, and Fernando Forga reading *The Adventures of Inspector Nichols* on the radio.

*

'Tonight we can eat with my friend Beser, at his San Cugat flat. I'll call for you. Be ready. This year you decided not to come to my place in the country for the slaughtering of the pig, so if Mohammed won't go to the Maestrazgo, then the Maestrazgo will just have to come to Mohammed.'

Fuster's phone call put him in a good mood. He went through the notes he had taken during his conversation with Teresa Marsé. He had circled the name of Nisa Pascual, the last teenager in Stuart Pedrell's known life. In the afternoons, she frequented an art school halfway along the road to Vallvidrera. The school was in a modernist tower which rose from the luxurious vegetation of a stream bed and looked conspicuously artificial amid the neatly kept greenery of mature and stately trees. Students were strolling on the grass, idly chatting and soaking up the moist fragrance with which the rain had endowed this earthly paradise. The first lights of evening were shining from refurbished classrooms that had once been the bedrooms of a private mansion. The retinal colours of primitive painting had taken possession of doors, windows, frames and windows, revealing a playful house given over to a life and culture of imagination.

Nisa was at an art-meditation class. The students seemed to be observing a minute's silence for someone or something. But the minute stretched into four . . . five . . . ten. Through the window, Carvalho watched the silence and the meditation and he had his doubts. Finally the bodies came to life again. A woman teacher dressed in more or less oriental style moved her lips and arms as if she were administering the last rites. There was a round of questions, and then the students made for the exit. Nisa came out with two other girls, as tall and fair-haired as herself. She wore long, plaited hair that cascaded down her slim back almost to her buttocks. There was a look of virgin innocence in those large blue eyes surrounded by freckles. Carvalho beckoned to her, and she came over with an air of curiosity.

'Can I have a word with you?'

'Sure.'

'I'm a private detective.'

'Have they hired you here? That's too much!'

She laughed with delight at her lucky find. So loudly that her two companions drew closer to ask her the reason.

'I'm just coming. I'll tell you all about it. Today's my lucky day!'

Carvalho met the girls' inquisitive stare with a look that was part admonitory and part provocative.

'A necklace has been stolen. It was very valuable. Are you meant to be looking for it?'

'Carlos Stuart Pedrell has been murdered, and I'm meditating on the case. By the way, what were you meditating about in there?'

'It's a new way of studying. It's as important to think about painting as it is to actually paint. Do you know how to think?'

'Nobody ever taught me.'

'It's something you have to learn for yourself. What were you saying about Carlos?'

A smile hovered on her pursed babyish lips.

'He's dead.'

'I know.'

'I've been told you were a good friend of his.'

'That was a long time ago. He went off on a trip and showed up dead.'

'Didn't he ever contact you after he disappeared?'

'No. To tell you the truth, he was very angry with me. He'd asked me to go along with him, and I'd refused. If it had been a short trip, for a couple of months or so, then I'd have gone. But there was no time limit. I was very fond of him. He was so kind of soft and helpless. But it wasn't my scene to go chasing after Paradise Lost.'

'Didn't he change his plans when you decided not to go with him?'

'He even began to say that he wouldn't go. But then he suddenly vanished, and I assumed that he'd finally made his mind up. He needed that trip. It was an obsession with him. There were days when he was quite unbearable. But he was a wonderful companion. One of the people who've most influenced me. He taught me a lot of things. He was so restless and full of curiosity.'

'At last! Someone with something good to say of Stuart Pedrell!'

'Has everybody else spoken badly of him?'

'Let's say that no one took him seriously.'

'He was well aware of that, and it hurt him.'

'During his long absence, did he never get in touch with you?'

'It would have been hard for him. I was pretty shaken up. I couldn't believe it was all over, that a whole part of my life was behind me. I got a grant to study art in Italy and I spent nearly a year there. In Siena, Perugia, Venice . . .'

'Alone?'

'No.'

'The king is dead, long live the king.'

'I've never had a king. Are you a moralist?'

'It's my role. I always have to be suspicious of people's morality.'

'Oh, I see . . . Fascinating! I've never met a private detective before. I saw one once on TV, and he wasn't at all like you. He spent the whole programme talking about all the things he couldn't do under the present state of the law.'

'Under the present state of the law, we can't do anything.'

'I've got to go to my project class.'

'Do you project projects? Or do you think about projecting projects?'

'I enjoy it a lot here. Why don't you enrol. You could bring a bit of mystery into the place. Maybe we could plan a crime, and you'd investigate it.'

'Who would you like to kill?'

'No one. But we could sell the idea to the victim. The people here are very imaginative.'

'Did your refusal leave Stuart Pedrell very disappointed?'

'Very. Almost desperate.'

'But he still . . .'

'But he still what?'

' . . . still left you.'

'The relationship was already over. If he needed to go off, it was basically because he no longer needed anything from any of us: not from his family, nor from anyone else. If I'd gone with him, it would only have lasted a few weeks before he discovered my doubts . . . Our doubts.'

'The class has started,' said one of her friends as she passed by.

Carvalho's eyes lingered on the friend's small waist, and on the mane of curly blonde hair tumbling over her shoulders.

'Give me a ring one day and we can talk more about your job. If you like, I'll ask my friend along. I see she's taken your fancy.'

'She's my type.'

'Shall I call her over and tell her?'

'I'm expected at a meeting of veterans.'

'Veterans of what?'

'Of a secret war. It's never been in the books. If I have to talk to you again, I'll come back here and look her up.'

A few minutes later, he discovered that the art-meditation school was not visible from his house. Never mind – he'd get a good view from the Vallvidrera cable-car station. With a pair of binoculars, he could spend his time looking out the girl with the small waist and the curly hair. Until she finished her studies, that is, and set up a shop selling picture frames and decorated mirrors.

'What are you doing with the binoculars?' shouted Fuster, as he leaned from his car window.

'I want to see a woman.'

Fuster looked towards distant Barcelona.

'Where? On the Plaza del Pino?'

'No. At the foot of the cable-railway.'

'*Cherchez la femme*! Who's she killed?'

'She was a real stunner.'

On the hill, a woman was struggling under the combined weight of herself and her shopping basket. She stopped and listened as she got her breath back.

'My fellow countryman is expecting us. Don't forget your indigestion pills.'

As Carvalho went to get into the car, Bleda started barking behind the trellis gate.

'Ha! You've bought a dog! What's this – the male menopause?'

'My menopause can't be compared with yours. Where did your goatee end up, eh?'

Fuster stroked his lewdly bare chin.

'As Baudelaire says, a dandy must aspire to be ever sublime. He must live and sleep in front of the mirror.'

*

Beser lived in San Cugat, in a flat that seemed to contain nothing but books and a kitchen. He was like a red-haired Mephistopheles with a Valencian accent. He scolded Fuster for their late arrival, which had placed the paella in jeopardy.

'Today you'll have a real *paella valenciana*,' he informed Fuster.

'Have you followed what I told you?'

Beser swore that he had followed his mentor's instructions to the letter. Fuster began walking through the book-lined corridor towards the kitchen. Carvalho mused that with just half of such a stock, he could have a fire in his grate from now until the day he died. As if sensing what was in the detective's mind, and without turning round, Fuster warned:

'Careful, Sergio, this guy burns books. He uses them to light the fire.'

'Is that true?'

'Absolutely.'

'It must give extraordinary pleasure.'

'There's nothing to beat it.'

'Tomorrow I'll start to burn this shelf. Without even looking at what books are there.'

'It gives even more pleasure if you choose them.'

'I'm a sentimentalist, though. I'd be sure to reprieve some of them.'

In the kitchen, Fuster marched up and down like a sergeant major inspecting Beser's work. The ingredients had been cut into pieces that were too large. He groaned, as if wounded to the quick.

'What the hell's this?!'

'Onion.'

'Onions in paella! Where did you get an idea like that! Onion makes the rice go soft.'

'That's ridiculous. They always use onions in my village.'

'In your village, you'd do anything to get yourselves noticed! Onion can be used in a fish or salted-cod *arroz* cooked in a casserole. In a casserole, do you hear?'

Beser stormed out and returned with three books under his arm: the *Valencian Gastrosophic Dictionary*, *Gastronomy of Valencia Province*, and *A Hundred Typical Rice Dishes of the Valencia Region*.

'Don't come to me with any book that's not written by someone from Villores. To hell with you Morellanos. I go by the memory of my people.'

Fuster raised his eyes to the kitchen ceiling and held forth:

'O noble symphony of all the colours!
O illustrious paella!
O polychromatic dish
eaten by eyes before touching the tongue!
Array of glories where all is blended.
Divine compromise between chicken and clam.
O contradictory dish

both individual and collective!
O exquisite dish
where all is fair
where all tastes are as distinct as the colours of the rainbow!
O liberal dish where a grain is to a grain
as a citizen to the suffrage!

Beser pored over his books, ignoring Fuster's poetic outburst. Finally he closed them and laid them aside.

'Well?'

'You were right. Onion isn't used in the paella of the people of Castellón. It was a lapse. A catalanism. I'll have to go to Morella. I'm in urgent need of a refresher course.'

'Ha!' exclaimed Fuster, as he threw the onion into the rubbish bin. 'I made myself quite clear. Half a kilo of rice, half a chicken, a quarter-kilo of pork shoulder, a quarter-kilo of peas, two peppers, two tomatoes, parsley, saffron, salt, and nothing else. Anything else is superfluous.'

Fuster set to work, while Beser plied him with little pieces of fried bread with chorizo and Morella blood sausage. Beser took out a bottle of Aragón wine, and glass followed glass like a chain of buckets damping down a forest fire. Fuster had brought from the car a greasy cardboard box which he handled as if it contained precious objects. Beser, impatient to discover the contents, suddenly shouted with enthusiasm:

'*Flaons*! Did you make these for me, Enric?'

They embraced like two compatriots meeting at the South Pole, and explained to the by now inebriated Carvalho that *flaons* are the absolute best patisserie to be had in all the Catalan lands. Throughout the Maestrazgo, they are made with oily dough, aniseed and sugar, and filled with curd cheese, ground almond, egg, cinnamon and grated lemon peel.

'My sister sent them yesterday. Curd cheese is very awkward and goes off very quickly.'

Beser and Fuster caught the aroma coming from the paella.

'Too much pepper,' Beser suggested.

'Wait till you taste it, idiot,' replied Fuster, bending like an alchemist over his retort vials.

'A few snails to add the final touch. That's what's missing. Pepe, today you'll have a real paella from its homeland, the one they used to make before fishermen corrupted it by drowning the fish in roux.'

'It's a good thing you eat it yourself.'

'It's because I'm studying anthropology.'

They put the paella on the kitchen table, and Carvalho prepared to eat it country-style, without plates, simply demarcating a portion of territory within the container. In theory it was a paella for five people, whose only effort would be to keep themselves well lubricated. They finished the five-litre bottle of wine, and began another. Then Beser brought out a bottle of Mistela de Alcalá de Chisvert for the *flaons*.

'Before you can no longer tell a sonnet from a piece of the telephone directory, you must solve the problem my detective friend wants to consult you about. By the way, I still haven't introduced you. On my right, Sergio Beser, a mean, red-haired son of a bitch weighing in at seventy-eight kilos. On my left, Pepe Carvalho. How much do you weigh? Sergio's the man who knows more about Clarín than anyone. So much so that if Clarín came back to life, he'd slaughter him. Nothing literary is beyond him. What he doesn't know, I do. "Robust slaves, sweating from the kitchen fires, left the first-course delicacies on the table, on huge plates of red Sagunto terracotta . . ." Who's that by?'

'*Sónnica the Courtesan*, by Blasco Ibáñez,' said Beser petulantly.

'How do you know?'

'When we're going to get drunk, you recite Pemán's ode to paella; and when you are drunk, you come out with the banquet that Sónnica organized in Sagunto for Acteon of Athens.'

' "Each diner had a slave in attendance behind him, and from the crater they filled the cups for the first libation." ' While Fuster continued with his solitary recitation, Carvalho produced the sheets of paper on which he had typed Stuart Pedrell's literary hieroglyph. Beser suddenly assumed the gravity of a diamond specialist, and his diabolic ruddy eyebrows rose, bristling, to the challenge. Fuster stopped to fill his mouth with the last *flaon*. Beser rose to his feet and walked round his guests twice. He drank his Mistela, and Fuster refilled his glass. The professor recited in a low voice, as if trying to memorize the lines of verse. Then he returned to his chair and left the paper on the table. His voice was as cool as if he had been drinking iced water all evening, and as he spoke he rolled himself a cigarette of light Virginia tobacco.

*

'The first line is no problem. It comes from T.S.Eliot's *Waste Land*. My favourite line in the poem is: "I will show you fear in a handful of dust." But that's not got a lot to do with the business of going south. I don't want to bore you, but I should say that the myth of the south, as a symbol of warmth and light, of life and the rebirth of time, is a very common theme in literature – particularly once the Americans discovered it as a cheap place to spend their holiday dollars.

'The second fragment is also rather obvious. It's from *The South Seas* – the first poem published by Pavese, an Italian poet much influenced by American literature. He never actually went to the South Seas, and he wrote this poem under the influence of reading Melville. Have you read Melville? Don't give me that book-burner's look! Reading is a solitary and perfectly harmless vice. In this poem, Pavese writes of an adolescent's fascination with a sailor relative who had travelled halfway round the world. When the relative returns, the boy asks him about his travels in the South Seas, but the sailor's answers are full of disillusionment. For the boy, the South Seas are a paradise; for the sailor, they're just another landscape marked by the daily routine of work. In my opinion, poets are a disagreeable bunch. They're like women. They trap you and leave you not knowing where you are. They're prick-teasers.

'As for the third fragment, it's difficult to say where it's from. It's a perfect hendecasyllabic, and could have been written by any Italian poet since the sixteenth century. But that nostalgia for the south gives it a more modern ring. Maybe it's by a poet from the Italian south, and maybe he's referring to Sicily or Naples. *Più nessuno mi porterà nel sud*. Something tells me I know it. *Più nessuno mi porterà nel sud*. In any case, the three fragments suggest a full cycle of disenchantment: the intellectual's self-image of reading all night and then going south in the winter, so as to cheat coldness and death; then the fear that this mythical south might turn out to be just more routine and disenchantment; and finally, total disillusionment . . . No more will anyone carry me south.'

'But he put together these three fragments when he'd decided to go south. When he even had the tickets bought, and the hotels booked.'

'Which south, though? Maybe he discovered that although he was in the south, he would never actually reach the south. As García Lorca once wrote: "Although I know the road, I shall never reach Córdoba." Do you understand? Poets like to pay tricks on us, and on themselves. Did you hear that, Enric? The little pansy knows the road, but doesn't go to Córdoba. Poets really are the dregs. Like his compatriot, Alberti, who says he'll never go to Granada. He took it into his head to punish the city. I myself have a different conception of poetry: it should be didactic and historical. Do you know my scenic poem on El Cid's campaign through the kingdom of Valencia? Enric and I will act you a little extract from it, when we've drunk a few more bottles and Enric is willing to play the fool. *Più nessuno mi porterà nel sud*. I'm going to go and read the spine of every poetry book on those shelves, and then I'm sure it'll come to me.'

He climbed up a little library ladder and began to look down the shelves. Every now and then he took a book down, leafed through it, and occasionally exclaimed in surprise: 'I didn't even know I had this book!' Fuster, meanwhile, was listening mournfully to a record of Gregorian chant that he had put on for his own pleasure. 'Getting warm! Warmer!' Sergio Beser was now actually perched on a bookshelf, looking for all the world like a pirate in a boarding party. 'Can't you two smell the South Seas? I can hear the surf.' He pulled out a slim, tattered volume. First he flicked through it, barely pausing to read. Then he swooped on one of the pages.

'I've got it! Here it is!'

Fuster and Carvalho jumped to their feet, excited at the prospect of a revelation now so close to hand. All the warmth of the food and alcohol rose with them, and through clouds of emotion, they saw Sergio standing at the masthead, with the missal between his hands. He had the solemn face of someone about to unveil a dramatic denouement.

'*Lamento per il sud*, by Salvatore Quasimodo. *La luna rossa, il vento, il tuo cuore di donna del Nord, la distesa di nave . . .* It's like Vendrell's *L'Emigrant* or Juanito Valderrama's *El Emigrante*, but with a Nobel Prize attached. Here it is: *Ma l'uomo grida la sorte d'una patria. Più nessuno mi porterà nel sud.*'

With an audible cracking of much-abused knee-joints, he jumped down from the bookcase and handed the little book to Carvalho. *La vita non è sogno*, by Salvatore Quasimodo. 'Life is not a dream.' Carvalho read the poem. The lament of a southerner who realizes that he is powerless to return south. His heart has remained in the green fields and overcast waters of Lombardy.

'It's almost a social poem. Very little ambiguity. Not very polysemic, as *Tel Quel* would say. This collection was published shortly after the war, at the height of critical neo-realism. Just think: "The south is tired of carting round corpses . . . tired of loneliness, of chains . . . tired of the blasphemies of those whose shouts of death have echoed in its wells, who have drunk the blood from its heart." There is also an amorous counterpoint to the poem: in revealing his sadness as an uprooted southerner, he is speaking to the woman he loves . . . Is all this of any use to you?'

Carvalho re-read Stuart Pedrell's sheet of paper.

'Just literature, in other words.'

A drop of contemptuous spittle flicked from his lip.

'Yes, I would say so. Just literature. It's amazing the obsession that people have about the south. Maybe it meant something before the days of tour operators and charter flights, but now the south no longer exists. The Americans have built a literary mythology out of nothing, and the south owes its very existence to them. The word "south" has a primal meaning for every North American. It's their accursed place, their vanquished territory in a land of conquerors; the only defunct white civilization in the United States – the Deep South. Everything else follows from that . . . Do you really not know our Valencian theatre cycle? In a moment, Enric and I will perform it for you. You'll see the difference between a literature of posed sentiment and a genuine popular literature. I'll be El Cid, and you, Enric, the King of the Moors.'

'You always take the best parts.'

'Not another word! I shall now set the scene. Here is El Cid – although some people say that he wasn't actually the Cid. Anyway, here is the lord of Morella at the city gates, and he sees the approach of the Moorish troops. He goes to the Moor commander and says:

'CID: Who are you that watches me from atop your horse?
MOOR: I am king of the Moors, come to conquer this town.
CID: You shall not succeed.
MOOR: Then we're going to fuck your women.
CID: Then there will be war.
MOOR: Then let there be.
CID: Trumpeter, blow your horn!'

Beser and Fuster began singing and jigging around:

'Ox shit
When it dissolves
Melts away.
So does cow shit.
Donkey shit doesn't, though.'

When they finally came to rest in front of Carvalho, he clapped until his hands hurt. The professor and the manager bowed gravely.

'That first piece could be called "The Defence of Morella". The next one takes place before the gates of Valencia.'

Fuster went on all fours, and Beser sat on top of him.

'I'm El Cid, riding on his horse Babieca. A Moor, whom you will have to imagine, exclaims:

'MOOR: Why, by heaven, it's the Cid!
ANOTHER MOOR: Why, it's the whore!
FIRST MOOR: Not the whore, but Ximena.'

'That's it,' said Beser, dismounting.

'Popular theatre is always short. Do you know *David and the Harp*?'

Just as Carvalho was saying no, a hot belch came up from his liver. Beser rolled another cigarette. Fuster was dozing, face down, on the kitchen table.

'You have to imagine the palace of Jerusalem. David is furious with Solomon for reasons we don't need to go into. But he is clearly furious. Imagine all the Asiatic luxury you can, and whatever kind of harp you like. Have you ever seen a harp?'

Carvalho drew the form of a harp in the air. Beser examined it with a critical eye.

'More or less. Anyway, David is furious with Solomon for reasons we don't need to go into. Solomon says: "David, play the harp." David looks at him, and frowns. He takes the harp and throws it in the river. That's all. What do you think of it?'

Carvalho stood up to applaud. Beser gave the half-smile of a victorious toreador feigning modesty. Fuster lifted himself off the table and tried to clap, but had difficulty making his hands meet.

Then the little light remaining in Carvalho's head went out. He felt himself being dragged into a car, and amid false images and memories, he found himself heaped with Enric Fuster in the rear seat of a car that was neither his nor Fuster's. The professor's ruddy face extended into the glowing tip of a lighted cigarette which helped him to see the road down which the car was travelling in an attempt to prove that a straight line is the shortest distance between two points.

*

He pictured his liver as some kind of animal half consumed by sulphuric acid. A purée of shit and blood. His head and legs felt slow and heavy, and he had a Saharan thirst. Water. The thirst swelled from his mouth and took over his chest. As he groped for the refrigerator in the dark, he patted his liver in an attempt to gain its indulgence and calm its fury. Never again. Never again. Why did he do these things? One drinks in the hope or expectation of that click that will open ever-closed doors. He picked up the bottle of ice-cold mineral water and filled his mouth, letting the liquid dribble down his pyjama front. Then he looked for a particular crystal-cut glass which he used only for bottles of champagne costing over five hundred pesetas. He filled it with the same cold water that had just served him as a shower. This, he decided, would be his early morning champagne.

'You're like a pensioned-off duke. With haemorrhoids. This very morning you'll be trying to get a passage to the South Seas. Waiter, please commission my fellow countryman, the Valenciano, to make me an ice-swan filled with fresh lychees . . . What the hell is a Valencian waiter doing in this story?!'

He had read it somewhere. Or maybe he would make a sailing

boat for his shipwrecked companions. Read until late in the night, and then all go south in the winter. Do you all really have any idea where the south is? But when I tell him that he is among the lucky ones who have seen day break over the most beautiful islands on earth, he smiles at the memory and replies that when the sun rose, the day was already old for them.

'The south is the other face of the moon.'

As he said, or rather shouted, the word 'moon', he felt grateful for the water's coolness as it assuaged the heat of the alcohol and the self-disgust inside him. The other face of the moon. A shower – first hot, then cold – refreshed the skin round his brain. Six in the morning. Day was trying to break through. Trees were already imposing their shape on the horizon.

'The other face of the moon.'

He was telling himself something. He caught himself looking for a street map of the city, that he kept for his more sordid investigations. The wife entered the furnished flat on Avenida de Hospital Militar at 4.30 pm. A surprising time, since adulterous women generally prefer to enter furnished flats after dark. A bit silly for you to ask me whether she was with anyone. The tatty street map lay open before him, like the tired skin of some overworked beast of burden, falling apart at the seams. He put his finger on the area where Stuart Pedrell's body had been found. His eye travelled across to the other end of town, to San Magín. A man is stabbed to death, and his killers have an idea. Decontextualize him. He's to be taken right across town, but to a human and urban setting where his death would still make sense.

'Did you travel to the South Seas by underground?'

As no reply was forthcoming from Stuart Pedrell, Carvalho focused his attention on San Magín. He opened the book which the man from Morella had lent him. A large number of speculative ventures were credited to Stuart Pedrell, of which the most important was the one in the *barrio* of San Magín. He thumbed through the reference book.

'In the late 1950s, as part of Mayor Porcioles's speculative expansion policy, the Iberisa Construction Co. (*see* Munt, Marquess of; Planas Ruberola; Stuart Pedrell) bought up areas of unused land at very low prices. The little remaining industry in the district was on its last legs, and the family market gardens of the "Camp de Sant Magí" came under the jurisdiction of the Hospitalet municipal council. Between the Camp de Sant Magí and the outer limits of Hospitalet, there was a large area of open ground on which the ring-development tendency of property speculation was once again in evidence. Development land was bought up quite a long way outside the city limits, so that the zone between the new urban development and the old city limit rose in value. Iberisa Construction built a whole suburb in Sant Magí, and at the same time bought up cheaply the remaining land between the new development and Hospitalet. In the second phase, this no-man's land was also urbanized, and the company's initial investment grew a thousandfold . . .'

San Magín was populated by a mainly immigrant proletariat. The sewage system was not properly completed until five years after they had moved in. Municipal services were completely lacking. There were angry demands for a health clinic. Between ten and twelve thousand inhabitants. A smart piece of work, Stuart Pedrell. Was there a church? Yes. A modern church was built next to the old San Magín hermitage. The whole development gets flooded when the Llobregat drainage system overflows.

Yes, Stuart Pedrell. The criminal returns to the scene of his crime. You went to San Magín to take a close look at your handiwork, to see how your coolies were living in their purpose-built hovels. A voyage of exploration? Researching true popular culture? What were you studying – the habits and customs of immigrants? The intervocalic pronunciation of the letter 'd'? Why the hell did you go to San Magín, Stuart Pedrell? Did you go by taxi? Or bus? No. Underground. You must have gone by underground, so as to achieve a closer identity of form and content on your long trip to the South Seas. And people say that poetry and adventure are impossible in the twentieth century! You only have to take the underground and you're off on a low-cost emotional safari. Someone killed you. They transported you back across the border. Then they dumped you on what, for them, was the far side of the moon.

The alcohol branched out through his veins like molten lead, and he fell asleep on the sofa. The street map finally tore beneath the weight of his body. He was awakened by the cold and by Bleda licking his face. He slowly retraced the logical steps of his journey earlier that morning. He tried to resuscitate his fragmented city map, but succeeded only in tearing it further. He was left holding the portion displaying San Magín.

Hazy memories came back to him. Of country houses and cement reservoirs. His mother coming towards him with a shopping basket full of rice and oil bought on the black market from one such house. They crossed the railway tracks. In the distance loomed a sparse, raggedy post-war town, full of grey wood and empty spaces.

They poured the oil from a musty wineskin and he watched it fill the bottle like a stream of green liquid mercury. This was real oil, not the stuff you got with ration coupons. He walked back. In his oilskin bag were five long loaves of white bread, as white as gypsum. Field after field. Stony tracks which bore cyclists coloured mauve by the setting sun, and carts drawn by horses as slow and heavy as their own manure. Then the streets of the town began to spread out into a suburb of dingy modern blocks which co-existed with little old turretted houses and homes expropriated by the Civil War victors to complete the punishment of the vanquished. Streets that changed from earth to paving stone, before finally being dissected by the splintering metal of tramlines. They trudged home, tired from the long walk, with adventure in their basket and the hope of a sated hunger in their eyes.

'I'll make up some red pepper, salt and oil, and we'll have butter on the bread.'

'But I like bread with oil and sugar.'

'It'll give you worms.'

But his mother could not leave the disappointment in his eyes for long.

'All right. But if you get worms, I'll have to give you a teaspoonful of Dr Sastre y Marqués syrup.'

*

The underground, any underground, is an animal resigned to its subterranean bondage. Some of this resignation rubs off on the passengers as they travel to their appointed destinations, their faces tinged by utilitarian lighting and their bodies gently rocking with the rhythmic motion of the brutish machine. For Carvalho, taking the subway was to experience once again the feelings of a young man going somewhere, contemptuous of this gathered mass of submissive, cattle-like humanity, while he himself only used the metro to reach the green grass of promotion and higher things. He recalled his youthful daily surprise at all the fresh marks of personal defeat on people's faces. He recalled how aware he had been of his own uniqueness and superiority, as he fought off the sickness that seemed to engulf the mediocre lives of these travellers. He was uncomfortable with his fellow-passengers. He felt that his journey was taking him forward, while theirs was simply taking them back.

Twenty years later, he found himself feeling only solidarity and fear. Solidarity with the old man in the two-tone suit and a three-day growth of beard, clutching in his hand a greasy wallet full of unpaid bills. Solidarity with the cubic, slant-eyed women from Murcia, chatting in incomprehensible dialect about Aunt Encarnación's birthday. Solidarity with all the neatly dressed children of the poor who had joined the freedom train of culture too late. *The Road to Confidence in Self-Expression . . . Anaya's Dictionary of the Spanish Language*. Girls dressed as Olivia Newton-John if you imagined Olivia Newton-John buying her clothes at an end-of-season sale in some Spanish department store. Boys with the masks of disco spivs and the muscles of the long-term unemployed. Here and there, the reassuring bone structure of a junior real-estate executive whose car was being repaired and who had therefore decided to use public transport in order to lose weight and save a bit of money which he would then spend on small, mediocre whiskies probably served by an inept barman with dandruff, dirty nails and ambitions that extended no further than the opportunity to call him Don Roberto or Señor Ventura as occasion demanded. The fear on all their faces, of being the victims of a banal, irreversible journey from poverty into nothingness. Their world was a landscape of filthy, latrine-like stations, covered with tiles stained black by the invisible dirt of subterranean electricity and the foul breath of the masses. As they shuttled to and fro, the people seemed to be performing a ritual transfer in justification of the machine's routine drudgery.

Carvalho went up the worn, jagged metal steps two at a time, and emerged at a junction of two narrow streets jammed with juggernaut lorries and battered buses. *Make your voice heard. Vote Communist. Vote PSUC. Socialism has no answers. Down with reformism! Vote for the Party of Labour.* The posters did not quite obscure walls of prematurely aged brick and flaking plaster. On the hoardings, the generously financed neatness of government propaganda flaunted itself like a tour operator's promotion: *The Centre Lives Up To Its Promise.* Above the makeshift left-wing posters, above the sophisticated propaganda of a government of young turks razor-trimmed by top class barbers, almost on a level with a sky the colour of cheap toy metal, a triumphant banner proclaimed: *You are now entering San Magín.*

It was not quite true. San Magín rose at the end of a street of irregular buildings, where the weatherbeaten functionalism of 1950s-style housing for the poor co-existed with the prefabricated beehives of more recent years. San Magín itself presented a symmetrical horizon of identical blocks of flats that advanced towards Carvalho and promised a labyrinth. The skyborne announcement added: *A new town for a better life. The satellite town of San Magín was inaugurated by His Excellency the Head of State on 24 June 1966*. The inscription stone was in the centre of an obelisk which had seemingly been placed there by a prodigious feat of strength on the part of some Herculean crane. The sharp concrete edges hurt the eyes, and were not softened by the humanizing presence of women in padded nylon housecoats, or by the dull sounds of humanity that emerged from every recess. The air smelt of frying oil and the dankness characteristic of fitted cupboards. Butane delivery men; women on their daily trail to the supermarket; fishmongers' shops displaying grey, sad-eyed fish. Two bars: El Zamorano and El Cachelo. One dry-cleaner's: Turolense. Sale – Big Reductions on All Fabrics. Graffiti: *Free Carrillo. The Fascists Are the Real Terrorists. Special Classes for Handicapped Children. Day Nursery at Hamelín*. Each of these phrases had survived by some miracle, as if they were vegetation growing from the concrete. Each frontage was like a face, complete with square, pupil-less eyes darkened by an advancing leprosy.

'Have you ever seen this man?'

The woman took a step back and looked at Carvalho, but not at the photograph he held out to her.

'What did you say?'

'Do you recognize this man?'

'I'm in a hurry.'

Without giving him time to explain, she moved off with the ease and resolve of a helicopter. Carvalho was left clutching the photograph and scolding himself for making such a dismal start to a quest in which he intended to leave no stone unturned until he was sure he was hot on Stuart Pedrell's Paco Rabane scent. As if watching from the outside, Carvalho saw himself going into shop after shop and showing the photograph time and time again. Only twice did anyone look at it, and only then because they thought it was some kind of free offer. Most of them did not even look. Instead, they scrutinized Carvalho, while their nostrils shied at his scent of policeman.

'I'm trying to find him. He's a relative of mine. Didn't you hear the appeal for information on Radio Nacional?'

No. They hadn't heard the appeal on Radio Nacional. Carvalho retraced his steps down streets with regional names that tried to convey the illusion of an immigrant Spanish microcosm that had been assembled there through the creative genius of the satellite town's developers. He followed a number of hard-hatted bricklayers into a bar-cum-restaurant, where upwards of a hundred workers were bent over the midday special of lentil stew and veal casserole. Carvalho wolfed down the set meal and used a fifty-peseta tip to establish a link with the waiter – a shy young man from Galicia, with a pimple on each cheek and a rash of festering chilblains on his hands. He answered Carvalho's questions without once looking him in the eye. He had been living in the area for two years. He was a nephew of the bar's cleaning lady. He had been told to come from his village. He ate and slept on the bar premises, in the room where they stored the empty drink crates.

'No. I've never seen this gentleman.'

'Is there a smarter restaurant in the area?'

'Smarter, yes. But I don't think you'll eat better there. The food here is simple, but it's good.'

'I'm sure it is. I was just thinking that my relative might have gone to the other one. People like variety.'

The air smelt of coffee laced with Fundador brandy. Young workers were laughing, talking in loud voices, pushing each other, threatening to crush each other's balls, or arguing over who was the better wing-forward, Carrasco or Juanito. The older ones were stirring the sugar in their coffee with the air of connoisseurs. They took the photo, held it at a distance from eyelids dusted with cement, and fingered it a little as if in search of some clue. The answer on the face of the collective was a consistent 'no'.

The landlord was loth to waste time that could be used to ring up another two hundred and fifty pesetas for two set meals. He glanced at the photo over his shoulder and shook his head. His wife was peeling potatoes with one hand while pouring coffee with the other and simultaneously giving her daughter a tongue-lashing. The girl, who had spots on her face and beads of sweat in her armpits, proceeded to clear the tables at the speed required by her mother. The next-in-line to inherit the business, a potato-nosed John Travolta, was meticulously pruning his fingernails. With his denim legs crossed and his small buttocks gently propped against the refrigerator, he was totally immersed in removing a tiny particle of flesh from the little finger of his left hand.

*

'Best wines from Jumilla.'

Carvalho went into the wine shop, which was architectually no different from any restaurant, chemist or dry-cleaner's in the area, and asked for a bottle of white Jumilla. The owner was a hundred and fifty kilos of white-skinned humanity whose pallor was relieved only by a dark pair of creased rings under his eyes. He and Carvalho were the only people in a shop dominated by a huge cold store. As its wood and chrome door swung open and shut, the noise reminded Carvalho of the refrigerators in the bars and taverns of his own end of town. It was a huge reproduction, built on the scale of its owner and lined internally with green tiles. The man sought to penetrate the zone of silence surrounding Carvalho.

'What a ridiculous situation! A disaster! I'd set them to work with a shovel and pick. And as for the rest of them – up against the wall! We're sixteen million too many. Not one more and not one less. It'll take a war to sort it out.'

Carvalho downed another glass and nodded without enthusiasm, but just sufficiently for the hundred and fifty kilos to shuffle over and spread themselves on the chair opposite.

'Do *you* think it's right? Obviously not. I'm a man who likes to get things straight. I like to be treated right. See the wood for the trees. But to be strung along by some smart-arsed talker. No sir! That's not for me. Like I say, there are sixteen million too many of us in Spain. Nobody's got the answers. *He* knew how to keep us knuckled down. If anyone stepped out of line – whoosh! Off with their heads! I never tire of saying it: I prefer to be told things straight. I like to know the truth. If that's the way you want it, OK. But don't start dressing it all up and pussy-footing around. No. That won't wash. As far as I'm concerned, they can all take a running jump. I've always spoken my mind, just like I am now. And I've had all I can take. Do you see what I mean?'

Carvalho nodded.

'Just the other day, we were talking about what needs to be done. You do this, I do that. Fine. We agreed it. But would you believe it – an hour later, everything was up in the air again. And he still went on laughing. So much that I thought fuck it, and gave him a kick where it hurts. Do I make myself clear?'

Carvalho emptied the bottle and deposited a hundred pesetas next to ten kilos of forearm.

'Stick to your guns, friend. Otherwise they'll walk all over you.'

'They don't know who they're messing with.'

The man barely lifted his eyes from the ring of wine that Carvalho's glass had left on the formica tabletop. Carvalho went into the street and entered the fanciest barber shop he could find. The walls were hung with photos of hairdressing models, over which was displayed a sign from the old days: *We sculpt your hair*. He asked for a trim and a shave. He kept a careful eye on the barber's hands – a habit he had acquired in prison, where the most one could hope for was a tolerable level of hygiene, and where the job was always performed by a convicted murderer.

Carvalho recounted the story of his missing relation, and held out the photograph. The barber viewed it rather than studied it, as if it comprised part of the visual field that he was slicing with his other hand.

The picture passed from one customer to the next, and then back to the barber. He studied it more closely.

'His face reminds me of something . . . But,' he added hastily, 'I don't know what.' He handed it back to Carvalho.

'Keep it and give it a look now and then. I'll pass by tomorrow.'

'I'm sure I've seen that face before, you know.'

Carvalho passed the Wines-from-Jumilla *bodega* again. The proprietor was taking the air. He was muttering to himself.

'Same as before?'

'Worse.'

'Don't give in.'

'I'd sooner die.'

Carvalho left him to his thoughts and continued his perambulation. The only dentist in the whole of San Magín had seen neither the face nor the teeth of Stuart Pedrell. He learned no more from the two doctors, either, whose waiting rooms were filled with toothless pensioners chewing over softly spoken words. He called into dry-cleaning establishments, and visited a boutique where silk ties jostled men's underwear. He left no chemist's shop or newspaper kiosk unturned. Occasionally the photograph seemed to stir a flicker of recognition. But only a flicker. Nor did anyone know Stuart Pedrell in the two night schools, managed by a couple of brothers who were teachers from Cartagena. His heart was slowly sinking, and only his previous investment in walking and talking persuaded him to pursue this suicidal investigation.

'Come to a mass rally this evening! Organized by the Socialists of Catalonia. Workers, if you want a San Magín in which *you* feel at home, and not the speculators, come to the Socialist rally at the Creueta Sports Centre! The speakers will be Martín Toval,

José Ignacio Urenda, Joan Reventós and Francisco Ramos. The Socialists have the answer!'

The voice was coming from loudhailers attached to a slow-moving van. The communication aroused little excitement among the local population – evidently aware that they should vote Communist or Socialist as some kind of bio-urban necessity, but not as a matter of great enthusiasm. A few children stuck their heads through the van windows and asked for leaflets. But they soon returned to their game: the UCD ones had been prettier. A cooked meat wholesaler put the photo down beneath a hanging leg of cured pork, and a heavy gob of Trevélez ham-fat splattered Stuart Pedrell's features. The wholesaler compounded his offence by wiping the photograph with his sleeve, so that it suddenly seemed to acquire the dark glaze of twenty years in an album.

Carvalho left the shop and began knocking on doors where the janitor's function had not yet been replaced by an entryphone. Old janitors, bleached white by years spent in gloomy interiors, appeared down dark passages lit by flickering TV sets. No, they said, they had never seen the man. One block. Two. Even if it takes me two weeks, he said to himself. But he was already thinking that as soon as night fell, he would flee San Magín and follow the logical thread in some other direction. It seemed like it was always the same janitor . . . always the same doorway . . . after a while they became indistinguishable.

Suddenly he realized that the pavements were full of children. The onset of dusk seemed set to greet their shouts and bustling laughter. Someone had given the order for pregnant women to appear, and they picked their way along the pavements like unsteady ducklings. He went up to the church that stood on a neat little hillock overlooking the built-up slopes of San Magín. It was a functional church, whose crumbling fabric had borne the full brunt of wind, rains, blazing suns across treeless landscapes, and the vile vapours of industrial effluent rising from dank reedbeds that hinted at the one-time presence of a stream long since extinct.

The priest's sacristy was littered with out-of-date posters calling for official amnesties. There was also a poster in Italian advertising the film *Christ Stopped at Eboli*. The priest himself sported a beard and a 1975 vintage Camacho pullover.

'I've seen this face, but not recently. It was some time ago. I really couldn't say when or where, though. Is he a relation of yours?'

All his revolutionary mistrust glinted from one eye that was more open than the other. Carvalho left under his watchful gaze and had to decide whether to plunge back into the labyrinth of the satellite town, or to head for a brightly lit hall from whence issued the sound of music. Above the door, a sign said: *San Magín Workers' Commissions*, and inside, someone was singing a sentimental song by Víctor Manuel about love between two mentally handicapped people. He showed the photo to the caretaker, who was using wood-shavings in an attempt to light a stove in the middle of the room. The room was furnished with two dozen assorted chairs, a small fridge, a blackboard, a bookcase, and several notice-boards displaying political posters and notices of various meetings.

'Of course I knew him. He used to come here, a few months ago, soon after the club opened. He came quite often.'

'What was his name?'

'You should know! I thought you said he was a relative of yours! Here everyone called him the Accountant. No. He never actually joined, but he used to come quite a lot. Then suddenly he stopped coming.'

'Was he very active? Was he a good worker?'

'No idea. I don't know what he was like at work.'

'No. Here, I mean. Did he put in a lot of work here?'

'No. He came to meetings, but he didn't really join in the discussions. Sometimes he'd stand up and make a point, though.'

'Was he very committed?'

'No. Only so-so. We get all sorts here. Half of them want to make the revolution overnight. But he was a moderate type. Obviously well educated, though. Very careful. He didn't say a lot, so as not to offend people.'

'Would you happen to know his proper name?'

'Antonio. His name was Antonio, but everyone called him the Accountant because that was his job.'

'Where did he work?'

'I don't know.'

'Didn't he make friends? Didn't he ever come with anyone else?'

'Yes, he did.'

A smile played round his lips.

'With girls?'

'One in particular. A metalworker from SEAT. Ana Briongos.'

'Does she still come here?'

'No. Or rather, not very often. But she's very, very radical – the kind who got all worked up about the Moncloa Accords, and I'm not sure that she's calmed down yet. Some people think everything's going to change overnight just because they want it to. They haven't got the years behind them. The experience. Like the civil war. That would have given them something to think about. Man is the only animal that trips over the same stone twice, you know. She's a real working-class girl, Briongos. Real guts. As committed as they come. But too impatient. I've been in the thick of it since '34, and I've been through many things, I can tell you. You win some, you lose some, that's what I say. But don't expect *me* to go round setting fire to letterboxes. Do you think that's the way forward? Have you ever heard Solé Tura speak? I heard him once say something that made me think a lot. It went something like this: the bourgeoisie took four centuries to come to power, and the working class has only had a century of historical existence as an organized movement. Word for word. I'm quoting from memory. It's obvious that it's not going to be easy. Some people seem to think that we can just turn up at the Winter Palace with our union cards in our hands and say: "Out you go. We're in charge now!" Do you see what I mean? There are plenty of people like that. But we've got to be patient. If we just start lashing out, we'll bring the whole works down on top of us. Because they're not blind, you know. Far from it. They've got eyes like hawks.'

'Where can I find Briongos?'

'That's not up to me to tell, and no one else here will tell you either. Talk to the guy in charge if you like, but nobody ever gives their addresses here. It's a responsibility, if you see what I mean.'

'And you don't know where the Accountant worked?'

'Not really. I think he worked by the hour, doing the accounts for some fellow dealing in glassware – bottles, lab equipment and so on. Somewhere around Block Nine, because that's where I used to see him. Always very stiff. This is how he'd walk. Very stiff. We didn't trust him at first. He seemed out of place, and no one knew where he'd come from. But the fact that he was going around with Briongos was a kind of guarantee. A real fighter, that one. She was in the Modelo Prison before she was out of pigtails. Her father went there to give her a telling-off, and she told him to go take a jump. Too many people like that just get tired though, and then they just dump all those years of work and effort. Now she goes around saying that she's through, and that the bourgeoisie's got everything under control. All that kind of rubbish. Just look at me. Do you think the bourgeoisie controls me? What the hell has the bourgeoisie ever given me?'

'Don't get carried away, Cifuentes,' shouted a young man from the back of the hall. His friends joined in the laughter.

'Don't be so stupid. And mind your manners. To think that even you have turned out a bunch of bums!'

'Come and have a joint, Cifuentes.'

Or maybe you'd prefer half a kilo of plastic explosive?'

'Just listen to them. It's all just a joke for them. But if the class enemy got to hear them, can you imagine what he'd make of it? It's the thoughtlessness of youth. You have to be on your guard as you go through life, and you have to wait for the right conditions.'

'The right conditions . . .' The phrase struck an ideological chord in Carvalho's memory. The conditions may be right objectively or right subjectively. The conditions . . .

'When the Accountant suddenly disappeared, didn't anyone think it strange?'

'No. He went the same way as he'd come. If we had to worry about all the people who move in and out of the workers' movement, we'd all end up in the loony bin. Especially nowadays. At the start, everyone was high as kites and new members were flocking in. Now the commissions have a good presence in the workplace, but you won't find a lot of people around here. The only time there's any action here is when the labour lawyers come here for their advice sessions. The Franco years miseducated us, you know. When I read that Spanish people are mature enough for democracy, it drives me up the wall. Mature, my arse!'

'Don't get steamed up, Cifuentes!'

'I'll get steamed up if I want to, you little sod. Hold your noise. I'm talking to this gentleman, not to you.'

He accompanied Carvalho to the door.

'They're good kids, but they do like getting me worked up. They'd give me the shirts off their backs, but they do love teasing me. That's life, I suppose. I put up with it because I'm retired. I just come here to save the Commission having to pay someone wages. I've been in prison six times in my life. The first was in '34. Then, each time we tried to organize the commissions again, there'd be a bust-up at the Graphic Arts faculty and Cifuentes would be off to the Vía Layetana cells again. Once, I told Superintendent Creix that if he'd rather, I'd happily move in there. And the old cynic laughed. What a nasty piece of work! Someone told me he's retired now.'

'Who?'

'Creix. It may be true. He must be my age. And you don't know the best part of it.' He took Carvalho by the arm, led him into the street, and said in a low voice: 'Creix and I are colleagues.'

He stood back, to savour the surprise which he expected to see on Carvalho's face.

'You don't understand? I'll explain. During the civil war, I went on a course for officers at the Party school in Pins del Vallés. Some of us were to end up as political commissars at the front, and some would go into the police. I was told that I should join the Republic's police force. It was Comorera himself who advised me. "Look, Cifuentes," he said. "We've got as many political commissars as we need, but we don't have reliable policemen. The force is full of fifth columnists." So I went into the police. Then it all turned out the way it did. I was based as a station in Hospitalet, and my boss was Gil Lamas. Do you know the name? He must have already been a fifth columnist, because after the war he still stayed on in the force.

'Anyway, when I got out of prison in '46, I bumped into him on the Ronda – the bit where the Olimpia used to be. I don't know what they call it nowadays. And he pretended not to recognize me, right? Anyway, I went through a great deal after that. But a couple of months ago, I received a letter informing me that I could claim my rights as a policemen in the Republic. So I go to see this official, a very polite, very professional gentleman. It goes before a committee, and that's that. No problem at all. They could have dreamed up all sorts of complications, but no, it went straight through. It's incredible. Look.'

He took a well-worn sheet of folded paper from a plastic wallet. ' "Your rights have been recognized as a retired police officer with the rank of Inspector."

'An inspector! Me! With a pension of thirty thousand pesetas a month. What do you say to that? As a retired doorman from a high-class store, I used to get fifteen thousand pesetas. And now another thirty on top! I feel rich. And what's more, I'm an inspector. It was about time something good happened to me. My wife still can't believe it. All our bad luck has made her a bit distrustful. I showed her the letter. I show her the thirty thousand every month. But she's still as obstinate as ever. "Evaristo" – that's my name, "Evaristo – nothing good will come of this." What do you think?'

He was seeking an opinion from a man of the world, who lived in the city-beyond from which he had been expelled.

'Cifuentes, once you're down in the books as a public servant, no one can take it away from you. Don't worry.'

'It's not the money that I care about. It's the principle. One of these days I'm going to go and visit Creix, and all the others who flayed me alive, and I'll stick this piece of paper right up their noses.'

*

The back room of a pharmacy for giants: fifty-litre flagons made for who knows what unmentionable potions; flasks; test tubes; glass containers packed in straw and woodshavings; bare wooden shelves stained by damp and darkness; carpets; sawdust on the floor; jumpy cats; bare light bulbs; an ageing white-moustached athlete juggling with cardboard boxes; a sad-eyed alsatian sniffing at each newcomer; at the end of a corridor, amid obsolete and abandoned giant-sized glass goods, a stern man using a calculator; beside him, a boy checking emery-polished syringes; Alfredo Kraus singing *The Pearl Fishers* through a loudspeaker perched in one corner of the ceiling. Above their heads, the sound of high-heeled shoes clicking across the mezzanine floorboards.

The man with the calculator said: 'Can I help you?' He didn't even turn his head until Carvalho held the photograph of Stuart Pedrell before his nervous eyes and twitching nostrils. He concluded his calculation, gave the boy a couple of orders about what needed to be done before closing time, and walked across the shop floor, his arms and high-set shoulders moving as if they were separate from the rest of his body. As he led the way up the wooden stairs to the mezzanine floor, Carvalho noticed a little office in which a girl was typing a letter and a short-sighted, heavily built woman with sad, narrowed eyes had stopped work to make a telephone call.

'Auntie,' she was saying in Catalan, 'Mother asked me if you'll be coming up to Garriga this Sunday.' She stopped at the sight of Carvalho and then continued in a lower voice. The boss sent the girl to do something, and sat down on an office table that was jammed up against metal filing cabinets. Next to the wastepaper basket a cat was eating a piece of liver. A spaniel looked at the newcomer with all the imperturbability of a Buster Keaton. A younger spaniel, the image of Lauren Bacall, imprudently sniffed him and tried to take a lump out of his ankle before the boss's shout drove her under a table. In a cage, two demented canaries were dancing the dance of servitude. The boss flicked a switch, and Alfredo Kraus faded away. They sat in the half-silence of a warehouse submerged between one of the hundred and seventy-two apartment tower blocks of San Magín.

'Why do you say that?'

'What would you make of a man who knows Placido Domingo's recordings by heart and gives a perfect description of the final scene of Strauss's *Salome*, as interpreted by Caballé? I'm very keen on opera, and I rarely get the pleasure of meeting a real connoisseur. He was one.'

'Did you only talk about opera?'

'Opera and business. But in fact we didn't see much of each other. I manage the warehouse from downstairs, and my wife runs the office up here . . .'

'. . . Míriam's fiancé will be there too. Look, Inès. Haven't you had a letter from uncle in Argentina . . . ?'

'Where did he live?'

'Very near here, but I don't know exactly where. Why? Has something happened to him?'

'He's a relation of mine, and he's gone missing.'

'I have to admit, it did all seem rather mysterious to me, but I don't like meddling in other people's lives. As long as they do their work properly. "Hello. Good morning. Goodbye. See you tomorrow." That's my idea of an ideal relationship.'

'In general?'

'Yes. And in particular. Especially with staff.'

'May I have Señor Vila's address? The man who recommended him.'

'I don't know it. He lives at the edge of town, in a little old tower. You can't miss it. It's got a garden at the back. Is there likely to be trouble? Like I said, he was a casual worker; I paid him by the hour, and he got on fine here. That's all there was to it.'

Lauren Bacall had left her hideout and cocked a cheeky eye at the stranger. Carvalho made a half-gesture to demonstrate a dog-owner's solidarity, but she started barking. Another crack of her owner's tongue sent her scuttling back to her refuge.

'I see you're running a zoo here.'

'You start by accepting a friend's puppy, and you end up with Noah's Ark. We've also got a hamster at home.'

'. . . By the way, Inès, did you know that Piula thinks she's pregnant . . . ?'

The woman gestured goodbye to him without detaching herself from the phone. The man then saw him to the door and watched him as he went down the street. He must have switched on again, because Kraus's voice drifted out onto the road. It glided along the towering walls, tapped on closed windows, lifted the dust from melancholy geraniums, and, like a gentle breeze, fluttered several sunshades hunched on tiny balconies. Mercury street lamps as tall as palm trees cast circles of light that contrasted ever more sharply with the darkness gradually enshrouding San Magín, while a cold damp rose from the Prat and filled Carvalho's head with thoughts of blankets and a glowing fire. His steps carried him from one pool of light to the next, towards a distant floodlit banner stretched across the street. It announced the outer limits of this paradise: *You are now leaving San Magín. Come again soon.*

*

It had the air of a chalet designed by a top-notch architect and built during weekends by a team of immigrant workers on piecework. The owner, and their employer, could well have been a 1940s black-marketeer who had decided to invest his profits in a house with a garden, where he could pass an occasional day of rest far from the bustle of post-war life in the distant city.

The door was opened by a broad-shouldered, grey-haired man wearing a quilted dressing-gown and a pair of slippers lined with rabbit fur. The house smelt of bechamel. There was a sound of whining children and an angry mother. Vila took him up to his little study, where the arrangement of objects gave the impression that the room was never used. They sank into two brown leatherette sofas. Vila was visibly surprised at the photograph that Carvalho held out to him.

'Señor Stuart Pedrell.'

'You knew him?'

'Of course I knew him. I was in charge of building work in the area, first as foreman for one of the blocks, and then, after I had earned Señor Planas's trust, as general supervisor. I never had any dealings with Señor Stuart Pedrell, though. He didn't come near the building sites. What a horrible death! I read about it in the papers.'

'Does the name Antonio Porqueres mean anything to you?'

'No.'

'It seems that you recommended him to work for a local wholesaler.'

'Oh yes. But I never actually met him. It was Señor Stuart Pedrell who recommended him in the first place. He called me one day and said he needed to find work and accommodation for an old childhood friend. He asked me to be very discreet about it. I never got to see Señor Porqueres.'

'Did you say accommodation?'

'Yes.'

'Did you find him something?'

'Yes.'

'Where?'

'The company sets aside five or six flats on the estate, in case they're needed for company personnel. I handed one of them over to Señor Porqueres.'

'Without even seeing him?'

'Yes. Señor Stuart Pedrell's wish was my command. I left the keys at the caretaker's lodge, and I don't even know if the gentleman is still living there. Señor Stuart Pedrell told me he'd settle the rent directly with head office.'

'When the news broke about Stuart Pedrell, didn't it occur to you to inquire about Señor Porqueres?'

'Why? I don't see the connection. Anyway, I'd forgotten about the whole thing. My head is chock-full of a thousand housing problems every day. Do you know how many drains get blocked every day? How many toilets have to be cleared? It's as though these houses were made of paper.'

'But wasn't it you who built them?'

'I put up what they told me to.'

'I've been sent by Señora Stuart and the lawyer Viladecans. It's vital that I get to see the flat where Porqueres lived.'

'I'll give you a note to give to the caretaker. Or if you prefer, I'll get dressed and I can take you round myself.'

'Don't bother. There's no need.'

'I'll write you a note then.'

He tried three or four drafts, but wasn't happy with them and tore them up. Finally he wrote: *Señor García, do what this gentleman asks. Treat him as if he were me.*

'If you need anything else, you know where to find me. How is Señor Viladecans? Still busy in the courts? I don't know how he can stand it. Whenever I have to go there about some trouble on the estate, it always depresses me. It's so inhuman, don't you think? And how about Señora Stuart? What a tragedy! What a terrible tragedy! Señor Planas is the one I had most dealings with, because he's the one who came to the site most often. He's certainly got brains. He has this look, like he's not taking anything in . . . But it's all there in his head, from the first bit of string to the last bag of cement. This has been a very important project. I don't care how much stick we get: these people used to live in slums and overcrowded sub-lets. Now at least they've got a roof of their own. The reason the flats have started crumbling before their time is because these people don't know how to live in them. They think they're like the slum tenements they used to have. All the lifts are falling apart, because they kick them about. You can't find anything that's in proper shape. It all has to be patched up. In the end, these people will get more civilized. But it's very hard for them – a different kind of life.'

'You're lucky Zulus didn't move in.'

'You can laugh. But there are some blacks here. From Guinea and other places. It's quite impossible to keep the sub-letting under control. Homes that were just right for four have now got ten living in them. They say it's to pay the bills. But once you start, it's a slippery slope. If there's room for five, why not twenty? I've got a file full of anonymous complaints about Chilean and Argentinian sub-tenants whose papers aren't in order. Where have they all come from? I put it in the hands of Señor Viladecans. They run away from their own country, and they end up here. Well, if they run away, they must have done something, surely? The police don't go round chasing people just for the hell of it.

Believe me, it's a constant source of problems. And then they're always complaining. Nothing's ever good enough for them. I tell them: Barcelona wasn't built in eight years, or even in a century. Give it a few years, and you won't recognize the place. But we need patience. They don't seem to have heard of the word.'

García the caretaker apparently had all the patience lacking in other people. He emerged from the depths of his lodge, struggling to adjust to the air and light of the outside world. He slowly took and read the note, as if it were a dissertation on gastroenteritis.

'In other words . . .'

'In other words, I'd like to see the flat where Señor Antonio Porqueres used to live. Is anyone there now?'

'It's just as he left it. No one told me to do anything. And unless I get orders from above, I'm deaf, dumb and blind. Come in.'

On the glass-covered dining table, a young boy was doing his homework with one eye on the television. The janitor bent over the drawer of his desk, as if he had to ask his kidneys for permission. His kidneys were slow in answering. His arms matched the slow-motion gymnastic style with which the rest of his body moved through the world.

'Here's the key to the flat.'

'I'd like a key for the downstairs door too.'

'Are you staying the night?'

'I don't know.'

It took him a long time to realize that Carvalho's reply left him no option but to hand over the key. Yet he still held on to it until Carvalho snatched it away.

'It's bound to be pretty dirty. My daughter cleaned it a month ago, but since no one ever said anything to me . . . Don Antonio's things are in the bedroom and the bathroom. The other stuff was already there when he rented it. I won't come up with you. It's an effort for me to move at all.'

'So I see.'

'A draught. There's so many draughts in this lodge!'

It seemed impossible that any air could enter his crypt. The child suddenly shouted, 'eight fours are thirty-two,' and scribbled it down as if his life depended on it. Señor García shook his head and mumbled. 'Always making a noise. I can't stand noise.'

*

The lift had been patched up with sheets of plywood. The flooring bounced like a trampoline, and seemed likely either to catapault him through the roof or plunge him down the liftshaft. Carvalho hugged the walls. He got out into a cream-painted corridor thick with dust and brooding in the perpetual twilight of a row of twenty-watt bulbs encased in wire-mesh cages. Eight grey wooden doors marked the exits from eight flats. He stopped in front of 7-H. Someone had used a key to scratch the name Lola on the paintwork. The door opened with no more effort than turning the page of a book. He lit a match to help him find the fuse-box, but it was staring him in the face like some computer switchboard. Light shone down the hallway as he switched on, down the blankness of bare, smudgy walls. Then it revealed a dining room complete with a three-piece suite with faded tartan upholstery. A turned-wood lampstand with a waxed paper shade. A horseshoe on one wall; on another, a Valencian woman covering her breast with a fan. A regional flag from Bultace. A half-empty box of matches. An ashtray lying on a little table in the middle of the room, with ash still stuck to the bottom. A glass case holding sherry glasses and two books – *The Meaning of Ecstasy* by Alan Watts, and *The Happy Forties* by Barbara Probst Salomon. More books in a wooden crate next to a folding bed: *Citizens and Madmen: A Social History of Psychiatry* by Klaus Dörner; *Francis Scott Fitzgerald* by Robert Sklar; *Les Paradis Artificiels* by Baudelaire; *Man of Plaster* by Joseph Kessel; *Dialogue in Hell between*

Machiavelli and Montesquieu by Maurice Joly; a dozen or so little textbooks with titles like *What is Socialism . . .* , *What is Communism . . .* , *What is Imperialism . . .* and so on; a book by Father Xirinacs in Catalan; Cernuda's *Collected Verse*; Friedrich's *Structure of Modern Lyric Poetry*.

Pulling back the bedspread revealed folded sheets and blankets that smelt of dampness and months gone by. On the bedroom wall was pinned a map of the Pacific and the coasts of Asia and America. As ever, the mouth of Asia seemed about to take a bite out of America's backside. Yellowing and near-illegible newspaper cuttings were stuck here and there on the wall with drawing pins. Political articles on the Moncloa Accords. News items that were dated no later than early 1978, as if by then Stuart Pedrell had managed to overcome his initial urge to provide himself with points of reference on these alien walls. In a wardrobe, a dark-grey suit bought from a Hospitalet tailor; a jacket with matching trousers from the same shop; underwear; a tie and a pair of straw and canvas summer shoes.

The kitchen was a desert, inhabited only by half a dozen plates on the drying rack, a coffee pot, two coffee cups, a jar filled with a compacted mass of sugar, and another half full of curiously discoloured ground coffee. The fridge was switched off, and in it a slice of honey-roast ham had been miraculously preserved in a mummified state. A jar of French gherkins pickled in peppercorns and white-wine vinegar added an exotic touch at the far end of the refrigerator shelf, next to a half-slab of butter wrapped in tin foil. In the glass-doored kitchen cupboard, a pack of Uncle Ben rice sat next to a packet of dried soup, an unopened jar of coffee, two beers, two bottles of sparkling mineral water, half a bottle of cheap white sherry and a bottle each of Fundador brandy and Marie Brizard anis.

In the other tiny room, he found a shoe-cleaning kit and a cardboard medicine-chest full of basic medicaments: aspirin, antiseptic cream, sticking plasters, hydrogen peroxide, a bottle of neat alcohol and a blade for treating corns. In the bathroom he found a full set of towels; a bottle of *Moussel Moussel Moussel* bath gel produced by the Paris firm of Legrain; a pumice stone; a white bathrobe; a pair of Arab-style slippers; and a much-used floorcloth. He went through the flat three more times, making a mental inventory of everything.

Then he left, without switching off at the mains. He looked for a phone box in the street, but the only two in sight were out of order. He ventured into the Jumilla wine shop. The owner was sitting alone in front of a large glass of fruit brandy. He didn't bother looking up, but said that he could use the phone. Carvalho called Biscuter and asked him to go up to Vallvidrera and feed Bleda.

'I don't have anything for a dog.'

'There are things up in Vallvidrera. What did you make for me?'

'Hake in cider.'

'Where did you get the cider?'

'The man who runs the grocer's on the corner is from Asturias.'

'Give Bleda hake in cider. Make sure you take the bones out, though.'

'Hake in cider? For a dog?'

'We've got to train her palate. Did anyone ask for me?'

'The usual.'

'The girl?'

'The girl.'

'I'll call in at the office early in the morning.'

'Shall I tell her if she rings again?'

'No. Take care with the bones. Don't get one stuck in her throat.'

'You really mean that, about the hake in cider?'

'Do what you like.'

'Can't you give me any idea where you are?'

'I'm afraid I forgot my compass, so I couldn't tell you . . .'

Bon appetit, Bleda. Try some good cooking, and see what the civilized human world is all about. When I'm dead and gone, remember that I once gave you the dinner that Biscuter had lovingly prepared for me.

'How much do I owe you?'

'No one owes me anything. I'm the one who owes things . . . to everybody . . .' replied the man, from the depths of his self-absorption.

Carvalho scoured the area for a bar that was still open. They made him up a sandwich of tuna in oil, and to go with it, a portion of potato tortilla. He bought a bottle of chilled white wine of indeterminate pedigree, and then went back to Stuart Pedrell's flat and switched on the water heater. He took a shower, soaping himself with *Moussel Moussel Moussel* and wrapping himself in the musty bathrobe. He paced the flat until the empty tomb-like smell got too much for him. He checked that the sheets and blankets were clean, made the bed, and finished the wine, while leafing through every page of the books that Stuart Pedrell had rescued from his shipwreck. They were not so much carefully chosen as indicative of an intellectual thirst that Carvalho considered morbid. All he found was a scrap of paper among the pages of Cernuda's *Collected Verse*:

> I remember that we reached port after a long crossing,
> and, leaving the ship and the quay, through little streets,
> (amid dust mixed with petals and fish scales),
> I came to the square where the market stalls were.
> Great was the heat, and little the shade.

The poem was called *Islands*, and it related the adventure of a man who went to an island, had it off with a woman, and later reflected on the nature of memory and desire. 'Isn't memory the impotence of desire?' Carvalho closed the book, turned off the light and lay down on the bed. The darkness transmitted the smells of stale air, the far-off sounds of cars, a voice, a trickling of water in next-door's bathroom. Stuart Pedrell had spent the nights of a long year in that room. He had only to travel a few kilometres to get back to all that he had been for the past fifty years. But he stayed in that darkness, night after night. Playing out the role of a Gauguin distorted by a fanatical socialist-realist writer intent on punishing him for all the ruling-class sins he had committed. And the writer was none other than himself. Incapable of extracting language from himself, he had decided to convert himself into language. He lived out the novel he couldn't write, the film he would never be able to direct. But who was the audience? Who was there to clap or whistle at the end of the performance? Only he himself. 'He's an incurable narcissist,' the Marquess of Munt had said. He must have had a supreme capacity for self-contempt to have tolerated living night after night in that anonymous, amnesiac solitude.

Did you at least look in the mirror, Stuart Pedrell? He jumped out of bed, went into the bathroom, switched on the light and looked at himself in a mirror dirtied by spatters of water and toothpaste. 'You've aged, Carvalho.' He took a piece of toilet paper and went back to bed. Thinking of the Stuart widow, he masturbated as furtively as if he had been in a school toilet or behind a tree. He cleaned himself with the paper and dropped it on the floor. He was surprised at the similarity of smells between sperm and empty tombs. Then he fell asleep.

*

He woke up two hours later. He took a while realizing where he was. He tried to get back to sleep, but the musty smell and damp texture of the sheets were irritating him. He made some coffee. What can a person do in San Magín at five in the morning? Catch the bus and go to work. Halfway through the coffee, it occurred to him that Ana Briongos would soon be taking the bus to the

SEAT plant. He downed a shot of coffee. Then he thought once, thought again, and decided to try one of the pickled gherkins. It was revolting.

The lift moved slowly upwards, like a maggot climbing up the nest in which it is trapped forever. Deserted sidewalks. Down the block, though, scattered human figures could be seen moving doggedly, almost obsessively, towards the exit to Barcelona. He quickened his step in order to catch up with one of the early risers. A young man, huddled in a black leather jacket, told him that the SEAT bus left from the little square next to the obelisk which read: *A New Town for a New Life*. There were two buses waiting. Their interior lights threw their passengers into sharp relief. The buses offered a homely shelter from the sharp hostility of the early morning.

'She always takes the one behind,' said the driver of the first bus. No, she hadn't arrived yet.

'She's on the next shift. She won't be along for another hour yet.'

'You don't happen to know where she lives, do you?'

'No. But she always comes from that direction.'

Carvalho stood and watched the buses fill up and leave, as if he were the Lord of San Magín despatching his argonauts on their quest for the golden fleece. He had a choice – either to take an early-morning stroll, or to return to Stuart Pedrell's flat.

In the event, he decided to stay where he was. But then the cold drove him off in search of a cafe that might be open at that hour – a fruitless search which took up half an hour and allowed him a second look at the neighbourhood. The cement cliffs began to display a sprinkling of lighted windows. The sun broke behind the tower blocks, forming an aurora around the heads and shoulders of these grey pachyderms.

He returned to the little square, hoping to be in in luck and find Ana Briongos waiting, with enough time for a conversation. Empty buses waited in line. The early-morning workers were now arriving in groups and the advancing daylight emboldened them, so that some were talking and some even laughing. As Ana Briongos drew nearer, she assumed the shape of a short, solidly built young woman with dark, striking features, whose hair had been badly mauled by some local hairdresser. On the lapel of her quilted jacket, she wore an old badge in defence of free speech and a newer one with a slogan against nuclear power. She firmly held the gaze of the man who stopped her at six in the morning, in order to ask whether she was Ana Briongos.

'Yes. And who are you?'

'I'm looking for a missing relative. I've been through half the city, and in the end it turns out that he came to live here. Do you recognize him?'

With one eye on Carvalho and the other on the photograph, she made a move, as if to continue on her way.

'I'm sorry. The bus is leaving.'

'Not for another ten minutes. I know this isn't a good place to talk. Perhaps we could arrange something else – a meal this evening, for instance.'

'I eat in the factory canteen at the end of my shift.'

'What about later?'

'I have things to do.'

'All day?'

'Yes.'

'I'll wait for you at the end of your shift.'

'I've already told you that I don't know this gentleman.'

'Maybe you need to take another look. I was told that you used to know each other, and that you were going out together. I was told it by an old communist trade unionist – the type who never lie unless Moscow tells them to. At least, that's what I was taught as a kid.'

'OK, you don't need to keep on at me. I do know him. The sooner we get this over, the better.'

'Won't you miss your bus?'

'There's more than enough time for what I've got to tell you. The man's name in Antonio. He lived in San Magín. We got to know each other. We saw each other a few times. One fine day, he vanished, and that's all.'

'He might have vanished, but he turned up again. Dead. On an abandoned building site. He'd been stabbed.'

She turned her face to hide a rush of tears, and wept uncontrollably, with her back to Carvalho. Her woman companion rushed over.

'Are you all right?'

'Yes. I'll join you in a moment.'

She turned round and looked Carvalho in the eye. The tears had reddened her nose. Her fleshy lips were trembling as she said, 'Seven o'clock this evening. Here.'

She sat beside her friend in the bus, and must have said something about Carvalho, for the other girl listened, nodded, and looked at him in some alarm. He turned away, crossed the square to the subway entrance, and allowed himself to be carried down by the stream of humanity hurrying down metal stairs worn smooth by millions of tired steps – steps burdened with the extra weight of a realization that every new day is just like the one before, and that the stairs that you came up at night are the stairs you'll that you'll be going down again in the morning.

'You should have got into a bank when you were young. By now you'd have twenty or twenty-five years' service behind you.'

That was what his father had told him on his deathbed, repeating one last time the theme that had become his obsession as it became increasingly clear that Carvalho would pass through university, prison, the country, and life itself without ever acquiring respectability.

'Even better if it could have been the National Savings Bank. There you get an end-of-year bonus.'

Carvalho would listen indignantly, until he reached the age of thirty; then with indifference; and more recently with a growing affection. His father had wanted to bequeath him security in life, symbolized in the use of the metro or some other means of public transport, every day, twice a day. The same metro that was now carrying him towards the heart of the city. He alighted at Paralelo, crossed the rambling intersection, and began walking down Calle Conde del Asalto, in the direction of the Ramblas. He passed familiar landmarks as if he were returning from a very long voyage. The ugly poverty of the Barrio Chino had a patina of history. It was completely different from the ugly, prefabricated poverty of a neighbourhood prefabricated by prefabricated speculators. It's better for poverty to be sordid rather than mediocre, he thought. In San Magín, there were no drunks piled in doorways, absorbing what little heat they could from those appalling stairwells. But that was not progress – quite the contrary. The inhabitants of San Magín could not destroy themselves until they had paid all the bills outstanding for the little corner they occupied in the 'New Town for a New Life'.

The front page of a newspaper announced that the United States would experiment with zero growth in 1980. President Carter's photo confirmed the news – looking like the branch manager of a bank, continually surprised that one of his functions might be to bomb Moscow, or to stuff himself all day with apple pie. What would you do if you were President of the United States? You'd screw Faye Dunaway, for starters. Assuming she allowed it. I must advise you that I'm the President. Faye Dunaway would look at him with wild eyes, pretend to kiss him, and treacherously bite off his nose. I must advise you that you've just bitten off the nose of the President of the United States. Carvalho entered his office without making a sound.

Biscuter was snoring on the folding bed that he got out every night after he had prepared the elements of Carvalho's surprise meal for the next day. He was sleeping curled like a foetus, with one eye half open. Curls of lank, fair hair stood out, like stunted, misplaced antlers on the sides of his skull.

'Is that you, boss?' said the eye, since the mouth was still in mid-snore.

'In person. What a din! You certainly have a way of snoring!'

'But I'm awake, boss.' And he went on snoring.

Carvalho climbed over the bed and prepared to make some coffee. But Biscuter was already up, rubbing his strained and bulging eyes. He smiled from a far and distant world, like an ugly angel wrapped in yellow pyjamas.

'Out on the town? You're quite a raver, boss. You've had some phone calls. One from that loony girl. One from Charo. And one from a lady. At least, she sounded like a lady. I wrote it down in the office book.'

Carvalho checked his suspicion – that the lady's voice belonged to the widow.

Señora Stuart Pedrell invites you to take an aperitif at the Vía Véneto.

'What's the celebration?'

'Señor Planas's victory in the elections for the CEOE vice chairman. It's the only spare moment Señora Stuart has. Don't forget to wear a tie. They're very strict at the Vía Véneto.'

The note reminded him that the appointment was for one o'clock.

'Have you got a tie, Biscuter?'

'I've got the one my mother gave me as a present twenty years ago.'

'That'll do.'

Biscuter came back with a big cardboard box. It was full of mothballs, which covered a blue and white polka-dot tie.

'It stinks.'

'I'm very fond of it. It's a memento.'

'Well, hang your memento by the window, to get rid of the stink a bit. If I go in smelling like that, they'll take me off to the hospital for infectious diseases.'

'Things like this have to be kept in mothballs.'

Biscuter half opened the window, hung a string between the two frames, and, caressing more than constricting, pegged the tie to the line. Carvalho phoned the Stuart Pedrell house.

'No, don't wake Señorita Yes. Tell her I called. I'll meet her at two at the Río Azul restaurant on Calle Santaló.'

As soon as he put it down, the phone rang again. A male tenor voice asked, 'Is this the number for the private detective?'

'It is.'

'I'd like to consult you on a confidential matter.'

'Has your wife run off?'

'How did you know?'

'Intuition.'

'It's not the sort of thing one can discuss over the phone. It's very delicate.'

'Come round straight away.'

'I'll be with you in a quarter of an hour.'

He saw the look of surprise on Biscuter's face as he hung up.

'How did you guess?'

'By the voice. Ninety per cent of voices like that belong to men whose wives have run away. Probably because they are tired of hearing them.'

Biscuter went to the shops, while Carvalho amused himself drawing flowery monsters on a sheet of paper. The man knocked almost furtively. He was wearing a crumpled suit on a no less crumpled body. His bald patch would not have shamed the front row of a military parade, and his voice was midway between tenor and soprano. Some people are born to look like deserted husbands, thought Carvalho, although the real misfortune is probably to be born to become a husband.

The visitor delivered a rehearsed speech, and then burst out crying. He got as far as saying that his wife's name was Nuria, and that she was blonde. But then he broke down.

'Have a drop. It's orujo.'

'I don't drink on an empty stomach.'

'It shouldn't be empty at this time of day. Would you like a sandwich? There may even be some hake in cider left.'

The man had one eye fixed on the hanging tie, and the other fixed on Carvalho.

'I'm a modest bread manufacturer. I have a little factory.'

'Absolutely disgusting. How can anyone run a bread factory?'

'I've been in the trade all my life. My parents had a bakery in Sants, and I've always been in the bread trade. What more can I say? It's my life.'

'And is your wife also in the bread trade?'

'She lends a hand with the accounts. But she comes from a different background. Her father was a judge.'

'Do you know where she is?'

'I have my suspicions.'

'Where?'

'I'm ashamed to say.'

'So you know who she's with?'

'Yes. Listen, it's very embarrassing. She's living in one of the streets around here. She's gone with a man called Iparaguirre, a Basque pelota player who's a big-mouth, always boasting . . .'

'About what?'

'Forget it. Let's just say certain eccentricities. I don't know what women see in people like that.'

'But what does he boast about? Tell me.'

'Of being in ETA. He used to rent a flat in the building where we have our offices. He was always chatting with me or my wife – about how the Basques have balls, how they're tough, and so on. They set off a few bombs, kill a few poor sods, and then they think they're Kirk Douglas or Tarzan or something.'

He laughed tearfully at his own joke.

'You're lucky. She could have run off with someone from GRAPO.'

'How does that make me lucky?'

'Because ETA is a different kettle of fish. It's a much more solid organization. I had another case recently of a husband deceived by someone claiming to be a member of ETA.'

'And he wasn't?'

'No.'

'The nerve of them . . . !'

'Anything goes, when it comes to picking up women. In my day, you'd carry half a dozen leaflets and you'd lower your voice when you talked about politics. You stood a fair chance. But nowadays, women are more demanding. They need something a bit stronger to turn them on.'

'But my Nuria was never involved in politics. Her father was a real right-winger: one of those judges who came to Barcelona with the *nacionales*. My God, the things they did! So why should this guy bother my wife? I'm not interested in politics either. Politics doesn't butter your bread.'

'Right. You know where your wife's gone, and who she's gone with. So what do you want me to do?'

'Go and see her, and make her see that she's acted wrongly. She's abandoned the kids. Two little girls.'

More tears.

'I can't do anything for you for the next couple of days. They should be left alone . . .'

'But if we wait too long . . .'

'What?'

'It's immoral.'

'The immoral bit has happened already. It'll take time to bring the morality back.'

'I'll pay whatever's necessary.'

'I should hope so.'

'Here's my card. I hope you'll look on me as a friend rather than a client. What should I tell my daughters?'

'What have you said so far?'

'That their mother's gone to Saragossa.'

'Why to Saragossa?'

'She goes there sometimes.'

'What for?'

'One of our flour suppliers is there, and we do a lot of business with them. I don't know. I even thought of telling them . . . At times like this, you think of the wildest things . . .'

'What did you want to tell them?'

'That she was dead.'

He looked at him with watery eyes – resolute, almost heroic, as if holding forth the dagger with which he had slain the adulteress.

'She'll come back one of these days, and that would give the kids a fine shock! Affairs with pelota players never last long.'

'This one doesn't just play matches here and there. I think he's on a fixed contract with a Barcelona team.'

'That kind of person is not to be trusted. Did you say they're living locally?'

'Yes.'

'How do you know?'

'He moved out two months ago, and Nuria started coming home late. One day, I couldn't stand it any longer, and followed her. She met him in one of the streets near here, and they went into a rundown boarding house nearby. They went up the stairs. I asked the caretaker if the Basque was living there. He was. I suppose they're living there together now. I'll leave you the address. I'm asking you to take on the case – you've only got to name your price. I know the value of good work. Shall I give you a cheque? What'll it be? Ten thousand? Twenty?'

'It'll be fifty thousand.'

'Fifty thousand,' the man repeated, as he registered the amount and reached for his wallet.

'Don't pay me now. In a week, when Nuria's back home – that'll be the time to pay.'

The man was as profuse in his gratitude as he had been in his depression. As Carvalho closed the door behind him, he said to himself: 'Nuria, I'll give you a few more days to let off steam. You need a break from matrimony.' He noted in his diary the day on which he would free the unhappily married woman from the arms of her terrorist. He took the tie from its gibbet and sniffed to check that the smell had subsided. Biscuter arrived just as Carvalho was attempting to wrap the tie around his neck.

'Biscuter, I can't manage it.'

'Careful, boss. Don't destroy it.'

Biscuter tied a knot with the delicacy of a viola player.

'Look in the mirror, boss. It suits you.'

⋆

The tsar was not there, but the place had been decorated as if to please the tsar of (nearly) all the Russias. Two or three hundred smartly dressed men were gathered there, all wearing ties, and their features seemingly moulded by some sculptor specializing in company directors. There were also fifty women evidently dedicated to a fierce, daily struggle against cellulitis, varicose veins and traffic wardens. And thirty or so waiters, carrying trays of assorted delicacies that reminded him of mushy one-for-mummy-one-for-baby spoonfuls served up to children when they have no appetite. Fingers with no appetite, but insatiable jaws devouring little corners of heaven at two hundred pesetas a square centimetre: Russian caviare, Asturian salmon, dates wrapped in Parma ham, potato tortilla with prawns crawling in a field of mayonnaise, minced Russian crab with French dressing, Kalamata olives, rolls of Cumbres Mayores ham. And most of them ordered their drinks without alcohol, as they patted waists that had been mauled by masseurs full of class hatred. Alcohol-free beer, alcohol-free vermouth, alcohol-free wine, alcohol-free sherry, and alcohol-free whisky.

'A whisky with alcohol,' said Carvalho, and the waiter went to seek out a bottle of whisky with alcohol.

'This is a whisky with alcohol,' he said to the widow by way of presenting himself. She was wearing a turban of mauve silk that gave her a striking resemblance to Maria Montez and Jeanne Moreau.

'I needed to talk to you, and there was no other opportunity.'

'Fine. I'll be able to congratulate Señor Planas while I'm here.'

'My problem is that I've been waiting for you to ring and tell me how things are going, but there has been no call.'

'Things are still more or less where they were. I can't be expected in a few hours to solve a mystery that is over a year old.'

'Who have you spoken to?'

He told her nothing about the San Magín connection. Her face registered no emotion when he mentioned the names of Lita Vilardell and Nisa Pascual.

'Sergio Beser? Who's Sergio Beser?'

'An expert on Clarín's novel *The Regent*. But he's also very well up on Italian literature.'

'Why did you have to go to him?'

'I don't know everything, you know. Poetry isn't my forte, and your husband was very keen on verse.'

'So, what progress has there been?'

'None, and quite a lot.'

'When will you know something? I presume that I shall be the first to hear. And by the way, you can forget about certain other people that seem to have become involved. My daughter, for one. Yes didn't hire you – I did.'

'The criminal always returns to the scene of the crime.'

It was at this point that Planas joined the conversation.

'Does that mean that Señor Carvalho is expecting to find his man here?'

'It was I who asked him to come. There was no other way of talking to him.'

'I haven't congratulated you yet.'

'Thank you. As I said when I was sworn in, it's the kind of position which makes you its servant, not one that you use to serve yourself.'

'You're not making a speech now,' the widow interjected.

'I have to keep making the point until people believe me.'

He left in the direction from which he had come, carrying a glass of fruit juice. He received a slow, fulsome embrace from the Marquess of Munt, who was dressed like an admiral of the fleet from a country with no ships. With his arm around the shoulder of the successful candidate, the tall old man smiled and exchanged private whispers with Planas. Then Planas looked over his shoulder at Carvalho, and the Marquess's gaze acquired a critical edge as it came to rest on the detective.

'They're watching us.'

'So what?'

'In a film, when the hero says to the heroine: "They're watching us", she is supposed to blush and give a little laugh. Then she takes him by the hand and pulls him into the garden.'

'Here everyone looks at everyone.'

'Yes, but usually without making it so obvious. Your two partners are watching us, and coming our way.'

'Carvalho, why aren't you drinking white wine? Don't they have your brand here?'

'You're not drinking it either.'

'No. I'm drinking an idiosyncracy I discovered in Portugal. Port with a cube of ice and a slice of lemon. It's better than the best vermouth. His Highness the Count of Barcelona, in whose Council I had the honour of serving, recommended the combination during one of those endless sessions in Estoril. And Motrico agreed that it was excellent. Isidro, you ought to give up your diet, if only for a few minutes, and try a glass. Señor Carvalho, this man is impossible. When he goes on a diet, he doesn't waver for a second. The same with his gymnastics.'

The marquess stroked Planas's cheek with the back of his hand,

and the cheek slipped away, without wishing to give offence.

'Mima, you're superb, and you're looking younger every day. When I saw you across the room, I thought who can that radiant woman be? But who else could it have been?'

'Señor Planas, Señor Ferrer Salat is asking after you.'

Insistent hushing sounds enforced quiet. The chairman of the Employers' Federation expressed his pleasure that he had beside him such an efficient, hard-working and intelligent man as Isidro Planas. Meanwhile, Planas stood at attention, hands crossed over his kidneys, shoulders braced, and head erect, except when he declined modestly, in response to one of Ferrer Salat's jocular, eulogistic remarks. The first speaker drew an applause that was brief but intense, perfectly in keeping with the time and the place. Planas took the front of the stage, and his head moved with a forceful motion, as if the words were being driven out under the pressure of an internal water pump.

'I don't apologize for having been born. We entrepreneurs must stop apologizing for the fact that we exist. Much of the prosperity around us is due to our efforts – and yet, what a strange time this is, when the fact of being an employer, or of having been one, is seen as something to be ashamed of! I repeat, I do not apologize for the fact of having been born. And I was born a businessman.'

Applause. Munt took the opportunity to bend towards Carvalho and murmur, 'What a demagogue!'

'Not only will I not apologize for the fact that I exist, I also intend to fight to rebuild the morale that people are trying to deny us. There are a lot of suicidal types in our society who are woefully ignorant about the facts of life. They don't realize that if the employers go under, then the country and the working class goes under too. A free society means a society in which the market economy and free enterprise make their law. This is our law, because we believe in a free society. Freedom should only ever be sacrificed in the interests of survival; but surely the best solution is for freedom and survival to combine.

'You will be aware that this is the first time I have made a bid for office. Was that because it was politically inconvenient to do so previously? My friend the Marquess of Munt would say it was a matter of style. Perhaps so. But I believe that there have been, are, and will continue to be entrepreneurs under any political regime, and that our function is to secure a general prosperity which will be of benefit to all – which will guarantee peace and freedom. I place myself unreservedly under the command of our chairman, and as I take my place beside him, I say: Carlos, if you do not flag, then nor shall I, and nor shall we.'

The applause covered the sarcastic murmur with which the marquess greeted this outpouring.

'They're incorrigible. Can we never escape from rhetoric? And what about you, Mima? Why don't you stand in the elections for the National Association of Businesswomen?'

The widow's eyes gently rebuked him. Carvalho felt the marquess's hoary hand on his shoulder. He smelt the sandalwood perfume and felt confined in a prison of hypocritical confidences and civilities.

'You're a man after my own heart, Carvalho. Have you got anywhere with your investigations? I've been thinking over what we discussed the other day. Maybe it wasn't so stupid, what I said about his going to university. I remember that Stuart once spoke of a particular American scholarship that would have allowed him to move around the United States at will. To study anthropology, I believe. The Midwest fascinated him. But that was before the South Seas idea. What do you think, Mima?'

'Don't forget that after the scholarship and before the South Seas, there was also a project for going off to Guatemala to study Maya culture.'

'Every other week, some new scheme. But the South Seas project was on a different level. You were divine, Isidro! Absolutely divine!'

Planas let himself be embraced by the marquess.

'Pity about the ending, though. *Don't flag, Carlos!* Is this to be the new theme tune of our nation's businessmen?'

'You always treat everything as a joke.'

'Everything except the survival of my legacy! Don't flag, Isidro, don't flag! Shall we eat together? Mima? Señor Carvalho? Should we count you out, Isidro? Presumably you'll be dining with your new boss.'

'Indeed. A working supper. Tomorrow we're off to Madrid. Abril Martorell has invited us round to eat.'

'Your first steps along the road to Calvary. What about you two?'

'I already have an appointment.'

'Mima?'

'I'll eat with you if you'll leave me alone with the detective for a couple of minutes.'

'That's a fair deal. I'd be delighted, Mima.'

*

'Are they always like that?'

'How do you mean?'

'Playing to the gallery.'

'We all do it, in our own ways. I just wanted to say that I want your complete concentration on the business in hand. I want results as fast as possible. Don't let anything – or anyone – side-track you.'

'I have an appointment with your daughter in five minutes.'

'That's what I meant. Among other things.'

'It's not as if I go looking her out.'

'There are many ways of looking and not looking, but only one way of avoiding. I expect a report on this affair every forty-eight hours.'

'Your daughter's affair?'

'Don't play the fool.'

Yes was waiting him on a chair set slightly back from the table. She held her knees tensed together, and was gripping the chair as if in expectation of a release signal. Carvalho's appearance was the signal, and she stood up. Hesitating for a moment, she rushed forward and kissed him on the cheek. Carvalho took her by the arm, disengaged himself and sat her at the table.

'At last!' she said, looking at him as if he was newly home from the wars.

'I've just left your mother and her partners.'

'How ghastly!'

'That's not the half of it. Your mother suspects me of being a corrupter of minors intent on kidnapping you for the white slave trade.'

'And aren't you?'

'Not in the least. I think we should get a few things very clear. In about a week's time, my job with your mother will be finished. I'll deliver her my report, pick up my cheque and move on to another case, if one turns up. You and I will not be seeing each other after that. Not even keeping in touch. If you like the idea of going to bed with me now and again, during the next week, then that's fine. But that's as far as it goes. Don't build your hopes for anything in the future. It's not my job to keep sentimental teenagers company.'

'One week. Just one week. Let me live it with you.'

'I can see that nothing serious has ever happened to you.'

'Well, it's not my fault if nothing serious has ever happened to me, as you put it. Do I have to have suffered from birth for you to take me seriously? Just a week. I'll leave you alone after that, I swear it.'

She had taken Carvalho's hand on the table, and the waiter had to cough in order to draw her attention back to the menu.

'Anything.'

'You can't order just anything in a Chinese restaurant.'

'You order, then.'

Carvalho ordered up a portion of fried rice, two spring rolls, abalone in sauce, king prawns and veal in oyster sauce. Yes rested her chin on her left hand as she nibbled at the meal. Carvalho mastered the indignation he always felt when eating in the company of someone with no appetite. His satiated hunger made up for Yes's lack of interest.

'My mother wants to send me back to London.'

'Sounds like an excellent idea.'

'Why? I already know English, and the country too. She wants me to go so as to get me out of the way. Everything's working out fine for her. My brother in Bali isn't causing any problems; he spends less money there than he would here, and he's not forever sticking his nose in the business. The other two spend all day on their motorbikes, and only go to lectures under protest. The little one is completely under her thumb. I'm the only one who's a nuisance to her, just like my father was.'

Carvalho went on eating as if the conversation was passing over his head.

'She killed him.'

Carvalho began to chew more slowly.

'I can feel him. He's here, you know.'

Carvalho's chewing resumed its normal rhythm.

'It's a hideous family. My eldest brother got sick of it and just cleared off.'

'What was he sick of?'

'I don't know. He left while I was in England, but he must have been sick to death of her. Always the prima donna, always looking down on people. She treated my father like that too. She never forgave him his affairs, and never had the courage to have any herself. Do you know why? Because then she'd have had to forgive my father. No. She went on playing the virtuous woman so that she could feel morally superior to him. My father was a gentle and imaginative man.'

'The king prawns are excellent.'

'He learned to play the piano without ever being taught, and he played it as well as me. In fact, I'd say that he played it better.'

'Your father was as much of an egotist as any other human being. He lived his life – that's all.'

'That's not true. You can't go through life thinking that everyone's an egotist, that everyone's a shit.'

'I've managed to get through life with precisely that point of view. And now I'm convinced of it.'

'Am I a shit?'

'You will be. No doubt about it.'

'What about the people you've loved? Have they been shits too?'

'Now there's a trap. It's a basic human impulse to be kind towards people who are kind to us. It's an unwritten contract, but it's a contract all the same. We are accustomed to living life as if oblivious to the fact that everyone and everything is shit. The more intelligent people are, the less you're inclined to forget them. But I've never known anyone really intelligent to get very close to other people or confide in them. At most, he feels sorry for them. That's a feeling I can understand.'

'But not all people have to be either evil-minded or crippled. Is that the only distinction you make?'

'There are also idiots and sadists.'

'Is that all?'

'And rich and poor. And New Yorkers and Londoners.'

'What if you had a child? What would you think of him?'

'While he was small and helpless, I'd feel sorry for him. When he was your age, I'd start keeping a careful eye on him, watching for that moment when the young victim undergoes his metamorphosis and takes the first step to becoming an inhuman wretch. And when he'd become an inhuman wretch, I'd try to see as little as possible of him. If he was a successful inhuman wretch, he wouldn't need my help. If he turned out to be a failure, he would pay back with interest any help that I might give him. He'd pay it in the form of the colossal satisfaction that I'd feel in continuing to protect him.'

'You ought to get yourself sterilized.'

'No need. I take care of that myself. The first thing I expect from my sleeping partners is evidence that they have a coil or diaphragm, or are taking the pill. If I'm not satisfied, I put on a sheath. I always carry a packet in my pocket. I buy them at La Pajarita, a rubber shop on Calle Riera Baja. That's where I first started buying them, and that's where I'll carry on doing so. I'm a very routine sort of person. Do you want a dessert?'

'No.'

'Me neither. I save three hundred and fifty or four hundred calories like that. Planas has infected me with his diet mania.'

Yes screwed up her nose.

'You're not too keen on Planas?'

'Not at all. He's the opposite of my father. Rigid, cold, calculating.'

'And the Marquess of Munt?'

'Like something out of an opera.'

'You surprise me. You're very hard on other people.'

'They're the ones who hemmed my father in and surrounded him with mediocrity.'

'Your father had started looking for girlfriends not a lot older than you.'

'So what? He didn't have to pay them, did he? They must have seen something in him. You don't know how happy that makes me.'

'Who or what killed your father?'

'They all did. My mother, Planas, the marquess, Lita Vilardell . . . He was dying of disgust, just like me.'

'That could have been your mother saying that.'

'No. She's happy now. Everyone sings her praises. All the local gossip says how strong she is, how intelligent. And how she's doing better than her husband! Of course she's doing better. There's nothing to distract her. She's like a hunter obsessed with her prey. She sees everything in black and white. She's forgotten how to relax.'

She took the hand in which Carvalho was holding his cigar, and cigar ash fell into his steaming cup of jasmine tea.

'Let me come to your house. Just for one day. Today.'

'You're really obsessed with my house!'

'It's a wonderful house. It's the first place I've seen in which my mother would feel really uncomfortable.'

'It's obvious you've never been in one of the homes that your father built for other people. I'll expect you tonight at my place. Make it late!'

*

'It's you! I don't believe it! Must be Christmas! What an honour.' Charo was in the middle of putting on her make-up, and she barely gave him the chance to cross the threshold. 'I believe I know you from somewhere.'

'Are you going to let me in or not?'

'Who can stop the great Pepe Carvalho from entering? Consumed with a burning impatience, she waited for the gentleman to return from his expedition to the South Pole. Are there a lot of bears at the Pole?'

Carvalho re-established himself in the familiar surroundings with a series of routine, habit-formed movements. He left his jacket on the usual chair, dropped into a corner of the usual sofa, and automatically reached for the ashtray.

'It's a fortnight since these walls last had the pleasure of your excellency's company. They must have made him pope, I thought, what with all the popes that are dying nowadays. After all, my Pepe is a Jesuit, isn't he.'

'Charo . . .'

'Jesuit is an understatement. A mega-Jesuit. If Charo's needed, then she's supposed to jump. If Charo's not needed, then she can just be dumped. But Charo always has to make herself available, for whenever it suits his lordship. I tell you, Pepe, I've had enough. More than enough.'

'Either the scene ends here, or I'm off.'

With her legs astride and her arms akimbo, Charo closed her eyes and shook her head. Anger was seething in her small face, whitened by the foundation cream.

'Go back where you came from! I suppose it's all my fault, eh? I suppose I'm the imbecile?'

Carvalho stood up, took his jacket and walked towards the door.

'And now he's off. The gentleman can't be told a few home truths, because the gentleman gets offended. A woman can't get offended. Where are you going? You think you can leave, do you? Stay where you are!'

The woman outflanked him and locked the door. Then she burst out crying and turned to Carvalho for protection. In spite of the slowness with which he raised his arms, she fell into them and continued crying on his chest.

'I'm so lonely, Pepiño! Lonely! I start imagining things, and they scare me. Pepe, listen to me. You've grown tired of me because I'm a whore. I always knew it wouldn't last.'

'Charo, we've spent eight years like this.'

'But it's never been as bad as lately. You're having an affair with someone else. I can see it.'

'I've always had affairs with someone else.'

'Who is she? Why do you need other women? I have to go with other men to eat, to live, but you don't.'

'Come on, Charo, cut this out. If I'd known you'd be like this, I wouldn't have come. I'm in the middle of a difficult case. I have to move around a lot.'

'You didn't sleep at home last night.'

'No.'

'Because of an affair?'

'No. I went to sleep in a tomb.'

'In a tomb?'

'The corpse was away.'

'You're lying to me, Pepe.'

She laughed amid her tears. Pepe disentangled himself and made for the door.

'I came to fix something up for next weekend. But if you don't fancy it, forget it.'

'Me? A whole weekend? What did you have in mind?'

'I've heard of a restaurant in La Cerdanya that's been opened by a retired couple. She cooks very well. We could make a little trip at the same time. To France, maybe. Buy some cheese, pâté . . .'

'And I could buy some cream for these spots that I've started getting. Look, Pepe, look how ugly I am. Look at these spots.'

'I'll call you at midday on Friday. We could leave in the evening.'

'But I have to work on Friday evenings.'

'Well, Saturday morning then.'

'No, Pepe. Friday. To hell with the work.'

She kissed him on the mouth, as if she were drinking him, and only detached her body at the last moment. The images of the Stuart widow and her daughter erased that of Charo in Carvalho's mind. In the street, whores were already trawling for customers at an hour that would have been unthinkable in times of prosperity. That's the power of market forces! An old whore, steeped in alcohols of every vintage, stood beside a younger one who, in a fortnight's apprenticeship, had learned not to mourn the passing of her lost moral prejudices. There was more cynicism in the eyes of the younger woman. 'You'll have a good time with me. I fancy you, you know. Let's screw, eh?' The part-time whore, fresh from doing the dishes at home, glancing at her watch in case she's late home to cook for her husband and children. She tries to appear nonchalant by gazing into shop windows in which there is nothing to see.

He had first met Charo in front of a shop displaying travel goods. The girl had started on full-time prostitution in Venezuela, and was now a self-employed call girl working from the top floor of a new house in the middle of the Barrio Chino. Carvalho was drunk at the time, and had asked her how much she charged. She said he must be mistaken. 'If I've made a mistake, then I'm willing to pay a lot more.' He then saw for the first time the flat that would often be his home until seven in the evening – the hour when Charo began to receive her regular customers. 'Wouldn't you be better off with a flat in a smarter part of town?' No. The rents would be higher, and anyway her customers liked the mixture of old-style squalor and modern sophistication. Barrio Chino plus a phone. 'Ring next time. I don't like doing business in the street. I'm not a street-walker and never have been.'

Carvalho grew used to her schizophrenia, to her double life as the jealous girlfriend by day and the telephone whore by night. At first, he'd suggested that she retire from the game, but she said that she was no good at anything else. 'Supposing I was a shorthand typist – the boss would still put his hands on me. If I got married, it would be my husband, my father-in-law, my brother-in-law, and God knows who else. Don't laugh! In my village, a married woman gets pawed by everyone, particularly her father-in-law. Does it bother you if I do this kind of work? No? Well, leave things as they are. I love you, that's all there is to it. When you need me, I won't let you down.'

She never spoke of her work or her clients. Only once did Carvalho have to intervene. 'There's some filthy creep who wants to pay to see me shit, and he threatens me with a gun if I refuse.' Carvalho waited for him on the stairs and threw a bottle of piss over him. 'It'll be shit next time, and at home – in front of your wife.' Too many women in his life recently. The widow, who was prepared to sell her soul in a world shaped by the likes of Planas and her husband. The neurotic daughter who had suddenly discovered sorrow and death. Charo, presenting a bill for long-term services rendered by way of sex and company. The next would be Ana Briongos, from whom he would have to wrench the secrets of life, love and death with Stuart Pedrell. And as if that wasn't enough, there was also Bleda.

He found his mind occupied by the image of the little dog, alone in the garden in Vallvidrera, chasing sounds and smells, putting her nose into everything to see what it was and whether she could trust it. He had more than an hour before his appointment with Ana Briongos. He climbed into his car and without thinking began driving towards Vallvidrera. He was already halfway there before he realized that this sudden impulse had been motivated by a wish to see the dog and even take her along to the rendezvous in San Magín. What a figure you cut, Pepe Carvalho! You'll go down in history as Pepe Carvalho and Bleda, like Sherlock Holmes and Doctor Watson. He was angry at his own weakness, and turned the car around. But Bleda's almond-shaped eyes haunted him for mile after mile.

I must be a racist. I'd have sacrificed myself for a human being. But in the end, what's to say that a man and a woman are human beings, and a dog is not? I'll put her in for her exams. I'll take her to the Lycée Française and tell them that I want my dog to become manager of the city trade fair, or chairwoman of the National Association of Canine Employers. Or a cosmonaut. Bleda could study to become a cosmonaut. Or a prima ballerina at the Bolshoi. Or general secretary of the CPSU. No dog has ever built a San Magín. No dog has ever unleashed a civil war . . .

*

Ana Briongos was pacing to and fro. Short, stocky legs, and the shape of her body concealed beneath her grey jacket. She must have smelt him coming. She suddenly turned as Carvalho drove up and drew alongside.

'Do you want to get in?'

She sat in the car without looking at Carvalho. The passing scenery of San Magín seemed to reproduce itself endlessly, as if it were circular and infinitely repetitious.

'Let's talk here, in a bar. Do you have a place of your own?'

'I share a flat with two other girls.'

'And your family?'

'They're doing fine, thanks. How about yours?'

'No need to get uptight. I'm not used to these working-class ways. I'm not a cop.'

'You surely don't think I swallowed that missing relative story . . .'

'Fair enough. But I'm not a cop. The dead man's family hired me to investigate what happened to him. It's a job like any other. Don't you read detective novels?'

'I've got better things to read.'

'Gramsci read detective novels. And he even had a theory about them. Do you know who Gramsci was?'

'An Italian.'

'Very good. One of the founders of the Italian Communist Party.'

'Bully for him.'

The badges were still on her lapel. *Nuclear Power – No Thanks!* and the words *Free Speech!* below a tragic mask whose mouth was closed with a red gag. A lot of rain had fallen on the mask: a few letters had almost disappeared, and the whole badge was cracked and fading.

'I can't talk about this in the car – it makes me nervous. Let's go to Julio's bar. Near the church.

Julio's bar was like an old tearoom that could have been hired from the studios of Metro-Goldwyn-Meyer. Tables covered with red-squared plastic tablecloths. Strings of chorizo, garlic and ham. Barcelona's football teams posing for posterity. The sound of dominoes, and voices trying to fight their way through the cigarette smoke. A wooden porch at the rear was waiting for summer, when it would be jam-packed with families who would come seeking fresh air on the dusty, sweaty outskirts of San Magín. Carvalho noticed that the friend who had been with Ana Briongos in the morning was sitting at a table with a man and staring straight at them. Ana ordered a coffee, and Carvalho a peppermint cordial with ice. She looked at his drink in amazement.

'I thought that was a summer drink, or for women with ovary problems.'

'Who hasn't got ovary problems, these days? Look, kid, you and me need to talk.' He had addressed her with the familiar *tú* instead of *usted*.

'Don't you call me kid. And why are you using *tú*? That proves you're a cop. Only cops use *tú* like that.'

'Why don't you call me *tú*?'

'I'll use *usted*, and you use it too.'

'What was your friend's name?' he asked, returning to the formal style of address.

'Are you referring to Antonio? You already know. He was called Antonio Porqueres.'

'That's the first lie. Now for the second. Was he an accountant?'

'Why is that a lie? His name was Antonio Porqueres, and he was an accountant. Or rather, he did accountancy work at Nabuco's.'

'The second lie. Are you saying that you don't know who Antonio Porqueres really was?'

'If he had another name, what's that to me? I knew him as Antonio Porqueres.'

'How did you meet him?'

'At a public meeting towards the end of 1977. We had to organize a number of meetings to explain the Moncloa Accords. No one was happy with them, but we were supposed to say what we'd been told – that they would benefit the working class in the end. It wasn't long before we saw that the whole thing was a swindle. Anyway, I spoke at a meeting near here, in the Navia Cinema. At the end, Antonio came up to me and wanted to talk about it. He was against the accords. Why are you laughing?'

'Did you win him over?'

'More or less. He was a man who knew how to listen and have a real dialogue – not like some people I know. I don't want to run people down – I feel fine with my own people, precisely because they're my people. But he had manners, culture, and education. He'd read a lot, and travelled a lot.'

'He arrived here from the planet Mars. Didn't you realize that?'

'He told me he was a widower and had spent a lot of time abroad. He was tired and just wanted to live a quiet life, observing and experiencing this new stage in the life of the country.'

'Did you get on close terms with him?'

'Yes.'

'All the way?'

'What do you mean? Did I sleep with him? Obviously I did.'

'And then, suddenly, he went off. Without saying goodbye?'

'That's right. Suddenly he went off, without saying goodbye.'

'And didn't you try to find out what happened to him? Weren't you surprised?'

'No. He left as he arrived.'

'You women never learn. You still believe in tall, dark sailors coming to take you away.'

'I don't believe in sailors. I know what you're trying to say. But you've got it all wrong. Things have changed in San Magín too. A man and a woman can happily accept each other for what they are, live together and part on the best of terms. You're one of those who think that only the bourgeoisie can do things like that.'

'Are you still telling me that Antonio Porqueres was Antonio Porqueres?'

'I'm just telling you what I know.'

'You don't know much, or so it would seem. Your man's real

name was Carlos Stuart Pedrell. Does that ring a bell?'

'Yes.'

'Do you know who he is?'

'I've read something about him in the papers. An industrialist, wasn't he?'

'Correct. The man who built San Magín.'

Ana Briongos's eyes were not large enough to contain her surprise. She wanted to say something, but was lost for words.

'You lived with one of the people responsible for this heaven on earth.'

'It may not be heaven, but we're better off than we were in Somorrostro. Do you know what it used to be like there? I spent my whole childhood there. Antonio . . .'

She was resting against the back of the chair. Her open jacket revealed a full bosom beneath a flannel dress, and the bosom gave way almost without transition to the now-undisguised abdomen of a pregnant woman. She tried to cover herself with a mechanical gesture, but stopped as she realized that it was too late. She exchanged glances with Carvalho. The flood of sadness which gushed from her eyes hit home.

'Will it be a girl or a boy?'

'A girl, I hope. One less fucker in the world.'

She shrugged her shoulders and turned her eyes away to the ceiling of hams, chorizo, garlic and cowbells, all covered with a uniform layer of dust and cheap tobacco grime.

'Is Señor Stuart Pedrell the father?'

'I'm both father and mother.'

'Did you never suspect that Porqueres wasn't who he said he was?'

'I always suspected it. But it didn't matter.'

'He always opened doors for you; he bought you flowers sometimes; he'd read more than you; he used two or three thousand more words than you; he could describe the charm of an April day in Paris. Did he ever tell you that April was the cruellest month? Did he ever tell you that he liked to read much of the night and go south in the winter?'

'What are you playing at? Are you trying to paint me as a girl who's been seduced and abandoned? I explained to him why we were fighting. I explained what it's like in the police cells at Vía Layetana, and in the Holy Trinity women's prison.'

'Holy Trinity? That must have been a premonition. His body was found on a building site in Holy Trinity.'

A look of utter incredulity appeared on Ana Briongos's face.

'He'd been stabbed several times, apparently by two different hands. One was weak and hesitant, the other strong, the hand of a killer.'

'You obviously enjoy giving the details.'

'They dragged him to an abandoned building site, probably over the fence. But they hadn't killed him there. When he was found, he'd lost a lot of blood, but there was hardly any around him. He'd been moved from some other place. And that other place was San Magín. His killers looked for somewhere at the other end of the city, maybe not realizing that they'd be helped by his false identity. Or maybe they did realize it. You have to help me. You must know enough to point me in the right direction.'

'It was probably robbery.'

'Did he usually carry a lot of money?'

'No. Only as much as he needed. He was very generous with the little he had. Always wondering what presents to buy me. Not flowers, though. There aren't any flowers in San Magín. You were wrong there.'

'So, one day, he just didn't show up. What did you do?'

'I waited a few hours, and then I went to his flat. He wasn't there. But it looked like he was going to return.'

'Did you have a key?'

'Yes.'

'So you went back the next day.'

'And the next. And the next . . .'

'Didn't you leave a note, in case he returned?'

'Yes . . . No . . . No, I didn't leave a note. Why didn't I? It began to dawn on me that he wouldn't be coming back.'

'Did he know about the child?'

'Yes.'

'Did you think that was why he'd run off?'

'Not at first. Because I told him very clearly that the child was mine and mine alone. But then I started putting two and two together. Maybe he would feel responsible. But what am I saying? I'm talking as if he ran away, when in fact he was murdered.'

'Didn't you think of phoning the hospitals, or the police? Didn't you think it strange that the flat remained empty for weeks and weeks?'

'I soon stopped going there. Besides, he didn't have many things. It was a rented flat. Just a few books. The rest belonged to the company, or the previous tenant.'

'If I go to the police and tell them of Stuart Pedrell's double life in San Magín, you'll be their only link. You realize they'll be down on you like a ton of bricks?'

'That doesn't frighten me. I've had dealings with the police since I was fourteen. I've nothing to hide.'

'Everyone always has something to hide, and the police know that.'

'I know my rights. I'll be OK, don't you worry. Go and tell them what you know. I'll go and tell them myself, if you like.'

'The police are neither here nor there. This is a private investigation that I'm conducting for the widow.'

'The widow. What's she like?'

'Older than you, and much richer.'

'Did they get on well?'

'No.'

'He seemed a sad man.'

'And you gave him happiness.'

'Not exactly.'

'Just one last question for today. Don't you remember anything, any event or any person, that might set us on the trail of the murderer?'

'The last question for today and any day. And this is my last answer. No.'

'We'll be seeing each other again,' said Carvalho, as he rose sharply to his feet.

'I hope not.'

'Tell your friend and her chum to disguise themselves better next time.'

'They've nothing to disguise. They came because we agreed that it would be a good idea.'

Carvalho got into his car and drove off to meet Señor Vilas. He was sitting in front of the television with his grandchildren, watching a programme about horses. He took Carvalho up to the office.

'Do you keep information about people living in San Magín?'

'Not everyone, but just about everyone.'

'Do you have files?'

'Señor Viladecans asked me to keep them. There's an administrative file, which is pretty complete, and a much patchier one for specific incidents.'

'What kind of incidents?'

'If someone gets into trouble. After all, you have to know your enemy. It's a jungle out there.'

'I want everything you have on Ana Briongos.'

'I can tell you that without a file. She's a red, but she hasn't been causing much trouble. Not for some months, anyway. She seems to have been lying low for the past year. I hear she has a sweetheart.'

'Where she lives, who she goes around with, what her family does, everything you know.'

'I'll see what I can do.'

A small cupboard that appeared to promise little of interest opened, to reveal Señor Vila's cardboard files. He searched around, pulled out three or four folders, and held them at a distance from his longsighted eyes.

'I can't see a thing without my glasses.'

The file contained Ana Briongos's address and that of her family – her parents and six brothers and sisters. The parents and the oldest brother had come from Granada. The others were born in the immigrant areas of Barcelona; the youngest in San Magín. The father: a cinema usher in La Bordeta. The mother: a cleaner at the same cinema. The eldest brother was married and working at a pipe factory in Vic. Ana was the next in line. Next came Pedro Larios . . .

'How come one of the Briongos kids is called Larios?'

'He's a half-brother. That's all I can tell you.'

One of the girls worked at a hairdresser's in San Magín. The youngest two were still at school. Ana's file had a long list of political activities. Next to the name of Pedro Larios 'Briongos' was a note about a motorcycle theft at the age of fourteen.

'What else is known about the guy?'

'This isn't a police file. I only record what people tell me.'

Carvalho jotted down a few notes.

'I'll be absolutely discreet.'

'Don't worry. Are they in some sort of trouble?'

'I don't think so. It's just routine.'

'It's not very pleasant to have to keep an eye on people. But these days, it's more necessary than ever. All this freedom is all very fine, but it has to be freedom with responsibility, and therefore with vigilance. Does this have anything to do with the tenant you were asking me about the other day?'

'Probably.'

'I repeat, it wasn't my responsibility. It was a direct order from Señor Stuart Pedrell, may he rest in peace. I'll make that clear to Señor Viladecans.'

'Don't mention anything for the moment. I'll have to give him a report myself.'

'Whatever you say. Would you like a drop of something?'

'Of what?'

'Whatever you fancy. Calisay, a liqueur, cognac, anis, Aromas de Montserrat . . .'

He drank a glass of Aromas de Montserrat while they sat and watched the sad story of a Mexican rancher who deserted his beautiful wife because of his obsession with horses.

'Iaio, what's a *xarro*?'

'A *xarro* is a gunman, a cowboy.'

'A western cowboy?'

'Yes. But from the west of Mexico . . . These kids are at the age when they want to know everything, and you don't necessarily always know the answers.'

'Almost never, in my experience.'

'It's true, what you say. Very true.'

'I heard that the Briongos family didn't much care for Ana's political activities.'

'No. She used to just take off, and no one ever knew where to find her. She's been in trouble of one sort or another ever since she was a kid. Even under Franco. I'm telling you. They'd give her a thrashing because the police were after her. I had words with her once, when there was that fuss about the clinic. She said that I'd been a Franco supporter. But I've never been anything. I fired a few shots in the civil war, on the side of the reds, but that was only because I was in Barcelona at the time. Anyway, I told her she was a troublemaker – and that you convince people by talking to them, not by shouting at them. So, she goes and says I supported Franco. I don't owe anything to Franco – well, nothing except peace and work. People have a lot of bad things to say about Franco, but in those days, things weren't like they are today. No one wants to work any more. They turn up from Almería and they think someone's going to pay them a thousand pesetas for bending down and picking up a bit of paper.

'Look, I'm no dictator, but I say we're in a complete mess now. We're heading for disaster. I've worked like a dog to give myself a peaceful old age. No one's given me anything. My children are married and well set up. I've got my health and a bit of cash for when I can't work any longer. What more could a man want? Am I going to let a few crackpots spoil everything because they decide they want the moon? No, sir. The parents are a different matter. Good, hard-working people. I went to see Señor Briongos, to ask him to get a grip on his daughter. One day she was demanding a health centre; the next she was making a fuss about the drains; and the next day it was about schools. Well, hold your horses, girl! We're not made of money, you know. And anyway, I just take orders. Thank God she's not been making much trouble lately. You can tell the difference. Her new boyfriend must have calmed her down. That's what I say: God save us from women who don't get a proper fuck.'

Winking as if to excuse the strong language, he raised his elbows as if preparing for take-off, and let out a laugh that sounded more like a sneeze, thereby annoying his grandchildren, who could not hear the sad story of the beautiful Mexican woman abandoned for half a dozen horses.

*

Señor Briongos smelt of omelette, and the trace of oil that he wiped from his chin had obviously been used in frying the omelette in question. He looked like a croupier from a Mississippi steamboat who had been brought down in the world by the effects of a stomach ulcer. A bald, emaciated man with long sideburns and eyes as large as his daughter's. Incisive arm movements dealt people and spaces into their allotted portion, and it was as if he were inviting Carvalho into some huge castle and instructing his family and servants to retire to their quarters. The main room was an exact copy of the one occupied by Porqueres's three-piece, tartan suite. There was hardly any space to move between the aerial-topped television, the outsize neo-classical dining table, the chairs, the glass cocktail cabinet, and two green imitation leather armchairs occupied by two boys and a girl who had her fingers in a jar.

'Switch the telly off, and go to your room. I have to talk to this gentleman.'

The father's withering look cut short their gestures of protest. By now the Mexican lady had decided to learn horse-riding, so that she could follow in the footsteps of her cowboy husband. Back in the room, a bell-shaped woman whose hair had been badly dyed in platinum-chestnut tufts was beginning to clear the dirty plates from the table.

'Is the girl in trouble again? I must explain that I no longer have anything to do with her. She has her own life, and I have mine.'

'God help us!' the woman muttered, without pausing in her task.

'That girl has given us a lot of worry, and no pleasure. Not that we haven't tried to set her on the right road. But what can parents do, when they've got a lot of children, and they both work.'

'Too much reading, and bad company,' the wife shouted from the kitchen.

'Reading's not a bad thing. It depends on what you read. But I won't argue about the bad company. So, tell me what she's done now. I'm prepared for the worst.'

'I don't think she's done anything. It's not really about her that I wanted to see you, but about a fellow she was going round with last year.'

'She's had so many – I'm ashamed to talk about it. I don't know what makes me more ashamed: that she's messed about with politics; or that she goes to bed with anyone who wants it, ever since she learned that it wasn't just for pissing with. Excuse me, but that daughter of mine brings out the worst in me.'

'This was quite an older man. His name was Antonio Porqueres.'

'Ah, yes. The musician. Amparo, he's come to ask us about the musician.'

'The musician!' shouted Amparo from the kitchen.

'Was he a musician?'

'We call him that because he came here one day and spent the whole time talking about music. I'd just bought a record by Marcos Redondo, and when he saw it, he suddenly began talking on and on about music. When he left, we all cracked up. Sole, the girl you saw just now, is a born comedian, and she began imitating him. You'd have died laughing. A very stuck-up sort of bloke, he was. She brought him here because her mother was dying of shame. The whole neighbourhood was asking who her daughter was engaged to. So I went looking for her at the bus stop, and told her straight that she had to introduce us to the man, if only for her mother's sake. And one day she brought him round. Then he went off, and left her with what she's got now.'

'So you know what she's been left with.'

'And how can I look people in the eye, now . . . ?'

'May the Lord help us!' added Amparo from the kitchen.

'I went back to the bus stop and told her, again quite plainly, that she'd have to fend for herself. I don't want to have anything to do with it. Pedrito has already been enough of a cross to bear.'

'Who's Pedrito?'

'My son. It's a very long story. When I already had Ana, I was given the chance of working on a dam near Valencia. I went there without my family, and I'm sure you can guess what happened.'

'How can this gentleman know what happened? Men aren't all the same. There are still some who have a sense of decency.'

'Shut up. Mind your own business, will you? Well, I had an

affair with this girl there, and she went and died on me in childbirth. The whole village was against me, and there was nothing I could do. She'd been through every man in the village, but they pinned the kid on me. So I came back with the little boy, and my wife, who's a real saint, accepted him into the family. It's a pity he turned out so bad – it must have been a bad seed to start with. How can you tell where he came from? He can't be my son – that's getting clearer all the time. But it's a funny business, all this stuff about seeds. Ana is mine, and look how she's turned out. There was no way of taming either her or Pedrito. And it wasn't that I spared the rod, either. In the end, on Amparo's advice, we put Pedrito into care. There was nothing we could do with him. But he managed to run away, and we were landed with him again. And it's still going on.'

'Does he live with you?'

'No,' the woman shouted emphatically from the kitchen. 'And he won't, as long as I have anything to do with it.'

'Funnily enough, though, the boy doesn't have bad feelings towards us.'

'He has no feelings, full stop. Neither good nor bad.'

'Don't exaggerate.'

'Don't let's talk about the monster. It only upsets me, and you know what I'm like.'

She was occupying the whole kitchen doorway, as if ready to fall upon them and hammer them into the ground.

'Was that the only time you saw Antonio Porqueres? When he was here talking about music?'

'Yes. Except for the time when I got him and my daughter tickets for the cinema where I work. I asked him if he wanted to join me for a drink, but he wouldn't. Just hello and goodbye. That was all. I never saw him again. Never.'

He tried to open his eyes and his face to the utmost, so that Carvalho would see that he was telling the truth.

'Could I talk to your son?'

'What for?'

'What for?' the woman repeated, now firmly esconced in the dining room.

'Maybe he had more contact with Porqueres.'

'He had no contact with him at all. He didn't even see him when he came here.'

'Ask Ana. She'll tell you.'

'Yes, ask Ana.'

I can see that you're both afraid. I don't know if it's the kind of fear that we all feel when we don't know what's round the next corner. But you're definitely afraid.

'Pedro didn't relate to anyone in the family.'

'Not to any of us.'

'We haven't seen him for months. I couldn't even tell you where to look.'

'He's living his own life. In our family, everyone's lives their own lives, except for us. We're always stuck with other people, aren't we, Amparo?'

The woman went off to the kitchen looking preoccupied. He stood up. The audience was over.

Carvalho left him a couple of telephone numbers.

'If your son drops by, tell him I'd be interested to meet him.'

'I doubt that we'll be seeing him. I'm almost certain of that.'

He accompanied Carvalho to the door.

'You always think you're doing the best for your kids, but either they turn out bad, or you find that you've made a mistake. I could never get anywhere with the girl. And what was I supposed to do with the boy? He was always a rebel. He was always answering me back, from when he was so-high. I'd give him a couple of good wallops, and he'd just stare at me, straight in the eye. I'd bash him again, and he'd still be staring.

'You know what he did with Amparo one day? He threw a plugged-in iron at her, so as to electrocute her. Dirty little swine! But to look at him, you'd think butter wouldn't melt in his mouth.

It seemed a rotten thing to do, putting him in a home, but what was the alternative? Some very decent men have come out of those places. Maybe he'll change too, when he grows up and has a family of his own. It's not true that he's rotten through and through. In his heart of hearts, he loves us, I know. When I threw him out last time, he came creeping back with toffees for the children. Maybe he'll come to his senses one day . . .'

If you're lucky enough to have a son who doesn't flinch when you give him a wallop, then it's possible that he'll turn out level-headed in the end.

'It's in his interest, and yours, that you tell him to contact me.'

'What do you mean?'

'Go and see if you can find him.'

*

'Bromide' the shoe-black was wielding a toothpick in desultory fashion, in an attempt to extract little pieces of squid from a brownish sauce. The skin hung from his wasted face, and the speckles and blackheads on his bald patch absorbed the witless attention of the waiter as he watched Bromide's skilful performance with the toothpick from the other side of the bar.

'You're not catching a lot today . . .'

'What do you expect me to catch, since it's all water? I don't know why you call it squid in sauce. It's more like the Mediterranean with a couple of bits of dead fish in it. Not even enough for a nibble. That's just what I needed to restore my lost appetite! Pour me another glass of wine. At least the waterworks are still functioning. Make it real wine, not that powdered garbage you mix with water.'

Carvalho touched Bromide lightly on the shoulder.

'Pepiño, you old son of a bitch. You're turning into a real

scruff lately. Look at the state of those shoes. Shall I clean them for you?'

'Finish your little snack.'

'Some snack! It looks more like the sinking of the *Titanic*. I've never seen so much sauce for so little squid. Hey, you, bring us the whole bottle, and a couple of glasses.'

Carvalho sat down, and Bromide bent over his shoes.

'I wanted to talk to you.'

'Fire away.'

'What do you know about flick-knife gangs?'

'Quite a lot. I know all the ones in this area. And that's saying something, because there's a new one every day. Any kid with two balls thinks he can set up on his own account.'

'What about other areas? Holy Trinity, San Magín, San Ildefonso, Hospitalet, Santa Coloma . . . ?'

'Hold on, now. I can't keep up with all of them! You're behind the times, Pepiño. Every area has its autonomy these days: things aren't like they used to be. Once I could know everything that happened in Barcelona just from the hundred square yards around here. That's impossible now. Anyone coming from Santa Coloma is like a foreigner.'

'Don't you have ways of finding out?'

'None at all. If they were the old kind of villains, like in my time or yours, I'd be able to find things out. But these knife-gangs are different. They go their own way. They have their own laws. You know what young people are like nowadays. Film stars. That's how they see themselves. Bloody film stars.'

'What are you wearing there?'

'A badge againt nuclear power stations.'

'Getting into politics at your age?'

'I've been saying it for years. They're poisoning us. We're forced to eat and breathe shit – in fact the healthiest thing about us is probably our shit, because our body keeps the bad and gets rid of the good. People laugh at you. They call me Bromide because I've been saying for forty years that they're putting bromide in our bread and water to stop us getting together and screwing all the time.'

'What's that got to do with nuclear energy?'

'It's the same thing. Now they've decided to *really* do us in. Not just piddling bromides. Mass murder. I don't miss a single demonstration.'

'So you're an ecologist?'

'Eco-bollocks! Drink some wine, Pepiño, and enjoy my company while I'm here, because one of these days I'm just going to get up and go. To another area. I'm feeling real bad, Pepiño. One day it's this kidney that hurts, and the next it's the other. Feel here. Can't you see the swelling? I'm keeping a close watch on it, because I like to keep an eye on myself. I'm like an animal. What does a cat do when it gets ill? Does it go to the doctor? No, it goes onto the balcony and eats a geranium. And it's the same with a dog. We should do like animals do. Anyway, I keep a close watch on myself, and this thing came up a couple of weeks ago. You don't know what it might be, do you?'

'No.'

'For weeks and weeks I was feeding myself on tinned cockles. I've a brother-in-law who works at a canning factory in Vigo, and he sometimes sends me a few tins. I was short of cash, and said to myself: Bromide, eat the stuff, because shellfish are very good for you. So, I went on eating the stuff until this swelling started. I ate nothing but bread and tomatoes and tinned cockles. I'd always eaten bread and tomatoes before, without getting any swellings. So, what's your conclusion?'

'The cockles.'

'Obviously.'

'You're letting me down, Bromide. I hoped you'd be able to solve my knife-gang problem.'

'This city isn't what it used to be. In the old days, a whore was a whore and a gangster was a gangster. Now there are whores everywhere, and everyone's a gangster. You know what I heard one day? That you'd been caught breaking into a ham shop. And I believed it. Evil is stalking the streets, with no order and no organization. Once you could just talk to a few guys and you'd know the whole set-up. Now you can talk to a hundred, and still not get the picture. Do you remember my gay pal Martillo de Oro, the good-looking one? Well, the other day they beat him to death. Who did it? It wasn't the competition, or the Marseilles mob. Just four Guineans who happened to get together and declared war. That couldn't have happened before. There was more respect. We're all rotten, all crazy. We need a strong hand.

'Men like Muñoz Grandes, my general in the Blue Division – that's what we need. There was a man who could impose respect! And he was honest, too. Paquito left a widow who didn't have to worry about making ends meet. But Grandes left the world with no more than he came in with. Anyway, what's up with you, Pepiño? Why are you so interested in knife-gangs? You're keeping pretty low company these days!'

'They used a knife on the husband of one of my clients.'

'That's a hard one – much harder than a gun killing. Everyone's got a knife.'

It's a cold death. You see the eyes of death. You move closer, you stop, and you can feel death inside as you open a little icy passage in the flesh. Carvalho felt the knife he always carried in his pocket. An animal which lived by nibbling at death, until it suddenly unleashed it in a full burst of pent-up fury.

'Steer clear of the knife-gangs, Carvalho. They're all young and crazy . . . with nothing to lose.'

'Thanks for the advice. Here, take this. Lay off the cockles and get yourself a steak!'

'A thousand pesetas, for nothing! No, I don't want it, Pepe.'

'Another time you'll give me some information.'

'Anyway, my stomach's fucked and I can't take meat any more. They pump it too full of water and hormones. You can't even breathe properly, these days. I'll buy myself a few bottles of good wine instead – the one you drink. That keeps you going and kills the bacteria.'

'Good luck in your fight for a world without nuclear power stations.'

'Luck never comes the way of the likes of me. Soon we'll have nuclear suppositories up our arses! Have you listened to these politicians? It's them who give the green light. Yes, and then they want popular approval, so that their democratic circus stays intact. A Muñoz Grandes – that's what we need. Even a Franco. I tell you . . .'

'It was Franco who put up the nuclear power stations in the first place.'

'Because Muñoz Grandes was dead! Otherwise . . .'

He rang Biscuter to say that he was going straight to Vallvidrera. Then he located Viladecans, after a telephone chase which ended in Planas's office.

'I need to talk to the policeman you mentioned.'

'Don't make too many demands on him.'

'I won't. It's absolutely essential.'

'I'll see what I can do. Stay in your office between ten and eleven tomorrow morning. If I manage to get hold of him, I'll tell him to call round. Just a moment, Señor Planas has something to say to you.'

'Carvalho? This is Planas. Is it absolutely necessary for you to go stirring things up in San Magín?'

'You've got loyal foremen! Nobody told me not to make inquiries in San Magín.'

'At this moment, any connection between Stuart's death and our business affairs would be very damaging. I'd like to have a private word with you. Would tomorrow suit you? We could have lunch together. Two o'clock at the Oca Gourmet.'

*

Yes had climbed over the garden gate. She was sitting on the steps, tugging playfully at Bleda's ears.

'Don't pull her ears. They're very delicate, and I don't want them falling off,' Carvalho called through the gate as he arrived. Bleda's tongue finished the job that Bromide had started on Carvalho's shoes, and then tried to continue the cleaning operation up his trouser leg. But Carvalho lifted the dog, looked her in the eye, and asked what she had been doing during the day. Bleda pondered the question with her tongue sticking out.

'I got here before you.'

'So I see.'

'I've brought some supper, too.'

'I dread to think. What is it, vichyssoise with cocaine?'

Yes waved a wicker basket tantalizingly under his nose.

'It's full of special treats. Four kinds of cheese that I guarantee you've never tasted before; a chicken-liver pâté made by an old woman in Vic, and a wild-boar sausage from the Arán valley.'

'Where did you get all this stuff?'

'From a cheese shop that somebody recommended, on Calle Muntaner, near where it joins with Calle General Mitre. I've written down the address for you.'

Carvalho seemed to approve of the girl's gastronomic initiative, and opened the front door for her to enter.

'I've also brought a book for you to burn. I don't know if you'll like it.'

'One book's as good as the next.'

'It's my mother's favourite book.'

'It'll burn.'

'It's called *The Ballad of the Sad Café*.'

'We'll burn the ballad, and the sadness, and the café, and even the hunchback too.'

'Have you read it?'

'Before you were born. You can start tearing it up.'

When Carvalho returned with an armful of firewood, he found Yes reading the book by the fireplace.

'It's very good. I feel a bit bad about burning it.'

'When you get to be my age, you'll be grateful for having read one book less. Particularly that one. The woman who wrote it is a miserable wretch who couldn't survive even by writing.'

'Take pity on her!'

'No. On the fire with it.'

'Let's swap it for one of yours, the one you hate most. Then I promise I'll bring ten more from home for you to burn.'

'Do what you like.'

'No. I'll tear it up.'

She began piling torn pages onto the old ashes. Carvalho lit the fire, and when he turned round he noticed that Yes had laid the table.

'What about the cocaine?'

'That's for later. It's much better after you've eaten.'

Carvalho brought out a bottle of Peñafiel red.

'Tell me about this wild-boar sausage.'

'I wrote down what they told me in the shop. It's called *xolis de porc senglar*. They make it in the Arán valley. It's very rare. This was the only piece they had in the shop.'

Goats' cheese, ewes' cheese from Navarre, Chester, and a mild cheese from the Maestrazgo. His praise for her selection obviously delighted Yes.

'Now that you've eaten, and sated the beast inside you, I'm going to tell you my plan. When you finish this job, if you decide to finish it, we'll take the car and go on a trip to Italy, Yugoslavia and Greece. Crete must be wonderful in spring. If it works out OK, we could cross the Bosphorus and go through Turkey, Afghanistan . . .'

'For how long?'

'All our lives.'

'That's too long for you.'

'We could rent a house somewhere and wait.'

'Wait for what?'

'For something to happen. And when it does, we'll carry on with our travels. I'd like to see my brother in Bali. He's a nice boy. But if you don't feel like seeing him, we don't have to go to Bali. Or maybe we could go there and not see him.'

'What if we ran into him in the street?'

'I'll pretend to be confused. "Yes! Yes!" he'll say. And I'll say: "You're wrong, pal!" "But aren't you my sister Yes?" "No, I'm nobody's sister." '

'Then he'll say that his sister has a scar under her left breast, and he'll want to check.'

'And obviously you won't let him.'

'What about Bleda?'

'We'll take her along.'

'And Biscuter?'

'No. Perish the thought! No, we couldn't take Biscuter.'

'And Charo?'

'Who's Charo?'

'She's like my wife. She's a whore I've been going round with for eight years. She's eaten with me at this table, and screwed in my bed. A few days ago, in fact.'

'You didn't have to say she's a whore.'

'But she is.'

Yes stood up, and knocked the chair over as she did so. She went into Carvalho's bedroom and closed the door. The detective went to put on a record of the Riego Anthem. The flames were fighting to escape up the chimney. Carvalho sprawled on the sofa, watching them. After a little while, Yes crept up and put her hands over his eyes.

'Why are you always sending me away?'

'Because you've got to go, and the sooner the better.'

'Why do I have to go? And why the sooner the better? I'm only asking for your company.'

'You're asking me to spend the rest of my life travelling!'

'But that life could last five years or just a week. What are you so afraid of?'

He stood up to put the Riego Anthem on again. He slowly undressed her and entered her as if he wanted to fix her to the carpet. She coiled gently around him. Reddened by the fire, their bodies enjoyed the moistness and the warmth. As they drew apart, they were each absorbed with their own desires and their own section of the ceiling.

'I've always had the horrors of becoming a slave of emotions, because I know it could too easily happen. I'm not keen on experiments. Live your own life, Yes.'

'What life are you asking me to live? What am I supposed to do? Marry a rich young heir? Have babies? Spend the summer by the sea at Lliteras? Take a lover? Two lovers? A hundred? Why can't my life be with you? We don't have to travel. We could just stay here, in this room.'

'When I reached forty, I reckoned up what my future held. Paying off debts and burying the dead. I've paid for this house and I've buried my dead. You can't imagine how tired I am. Now I'm realizing that I don't have the time to take on new debts. I could never pay them off. I've only got one corpse still left to bury – myself. I'm not interested in wild affairs with a girl who can't tell the difference between love and cocaine. You can't tell the difference, can you? Sleep the night here, but tomorrow morning you'll have to go, and we won't be seeing each other again.'

Yes rose to her feet. From the floor, Carvalho could see the precise lines of her body, her sexual parts moist after the advances of his voracious member. She moved her rounded buttocks towards the door, turning for a moment to tuck a strand of hair behind her ear. Then she went into the bedroom and closed the door. Moments later, Carvalho followed her into the room and found her snorting cocaine. Yes smiled from the depths of a waking reverie.

*

'Can't you survive without seeing me? I've already told you, I prefer to keep a low profile.'

'I needed to talk to you.'

'I'm nobody's servant. I told Viladecans. He's done me favours, but I've done plenty enough in return. A policeman isn't a servant.'

He paced the floor of Carvalho's office, nervously.

'I wouldn't like anyone in the force to know that I'm having dealings with a shit-stirrer. Pardon the expression, but that's what we call you people.'

'All right. I won't keep you long. When you were investigating the Stuart Pedrell case, I presume you started with the knife-gangs?'

'We did what we could. They say that there's one rat for every person living in this city. Well, for every rat there's also someone carrying a knife. We keep tabs on most of the gangs, but there are new ones springing up every day.'

'Did you get any tip-offs?'

'Our tip-off was that none of the known gangs was claiming responsibility. That didn't get us far. You know, people are surprised that there's a new knife-gang popping up every day. But it's not surprising at all. Did you know that the judge at the delinquents' court is a red? As fast as we send them to court, he puts them back on the streets. This job is getting more pathetic all the time. Now they're supposed to have a lawyer present during interrogation. How can you get something out of a villain without roughing him up a bit? The people who make the laws should have to deal with this riff-raff themselves. At least the lawyers don't come to the station very often. Not that they wouldn't like to. They're just scared.'

He had calmed down and was eyeing Carvalho from behind his sunglasses.

'I hope you're not expecting me to solve this case for you. It's your baby now.'

'Did you cover the whole city in your search?'

'First of all, we started round Holy Trinity. Then we contacted our informers all over town. But it was hard for us to get really stuck in, because of pressure from the family. We weren't even allowed to publish Stuart Pedrell's photo. Viladecans pulls a lot of weight. Things aren't like they used to be. Between you and me, I'm getting out of this job. But before I go, I'm going to set off a few fireworks. I'll knock off a few reds, and see if they come after me. A society of inadequates and cripples – that's what they're creating. Look.'

He took a wad of notes from his wallet.

'Forty thousand pesetas. I always carry ready cash, in case I suddenly get the urge to leave. That's what it would cost me to get to Paris and stay a few days while I enlist in a group of mercenaries. When I find I can't take it any more, I'll get the hell out and head for Zimbabwe.'

'There's already a black government in Zimbabwe.'

'There too? The world's gone mad! Well, I'll make it South Africa. At least *they've* got their heads screwed on right.'

'What were your conclusions about the Stuart Pedrell case?'

'That the truth will come out sooner or later. When you're least expecting it, a little birdie drops into your lap. You force him to eat a bit of shit, and he tries to get you off his back by confessing to something big. Now you're on the right track. But you'll never get anywhere without using rough stuff. One day, the killer will walk into the net. We'll stick him with the biggest thing around at the time, and he'll get shit scared and come up with something we can believe. A mutual favour, you might say. I like my job; I'd never say I don't like it. But it's getting harder and harder. The reds hate our guts, and they're afraid of us. They know that we're what holds this society up, and that if they want to take over, they're going to have to get rid of us first.

'You see this hand? It's had the pleasure of laying one on one of those MPs who's so much in the news nowadays. They'd got together a little group to present a petition to the head of the Council, but they hadn't got a proper authorization. This was when the Old Man was still alive. This guy started getting uppity, so I gave him one that he won't forget in a hurry. You don't happen to know a good publisher, do you? He'd have to have guts. You see, I keep a diary in which I write down everything I do, and everything I see and hear. There's a conspiracy all around us. You'd die of fright if I told you how many top knobs in this country are working for the KGB. I leave the diary with a woman friend of mine, in case anything happens to me. If you mention it to a publisher with guts, I'd happily give you a commission.'

'Fuerza Nueva has a publishing house.'

'They're all sold out. The government tolerates them, so as to keep them in line. What do they actually do? A few rallies, a few punch-ups, and it's all over. That way, they can keep the kids amused and stop them blowing everything sky-high. I'll publish it when I'm in South Africa or Chile. *Red Power Over Spain*. How do you like that as a title? I'll use a pen name – Boris Le Noir. Ever since I was little, I've been thinking up adventures for myself. And I've always been Boris Le Noir.'

'You do of course realize that Boris is a Russian name.'

'Not all Russians are communists. In fact, the great majority of them aren't. That's what I call an iron dictatorship. You can always get out of a fascist dictatorship, but what about a communist one? Tell me, how can people be so blind? The reds'll end up taking over everything. They start by castrating the men and masculinizing the women. They're getting their fingers in everywhere. There's not one virile country left north of the Equator. I've been giving this some thought: in the North, you have the countries where democracy and communism are ruining everything; in the South, you have the countries where there are still virile qualities, where the individual still has room to fight. Chile, Argentina, Zimbabwe, South Africa, Indonesia . . . Make no mistake. If you still want to die on your feet, with your balls in the right place, then forget all this shit and join up with the mercenaries.'

'Do all your colleagues think like you?'

'No. The force is rotten too. Socialists are springing up like mushrooms. I ask them where they were four years ago, and they can't even answer. They've got no sense of adventure. They're just pen-pushers. Talking with you has made me quite excited again, you know. This evening I think I'll go and get my ticket at the Estación de Francia. What do you think I should do about the book?'

'Take it with you and add some field observations.'

'Not a bad idea. But what if it gets lost? I'll make a photocopy and leave it with my woman. Let me give you some advice. Don't break your back trying to solve the Pedrell case. Try to find an explanation that sounds plausible. Give it to the family, and pick up your cheque. They haven't the slightest interest in finding out what happened. That guy was in their way, I can smell it. He was a nuisance to all of them.'

He clicked his tongue against his cheek, adjusted his glasses, and went on his way.

'I don't know how you can stomach all that garbage, boss. How can you stand people like that?'

'He's a good kid, and one of these days they'll do for him. He'll never make commissioner-in-chief.'

'He'll have asked for it all right. Now he's off to gun down blacks, because he can't kill reds. He's off his rocker.'

'Biscuter, I want to give you an assignment for the next three months.'

'At your service.'

'Chinese cooking is the healthiest food there is. It's tasty, but doesn't make you fat. I'd like you to specialize in Chinese cuisine.'

'Will I have to cook rats and snakes?'

'No. Just about everything else, though. Go and spend a couple of hours every morning at the Cathay restaurant. The owner is a friend of mine, and he'll initiate you into the secrets.'

'I've been working on Rioja cooking lately, and it hasn't turned out too bad.'

'Chinese is the cookery of the future.'

'Thanks, boss. It'll be an honour and a pleasure. The main thing in life is not to get into a rut. Cooking for you has shown me that I can be of use to someone. And I'd like to learn more.'

'If you do well, I may even pay for you to go to Paris and learn how to make French sauces.'

'I couldn't leave you here alone.'

'Who says you'd have to? I'd come too, and we could set up shop there for a while.'

'That would be really nice, boss. I won't be able to sleep for thinking about it.'

'Sleep easy, Biscuter. What's important is that we start planning for a change in our lives.'

'And Charo?'

'She'd come too.'

'And the dog?'

'Naturally.'

'In a flat? You do realize that dogs don't stay little for ever? They grow.'

'We'll rent a little house on the outskirts of Paris. By a lock on the river. We'll be able to sit and watch the barges passing.'

'When, boss, when?'

'I don't know. But you'll be the first to hear.'

*

'I hope you don't mind me joining you.'

The Marquess of Munt was wearing a tweed suit and a silk cravat tucked under his double chin. On a chair beside him, Planas was swirling what was certainly an alcohol-free beverage.

'Isidro asked me to come.'

Planas looked at him with surprise.

'A meal for two always turns into a dual monologue. It takes a third person to get a conversation going.'

'I thought you were in Madrid seeing some minister.'

'I was.'

'Isidro's like that. One day, I phone him at nine in the morning, and we arrange to see each other for supper. When he arrives, I discover that in the meantime he's done a day trip to London.'

'Señor Carvalho, I'll come straight to the point.'

'Isidro, Isidro. Such things should be discussed during the second course.'

'Well, I want to raise them now.'

'At least wait until we've finished the aperitif. Don't you agree, Señor Carvalho? Of course you do. As Bertolt Brecht put it: first the belly, then morality.'

Carvalho agreed not only with the Marquess's point of view, but also with his choice of white wine for the aperitif.

Two waiters congratulated Planas on his recent appointment, and he replied with a thank-you clouded by the frown with which he had greeted Carvalho.

'Grilled fish and a green salad.'

'He's quite impossible. All he thinks of these days is how to keep his muscles and his gut looking youthful. Have you ever seen him with no clothes on? He's like a Greek athlete. You can identify each muscle. And he keeps his insides in even better shape. His liver is like a little goat's.'

'You can laugh, but I'll have the last laugh.'

'That wasn't a very clever or gracious thing to say. I'm well over seventy, and I don't have to give things up to keep fit.'

Carvalho ordered a prawn mousse and bass with fennel. The marquess started with snails à la Bourgogne and then also ordered the bass.

'Now that our stomachs have something in them, I think I can begin. I was not at all pleased to hear that you've been sniffing around San Magín. If you insist on turning things up, then turn them up somewhere else – anywhere but San Magín.'

'No one ever set me any limits. Neither Viladecans nor the widow told me anything about staying away from San Magín.'

'Well I'm telling you now. Viladecans doesn't know what he's doing, lately. Yesterday he even objected to the fact that I won't allow San Magín to be turned upside down. I don't know what's the matter with him.'

'I've barely had the pleasure of meeting him, so I wouldn't know.'

'But if things start to get complicated, it'll affect you too. We're at a delicate moment. We've managed to stop rebuilding work in San Magín, and we've stymied the journalists who are trying to sully my good name with talk of a "property scandal". I'm in a difficult and very responsible position now, and I can't allow myself to be exposed to a publicity campaign.'

'I agree entirely with what Isidro is saying, Señor Carvalho. If I were a town planner, I would probably recommend the demolition of San Magín. But unfortunately, that is not a possibility. A scandal would serve only to harm Señor Planas and myself. I have used my influence with the head of the Metropolitan Council to obtain well-nigh impossible planning authorizations. A clear case of speculation, which I would not wish to conceal, and of which I am not in the least ashamed. After all, the whole economic miracle of the Franco regime was built on bluff. We all went in for speculating with the only asset we had: land. As there's nothing beneath the land, there wasn't much point in preserving it. Ours is a very unfortunate country. A lot of land, but very little else. And now the sea is starting to get over-polluted. Have you noticed how this bass has a faint taste of oil? Bass is the dirtiest fish in the sea. It sticks close to ships and swallows everything that comes its way, and that includes oil.'

'I'll give you a piece of advice, Carvalho. And when I give advice, it's rather more than advice.'

'Isidro.'

'Let me speak. I'm talking about the real world now, not *haute cuisine*. Finish your investigation as soon as possible, and give a plausible-sounding report to the widow. I'll pay you the same as she pays . . . You'll get double.'

'Isidro. That kind of thing is discussed over coffee . . . and a couple of glasses of brandy.'

'Would you have given me the same advice?' Carvalho asked.

'Basically, yes. In a different way, and, of course, after the liqueurs. But my general gist would have been much the same.'

'Have you consulted the widow?'

'No. We should reach an agreement among the three of us. All the widow wants is an explanation that will reassure her about the Stuart Pedrell legacy. Do you think it will be a reassuring explanation?'

'Probably.'

'Well, no more needs to be said. I'm sure that Señor Carvalho doesn't want to complicate matters for us or for himself. It's enough if Señor Carvalho can square it with his professional ethics. Am I wrong?'

'No, you're not wrong. I undertake to supply my client with the truth that I was hired to discover. The rest is no concern of mine.'

'You see, Isidro?'

'But this is an explosive business. What were you doing in San Magín? Who is Antonio Porqueres? Is he connected with Stuart Pedrell's disappearance?'

'Yes. I won't say any more. When the time comes, I'll deliver my findings to my client.'

'Don't forget that I've made you an offer. I could be your client too.'

'A detective who plays a double game. An exciting idea, Señor Carvalho.'

'No.'

'I thought as much, Isidro. You'll have to be content with Señor Carvalho's assurance that everything will stay in the family.'

'I don't trust assurances that are given gratis.'

'The same old Isidro Planas.'

'Anything you get for nothing usually ends up costing a lot. And don't you laugh. You weren't laughing last night. You were as worried as I was.'

'Today's another day.'

'The trouble is that you like to remain above everything and everybody. But you can't fool me with your airs and graces, your aristocratic detachment . . .'

'Isidro, Isidro . . .'

The Marquess was trying to pat him on the back. Planas jumped up and flung his napkin on the table, knocking over a crystal glass in the process. He bent over, so that his choking voice could not be heard by people sitting at other tables.

'I've had all I can take from you, do you hear? All I can take.'

'Don't say anything you might regret later.'

'I'm the one who's always had to face the consequences, while you go around pretending to be beyond good and evil. When there was dirty work to be done, I was always the one to do it. Who's worked himself like a donkey?'

'You have, Isidro. But don't forget that that's what we agreed. You were a sharp-witted pauper who could have accomplished nothing without our money. Without us, you'd be selling dish-washers.'

'It's thanks to me that you got rich. Thanks to me! And now I'm in a position to send you packing. I don't need you! I don't need you for anything!'

He made for the door so quickly that he failed to hear the Marquess call out: 'At least don't go off without paying for the meal. I've no cash with me.'

The Marquess chose a champagne sorbet for his dessert; Carvalho chose pears in wine.

'He's very agitated. It's because he's coming close to power. This morning, he was received not by a minister, but by a superminister. The ambition to exercise power may be his undoing. It's the Achilles heel of fighters. But don't take what he said lightly. In the end, I would agree with it myself. I have a certain social vanity, and I would hate to see my face appearing in the papers under a headline: "Gang of Property Speculators".'

Planas was back again, standing beside the table, his head bowed. He murmured, 'Please forgive me.'

'You've come back at the right moment, Isidro, as you always do. I haven't any cash on me. You'll have to pay, or charge it to your account.'

*

A general and a colonel had been shot dead, but nothing would stop the irreversible march towards democracy. Everybody said so. Even some generals and colonels said so. Young communists and socialists had worked through the night, leaving the Ramblas and their sidestreets plastered with electoral posters. *This Time You Can Win* promised some. About time too, thought Carvalho. *You Are The Heart of The City* proclaimed the government party.

A few evenings previously, a drunken homosexual, or a homosexual drunkard, had walked down the Ramblas proclaiming: 'Citizens, don't let yourselves be fooled. The heart of the city is the Plaza de Cataluña.' *The reconstruction of Catalonia must come through a democratization of the town councils* declared, or declaimed, a political leader with a thin beard, from the front of a magazine. Curiously, none of the election programmes said anything about tearing down what the Franco regime had built. This is the first political change that respects the ruins.

Each century builds its ruins, and the Franco regime built this century's quota. You wouldn't have muscles enough to knock them all down. There would have to be a nocturnal miracle. The city would wake up and discover that corruption had been happily carted away, and that the suburbs had been transformed into a felicitous site of levelled rubbish on which the citizenry could now build anew. Maybe Yes would no longer want to go round and round the world, like some lone satellite; maybe Charo would be content with her job, and Biscuter happy with his knowledge of Rioja cooking. Maybe he himself would again enjoy the routine of investigating, saving money, eating, walking the Ramblas two or three times a day, and by night pointlessly avenging himself on the culture that had isolated him from life. How could we love if we hadn't learned how to love from books? How would we suffer? We would certainly suffer less. I'd like to go to a health resort, full of convalescents, and meet Yes there. Begin a romance amid mud baths and herbal potions. A mountain spa where it would rain every evening and the thunder would silence us all. And I would not leave the resort, but follow the cycle of the seasons, grow used to the faint light, get my bearings from tiny cardinal points, be thankful for the warmth of blankets, and be aware of my body, conscious of the minutes passing. The relationship with Yes would be bitter-sweet and everlasting. The herbs would provide sufficient youth to remain ever young beside Yes, so that she would never feel drawn from the spa to follow the trail to the East in search of the sun's origins.

Once again he found Charo putting on her make-up. She embraced him and smiled with satisfaction as he fell on the sofa and lay there with the air of a man with time on his hands. She would soon be finished, she said, and then they could make love.

'Save your energy for the weekend.'

'This weekend will be . . . I don't even want to imagine it. We won't leave the bedroom. We'll throw the key out of the window, like they do in films.'

'I'd like to eat in the restaurant I told you about.'

'You can eat there five times a day, if you want. But in between, it'll be bed.'

She lifted his hands to her face. Carvalho caressed her long enough for her not to feel rejected.

'You're sad. What's the matter?'

'Indigestion.'

'That happens to me too. After eating. I feel cold and always get cross with myself that I've eaten too much. Sometimes I end up crying.'

He used her return to the bathroom as an opportunity to say goodbye.

'Going so soon?'

'I've nearly finished with this case. I'd like to solve it by tomorrow, so that I can leave with an easy mind.'

'Is it dangerous?'

'No.'

The phone message he was expecting was written on the notepad, together with a brief addendum from Biscuter to the effect that he had just heard his mother was in the Mundet Home and that he was going to see her.

Carvalho didn't even know that Biscuter had a mother. The note read: 'Señor Briongos says that his son will be outside the Navia Cinema in San Magín at nine o'clock. Señor Briongos's daughter also phoned, to say that you shouldn't go. You should get in touch with her.' Carvalho took the knife from his pocket. He pressed the spring-loaded catch, and the blade shot out with a click. The knife and Carvalho observed each other. It seemed to be awaiting the order to attack. He, on the other hand, seemed to fear the weapon and, having closed it, returned it to his pocket. He opened a drawer. His gun was sleeping like a cold lizard. Carvalho picked it up, examined it, and went through the motions of firing it at the wall. Then he took bullets from a cardboard box and carefully loaded them. When he had closed the drum, the lizard lay wide-awake and menacing. He frustrated its homicidal impulse by applying the safety catch and telling it to be quiet as he put it into his pocket. The gun drew warmth from his body. He took a knuckleduster from another drawer, and fitted it onto his hand. He flexed his fingers, and then struck out at an invisible adversary. Then he removed the knuckleduster and tucked it into his other jacket pocket. There it was: the Invincible Armoury. He took the bottle of white wine from the refrigerator, but changed his mind and looked for the orujo. He drank two glasses, and then dipped his fingers in the pot and ate some of the salted codfish with garlic that Biscuter had prepared for him. He bade farewell to his office. See you later. As he went down the stairs, he lingered slightly to listen to the sculptor's chipping hammer, the sound of bustle from the hairdresser's salon, and the muted trumpet of the boy in lilac. His path crossed that of two homosexuals dressed as boys going to their first communion – or perhaps they really were gay boys going to communion. They looked like Romeo and Juliet, with beard and moustache, fleeing the Montagues and Capulets.

'Pepe, Pepe, don't run off like that.'

Bromide drew alongside with his shoeshine box.

'Come and have a glass on me. Whatever you fancy. I'm rich, thanks to you.'

'I've got a date.'

'Give her two from the front, and two from behind – with my compliments.'

'It's not that kind of date.'

'Pity. You know, has it ever crossed your mind how little we men have, compared with what women need?'

'On occasion.'

'And doesn't it make you want to weep? When I served as a cavalryman under General Muñoz Grandes, I once had it off with a woman six times in one night. But she could quite easily have done it another six times. And that was my best night ever. Women are superior beings, far superior.'

He left Bromide pondering his male inadequacies. He picked up his car, so that he could travel at an easy pace towards San Magín. As he approached the posh part of town, he was surrounded by mothers driving to collect their kids from school. The Stuart widow must have driven like that, day after day, to pick up her children. Then they grew up and set off for Bali. Or limbo.

*

Ana Briongos arrived on the bus and was obviously relieved when she saw Carvalho. She was the first off, and hurried to meet him.

'Thanks for taking me seriously.'

They began to walk. You could almost hear the sound of the words that were piling up in her head. She looked at Carvalho, hoping for some gesture that would prompt her into speech. But he seemed lost in thought, and trailed along as if he had all day and all night to walk and be silent.

'Why did you go to my parents' house?'

'This is the second time today that someone's telling me I shouldn't come here. They should put up a sign on the main road: San Magín – Prohibited Area.'

'You don't know the damage you've done by coming here, and the damage you might still do.'

'You could say that the damage has already been done.'

'My parents are just two old people who are scared silly about everyone and everything. That's just the way they are.'

Carvalho shrugged his shoulders.

'Don't go and see my brother.'

'Why not?'

'It's not worth it.'

'I'll decide that once I've seen him.'

'My brother isn't a normal kid. He reacts unpredictably – like a child. A violent child. He's been the whipping boy all his life. My mother always hated him. She's wicked. She has that absurd, petty nastiness of the poor. And that's all she's got – the only thing that gives her any personality. My father has always been intimidated by her. He's had to pay for the sin of Pedro's birth.'

'This is some scenario!'

'He was only seven when they put him in a home for the first time. He'd stolen money from one of the neighbours to buy a few odds and ends. He came back two years later, behaving worse than ever. He was nine by then. The shops are full of books which say that adults should treat children with respect. But at nine years old, my brother was just fodder for my father's rage and my mother's broom handle. They sent him away again when he was eleven. Have you any idea what it's like in the Wad Ras reform school?'

'I come from a different generation. I grew up with the threat of being sent to the Durán Home.'

'In spite of everything, he's always thinking of the family. He's always seen himself as one of us. The minute he has a few coppers, he spends them on my parents or his brothers and sisters. He's eighteen years old, now. Just eighteen.'

'Just four or five years younger than you.'

'He's quite different, though. If he's done anything wrong, his whole life is to blame.'

'What has he done?'

'What are you after? Do you have to be one of those creeps

who come sticking their noses into a world that isn't theirs?'

'Like Stuart Pedrell. Like your Antonio. He was another one sticking his nose into a world that wasn't his.'

'Nothing compensates me for the pain of Antonio's death. And it does hurt. Here.' She pointed to her belly. 'But it was inevitable.'

'What happened?'

'Why don't you just go away? What are you looking for – weak victims for an easy victory? Is that the way you like it?'

'What can I say? I'll admit to the role you're casting me in. I'm my masters' servant, just like you are. But I don't like victims, easy or otherwise. They are simply the consequences.'

'They're people – and in this case, they're people I love and people who could be destroyed. Sometimes I can still see my brother as a child, when he didn't know that he carried the guilt for my mother's humiliation. I can see his little face, and then I suddenly see it twisted out of shape by all the brutality that he's had to go through.'

'It's in the logic of the case for me to meet your brother, and I always follow my cases through to the end – to what *I* regard as the end. When I've finished, I leave things in the hands of my client. I tell them what I know, and the client decides. The police would take him before a judge. But in my work, the client is the judge.'

'A rich, hysterical old woman who doesn't know the meaning of the word suffering.'

'She's rich, but not old. And everybody knows what it means to suffer. You have a lot going for you. You belong to the social class which has right on its side and spits it in everyone's face.'

'I tried to help him. I used to tell him don't do this, Pedrito . . . don't do that . . . ! When I was away from home, I was always in fear. What would Pedro do? And when I returned, he'd always done it. They always found some reason to hound him into a corner. I used to wait for him outside school, so that he'd go straight home and not do something stupid on the way. Can you imagine how the police treated him when they came about the motorbike business? How they treated us? To make things worse, I had a political record. Do you know how they treat delinquents at the police station? In prison?'

'I didn't create the world, and I don't want to be everyone's conscience. That's too big a role. I presume you didn't call me just because you wanted to tell me your brother's life story.'

'I wanted to stop you meeting him.'

'You won't succeed.'

'Do you know what will happen?'

'I can guess.'

'Isn't that enough to stop you? Why don't you wind your investigation up? Tell your client whatever you like. It's in her interest too, for me to keep my mouth shut.'

'You can sort that out between the two of you.'

She caught him by the arm and shook him vigorously.

'Don't be stupid! Something terrible could happen. If I talk to you and tell you everything . . . would you still go and see my brother?'

'I want to hear it from the horse's mouth. He's the one who has to tell me. Don't be silly – your conscience would never forgive you.'

Carvalho walked ahead, while she stood frozen at the crossroads, one hand held out towards him and the other clutching her jacket pocket. She ran level with Carvalho, and they walked on in silence.

'How easy it would be, just to clear out of here!'

'This place and its people would go with you, like the tortoise carries its shell.'

'I'm not thinking of leaving. You might find it strange, but I don't think I could manage anywhere else.'

'If it's a boy, don't give up hope. Some men have produced excellent results. In the future, men will be better than women. I'm sure of that.'

'I don't care if it's a boy or a girl. I'll love it just the same.'

'One of my first jobs was at a local primary school. It was an old neighbourhood with quite a history, but the people were a lot like the people who live here. One of my pupils was a dark, sad-eyed boy, who had the gestures of a wise old man. He always talked as if he was excusing himself. One day, I met his mother at the school gates. She had the gestures of a wise old woman. She also always talked as if she was excusing herself. She was very beautiful, even though she had white hair. The child could have come out of any part of her body: from her arm, her breast, her head . . . She was a single mother at a time when there was no longer any reason. The war had been over too long to serve as an alibi.'

'And what happened?'

'Nothing. I left the school and never saw them again. But I often remember them, and I sometimes have an odd feeling that the boy had white hair too. I was still young then and masturbating a lot. Some nights, I masturbated thinking of that woman.'

'What a pig!'

'Nature is nature.'

*

He was wearing denims and a black plastic jacket decorated with rings, zips and metal studs. Shoes with heels that gave extra inches to his nervous body; hands stuck deep in large jacket pockets; a neck arched high as if to spy on a threatening world; short, sleeked hair and the face of a young stallion. He looked at Carvalho and bent his head in a way that suggested he did not want to see him. A movement of his shoulder beckoned Carvalho to follow.

'We can't talk here. Let's go somewhere quiet.' He walked

ahead in sudden spurts, as if every step were a whiplash. 'Take it easy. No need to rush.'

Carvalho did not reply. Pedro Larios turned back every so often and smiled: 'Not far to go.'

As they turned a corner, the dark loneliness and San Magín backstreets fell around them. A church was outlined against the moon. The voice of Julio Iglesias came from a nearby jukebox. Carvalho and Pedro Larios stopped in a pool of light from a street lamp that swayed in the breeze. Pedro kept his hands in his pockets. With a smile, he looked left and right, and two young men emerged from the shadows to stand beside Carvalho.

'It's better to talk in company.'

Carvalho sized up the body of the man on his left. He was strong, and his eyes were opaque, as if he had no wish to see what was around him. He wasn't sure where to put his hands. The one on the right was more like a child. He looked at Carvalho with a curled lip, like a dog before it bites.

'Have you lost your voice? It was loud enough in my folks' place. Too loud.'

'Did these two help you?'

'Help me what?'

'Kill the guy who was going around with your sister?'

He blinked. The three looked at one another.

'I don't know what you're talking about.'

'Don't go too far, mister,' said the kid on the right. 'Watch what you're saying.'

'Listen, I don't know what my dad told you, but you'd better believe what *I* say. You were snooping too much for my liking, because I don't like snoopers.'

'He's got a snooper's face,' said the kid.

'Let's finish him off,' interrupted the Hulk.

'I don't like guys who stick their noses where they're not welcome. My friends don't either.'

They took two steps forward. Carvalho was now within reach,

and behind him lay the wall of a building site. The kid was the first to take a knife out. He waved it under Carvalho's nose. Pedro's seemed to be open even before it came out of his pocket. The Hulk threw back his shoulders, lowered his head, and made ready with his fists. The kid lunged at Carvalho with his knife. The detective ducked back to dodge it. While Pedro attacked from the front, the Hulk threw a punch at Carvalho that just grazed him. Carvalho managed to kick the youngster, who howled and doubled up in pain. He parried the thrust of the Hulk's body, and pushed him against the advancing Pedro. He had no time to reach for his revolver before the kid blindly returned to the charge, hurling a stream of insults. Carvalho caught his arm and twisted it until it cracked. The kid screamed in pain:

'The bastard! The bastard! He's broken my arm!'

The other two looked at the useless arm. Pedro rushed wildly forward and left a fine cut down Carvalho's cheek. The Hulk then found new courage and rejoined the fray. With clasped fists and a flash of his knuckledusters, Carvalho dealt him a backhander that immediately opened four gashes on the Hulk's face. Carvalho toppled him, punching his head and face with a swift one-two action, but as he went over, the big one grabbed Carvalho's legs and brought him down.

'Kill him! Kill him, Pedro!' shouted the youngster.

Pedro tried to plunge his knife among the writhing bodies. Carvalho emerged on top, pulling the Hulk's head back by the hair, and put his knife to his throat.

'Get back or I'll kill him.'

'Kill him, Pedro, kill him!'

The Hulk tried to speak, but Carvalho's arm was choking him.

'Get the brat out of here. You, you little arsehole, beat it!'

Pedro signalled to him to obey. The kid disappeared from the pool of light and began throwing stones from the darkness.

'Don't do that, idiot, you'll hit us!'

The stones stopped. Carvalho loosened his grip, rolled the

Hulk over and began battering at his face, chest and stomach. When he had him on his knees, he pummelled his head into the ground. Then he leapt over the body and stood facing Pedro. The boy retreated, using his knife to mark a distance between them. As he moved forward, the detective shed his knuckledusters and pulled the gun from his pocket. Legs astride, he steadied the gun across his right forearm and targeted Pedro's face. He wanted to speak, but for some time his gasping lungs wouldn't let him.

'Down! Get on the ground or I'll blow your head off! Throw the knife over here. Careful what you do.'

The knife detached itself from Pedro's hand. The boy sprawled to the ground, supported on one arm so as to watch Carvalho's movements.

'Kiss the ground, baby! Kiss it! Spread your arms and legs.'

Pedro stretched out beneath the streetlamp. The Hulk hobbled off in search of darkness. Carvalho let him go. Then he drew slowly closer to Pedro, trying to calm his breathing. He kicked at Pedro's legs.

'Spread them wider.'

The prostrate Pedro obeyed, and Carvalho began kicking at him furiously. The body wriggled like an electrocuted animal, but the blows homed in on his stomach and kidneys and feverishly sought out his face. From the ground, Pedro heard the wild and weary animal-panting coming from Carvalho's half-open mouth. A kick to the temple stunned him. The impact of the blows that followed seemed duller and somehow ineluctable. Carvalho pulled Pedro's head up by the hair. He made him kneel down, and then forced him to his feet.

Pedro had a moment to see the detective's face at close quarters, with blood flowing from the cheek, before he was dragged to a wall and battered against the brickwork. The detective was again panting like a weary animal, as if the air was shouting with pain as it left his lungs. Pedro heard him cough and retch violently. He tried to turn round, but his body wouldn't obey the command.

His legs were trembling, and his brain told him that he had lost. Once more, he felt the damp heat given off by Carvalho's body. The detective's voice sounded almost calm.

'Now get going to the place where your sister lives. Don't forget the gun. It's a miracle you're not a stiff by now.'

Pedro began to walk. When they reached the main streets of San Magín, he followed Carvalho's softly spoken instruction to keep close to the shopfronts. This was what his instinct already told him, because he knew he looked pretty bad and he didn't want to create a stir.

*

'It's not very deep.'

Ana Briongos applied a small amount of antiseptic cream to Carvalho's wound. She had told her flatmates to make themselves scarce. Her brother lay curled on a folding bed, and Carvalho told her not to let him fall asleep. Ana bent over to listen to what her brother was saying. She felt his finger joints, and Pedro let out a scream.

'This finger's broken, and the rest of him looks like mincemeat. Did you do this all alone? You're a big man when you're dealing with kids.'

'He was with his pals.'

Ana didn't know where to start. She cleaned the swellings on Pedro's face with hydrogen peroxide. She tried to remove his jacket, but he groaned for her to stop. The door opened, and their father appeared.

'Pedro! What have they done to you, boy?'

He stopped dead at the sight of Carvalho.

'Good evening.'

'Good evening.'

The man's voice was choking.

'I told you, Pedro. I told you, boy.'

He began to weep, and moved neither forward nor backwards, as if all his faculties were required for the business of crying.

'You didn't need to come.'

'Is he badly hurt?'

'A good beating. He asked for it.'

The father looked at Carvalho as if he were a god on whom his fate depended.

'What will you do with him?'

Carvalho sat down. For a few moments, he saw the scene as from a distance. He saw Ana from afar, as she nursed a wounded man who was not Carvalho but somebody else. The old man seemed to be standing in someone else's doorway, not daring to ask if he might enter. Carvalho was thirsty and heard himself asking for water. Ana brought him some. It was cold, but it tasted of chlorine.

'Give a glass to the gentleman. It'll bring him to.'

Briongos senior was still waiting for Jove's decision.

Carvalho stood up, took hold of a chair, and went to sit beside Pedro's bed.

'If you can't talk, just listen and answer yes or no.'

'I can talk if I want to.'

'Fine. So, you three went after Stuart Pedrell to kill him. You and your two pals.'

'We didn't know that was who he was.'

'You went out to kill him. Why?'

'Don't you know what he did to my sister?'

'You idiot!' shouted Ana Briongos, momentarily exasperated.

'They didn't mean to do it,' added Briongos senior. 'They didn't mean to go that far.'

'We only meant to put the wind up him. But then he started getting all excited. The dirty bastard put his hand on my shoulder and started lecturing me. The Shrimp – the kid whose arm you broke – let him have it with his knife. And then I got angry, and I had a go too.'

Briongos senior covered his face with his hands and was shaking visibly. Ana looked at her brother.

'You're a fool. Nobody asked you to do it!'

'You're my sister.'

'You see, sir, she's his sister.'

Briongos gestured expansively, as if to express the depth of the family bond that united his two children.

'If he hadn't started getting all wound up, nothing would have happened. But he began shooting his mouth off, telling me that I had to do this, that I had to do that, that my sister was a free woman, and that he wasn't the only man in her life. That's what he said, Ana, I swear it!'

'So what, you idiot? It's true, isn't it?'

Carvalho looked at Ana and her father.

'So, you found out what had happened and ended up becoming accessories to the fact.'

'I wasn't going to turn my own son in.'

'And you?'

'What was I supposed to do?'

Briongos senior summoned up his little remaining courage.

'He didn't belong here. He was an intruder. It was just a game to him.'

'Shut up, Dad.'

'So, you took him to a derelict building site at the other end of town.'

'No one took him to no building site.'

Carvalho looked at Pedro, bemused. The faces of the other two seemed to testify to the truth of his statement.

'Say that again.'

'Nobody took him to no building site. We left him bleeding, and he must have scarpered.'

'Pedro came home and told me that there'd been a fight and

that he'd wounded Antonio badly. My father and I spent the night searching around, but we couldn't find him anywhere.'

'Sure. He took the subway, because he preferred to die on a patch of waste ground in Holy Trinity. You expect me to believe that?'

'I don't expect anything, but it's the plain truth.'

Briongos junior's eyes glimmered with one last hope.

'So you've still got to find out what happened to him after that.'

'Stuart Pedrell died from the two stab wounds that he got from these two trainee butchers. Don't think you'll get out of it that easily, Sunshine. That Shrimp of yours is a maniac who kills for kicks, and the Hulk's got about as much guts as he has brains. Al Capone kept better company.'

'Bad company, Pedrito. What has your father always told you?'

Pedro was still flat on his back. When his eyes met Carvalho's, the detective saw in them a deadly and unrelenting hatred. Carvalho left the room, followed by Ana and her father.

'Señor, please. Don't bring any more misfortune onto this family. I'll try to sort him out. I'll tell him to go into the Foreign Legion. They make a man of you there. They'll soon take him in hand.'

'Shut up, Dad. Don't talk rubbish.'

Briongos lingered while Ana went with Carvalho to the door.

'What are you thinking?'

'I can't work out what the man did with two stab wounds in him. He wouldn't have lasted long. He didn't have a car. He couldn't get a taxi for fear of discovery. Why didn't he ask someone to help him get to a hospital?'

'Maybe he thought that by not asking he was helping me.'

'The question is, who took him and dumped him on the building site?'

Carvalho didn't wait for an answer. As he went down the street, the evening cool soothed his aching face and body. He left behind him the cement islands of that Polynesia into which Stuart Pedrell had ventured to search out the far side of the moon. The natives he had found there were a hardened race – the same hardness that Gauguin had discovered in the Marquesas, where the natives had come to know that the world was a huge market in which they too were up for sale.

He crossed the frontier and drove at full speed back to his den. He stood, lost in thought, staring into the hot embers in the fireplace. He stroked Bleda's velvet ears and scratched her belly, the dog pawed the air. Who did Stuart Pedrell turn to that night? He would have scanned his former kingdom to find a safe haven. He couldn't have gone home. If he had, this investigation would never have been necessary. Nor could he have expected much help from Nisa. The choice must have been between his business partners and Lita Vilardell.

At three in the morning, he called Lita Vilardell. A man picked up the phone. It was the lawyer Viladecans.

'Ask Señorita Vilardell if she has a piano lesson tomorrow.'

'Is that why you're calling at this hour?'

'Just ask her'.

She came to the phone herself.

'What are you trying to say?'

'That I want to see you tomorrow. Early, if possible.'

'Couldn't you have waited till the morning?'

'No. I thought I'd give you all night to think about what we're going to talk about.'

The woman pulled away from the telephone and had a whispered conversation with Viladecans. It was he who came back on the line.

'Couldn't you come round now?'

'No.'

Carvalho hung up. He slept fitfully for brief spells, tangling up the bedclothes as he tossed and turned. During the times when he was wide awake, he consoled himself with the thought that he was not the only one who wouldn't be sleeping that night.

*

They had just finished taking a shower. They asked Carvalho casually if he would care to join them for breakfast. The detective declined with a wave of his hand. They proceeded to butter their toast and to spread the jam with a curious air of childlike absorption. Drinking white coffee as if it were the elixir of life. Taking obvious pleasure in breathing in the morning air that entered through the half-open balcony door.

'Would you like a coffee at least?'

'Yes, please. Black, with no sugar.'

'Are you diabetic?'

'No. When I was young, I fell in love with a girl who was a coffee addict. Black with no sugar. I got used to it out of love and solidarity.'

'What became of the girl?'

'She married an Austrian who had a little aeroplane. Now she lives in Milan with an Englishman. She likes Englishmen, and she writes surrealist poetry in which I sometimes appear.'

'Just think. What an interesting life this man has had!'

Viladecans smiled broadly and lit up a cigarette.

Drawing deeply, as if bent on consuming the cigarette in a single puff, he immediately filled the room with smoke.

'Do you often phone people at three in the morning to fix appointments?'

'It seemed a reasonable time to me. One has returned home and just finished making love.'

'You must lead a very orderly life. I prefer the afternoon, personally.'

'So do I.'

Viladecans listened to their conversation in silence.

'I really don't see how I fit in here,' he said, finally.

'You will. In fact, maybe you fit in more than it seems. Now that you've satisfied your stomachs, let me tell you my little problem. Three months ago, Carlos Stuart Pedrell was stabbed in San Magín. He was left wounded. He thought he was probably dying, and so he tried to find help. He ran through the various possibilities, and finally decided on you. After all, you'd had a passionate relationship for the past eight years.'

'That's putting it too strongly.'

'As I was saying, a passionate relationship. Anyway, the fact is that he chose you. He told you that he was wounded, and asked you to go and pick him up. Maybe you were reluctant, maybe not. But in the end you went. Then you took him somewhere. Here? Yes, probably here. You must have called someone to help you. Or maybe that someone was already here. Would I be wrong in supposing that it was you?'

Viladecans blinked and smiled.

'Ridiculous.'

'If not you, then it must have been the guy with the Harley Davidson.'

'Which guy with the Harley Davidson . . . ?'

'She knows who I mean. So, you took a while checking that Stuart Pedrell was dying – so long, in fact, that he actually died right here. Then you and Viladecans, or you and the Harley Davidson guy, took the body back into the car. You looked for a suitable spot out of the city. You eventually settled on an abandoned building site. Viladecans might even have known about it from one of his dealings with the property companies. You pushed the body over the fence, and heard it fall to the ground and roll down the slope. You thought it would be weeks before the body was found, but the very next day a car thief was running from the police and tried to hide on the site. They fished him out. Stuart Pedrell must have said something before he died. He probably put together a few jumbled sentences about where he had been for the previous year. That year suddenly became a threatening black hole for you. Did he tell them that he was trying to get help from his former lover? From the girlfriend he had once arranged to meet in London at four in the afternoon, in the middle of Hyde Park? Or at the Tivoli Gardens in Copenhagen, at the Laughter Well?'

'You're very well informed about Carlos's erotic fantasies.'

'I've already said that everything about people like you is public knowledge. You needed to know where Stuart Pedrell had been – which were the Southern Seas that he'd travelled. So did the widow and her partners. After all, the interests at stake ran into millions.'

'I had no hand in starting the investigation. Mima acted alone. In fact, I thought it was absurd from the outset. But as her lawyer, I couldn't refuse.'

'As her lawyer, and as one of the parties involved. I'm no moralist, and I won't dispute your right to get rid of embarrassing dead bodies. Your chosen method wasn't particularly tasteful, but the value of a human being is and always has been a matter of convention. Maybe you could even have done something to save his life.'

'There was nothing that could have been done.'

'Lita!'

'What does it matter now? He knows everything and nothing. It's his word against ours. Your deductions are entirely correct, Señor Carvalho. It wasn't the Harley Davidson rider but my friend here. We were together when he rang – in bed, to be precise. Even if the call had actually been from the South Seas, it could hardly have seemed more distant, more absurd. At first I didn't want to go, but his voice sounded really scared. The two of us went to find him. He wouldn't go to a hospital. We offered to drop him outside one, and then we would have driven off. But he refused. He wanted a doctor who was also a friend. We thought about whom we could call. But he didn't give us enough time. He died.'

'Whose idea was it to throw him over the fence?'

'That's not important. We thought of how it would look: Stuart Pedrell's body showing up in his lover's apartment, at a time when she was having an affair with his lawyer. An *Interviu* article would expose the evil ways of the rich, and would probably also dig up dirt on the companies in which Carlos was involved . . . We had no choice.'

'You could have left him outside his own house. It would have looked as if he hadn't had enough strength to ring the bell. The wanderer returns home to die among his family.'

'That didn't occur to us. Neither of us has that much of a literary imagination. Do we?'

'Leave me out of it. I didn't agree to anything. I haven't said a word.'

'Shouldn't you be saying that you'll only speak in the presence of your lawyer . . . ?'

'Laugh if you like. We'll have to see how Mima reacts.'

'What will she do? Brandish her wounded love? She cares even less than I did about Carlos. What do you think, Señor Carvalho? Can we expect a happy ending?'

'You mean, can you expect a trouble-free ending?'

'Exactly.'

'It's not up to me. The widow will have the last say.'

'I would like to suggest, Señor Carvalho, without prejudicing anything, and strictly off the record, that there might be ways of resolving this business to everyone's satisfaction. Couldn't we be written out of the story? I'd pay handsomely.'

'I wouldn't pay anything. Don't be stupid. What do we have to lose?'

'The bill I give the widow will be quite high. I think I'll be paid handsomely enough, and the case has also given me the chance to examine a set of exemplary circumstances that almost make me believe in fate. Some things are against nature. If you try to deny your own age, to escape from your social condition, in the end it turns to tragedy. Think of that whenever you're tempted to go off to the South Seas.'

'If I ever go, it'll be on a cruise. But I'm not tempted by the idea. My sister has been there, and although it all looks marvellous, you daren't even put a toe in the water. If there aren't water snakes, then there are always sharks around. I prefer the Caribbean or the Mediterranean. They're the only civilized seas in the world.'

'Remember my offer when you go to see Mima. And by the way, remember that no gutter press will pay you as much as I can.'

The lawyer suddenly remembered that he was late for court. He should have been there an hour ago. Carvalho did not take the hint, not even when the lawyer opened the door for him. Lita Vilardell motioned for Viladecans to leave. Carvalho looked at her dynastic eyes, inherited from the last European and the first Catalan to have been a trader in black slaves. Gradually, she dropped the ironical curl of her lip and turned to gaze to the balcony, where a sudden breeze was fluttering the leaves of the banana palms.

'The wind is the salvation of this city,' she said.

Finally she decided to meet Carvalho's gaze.

'It may surprise you, but a lover can feel more humiliated than a wife when she becomes an old and forgotten part of a man's harem.'

*

Carvalho was on the fast lane to drunkenness. In the course of preparing his report, he had emptied a bottle of Ricard and all the iced water that Biscuter kept in the fridge. With his stomach turned into a sea of watery aniseed, he now required tons of food to soak up the liquid. He finished off the salted codfish with garlic, and Biscuter's improvised onion and potato tortilla. Then he demolished one of Biscuter's soused sardine sandwiches, a speciality wherein oregano had primacy over the bay leaf. He called Charo to confirm the arrangement for the weekend, and to check what time she would pick him up from Vallvidrera.

'What's up with you? You sound constipated.'

'I'm drunk.'

'At this time of day?'

'Can you think of a better time?'

'I hope you're not going to stay drunk all weekend.'

'I'll stay any bloody way I like.'

He hung up, and dulled the pangs of remorse by eating the bananas with rum that Biscuter had prepared as he watched the detective's stupendous display of gluttony.

'Biscuter, go down to the Rambla and get them to send a bunch of flowers to Charo. Today.'

He finished the report, put it in an envelope, and slipped it into his jacket pocket. Then he took another sheet of paper and wrote on it:

'Maybe it *would* be a good idea for you to make this trip – but alone, or with someone other than me. Find a nice boy whom you'd be doing a favour by inviting him along. A sensitive young man with some culture and not much money. You'll find dozens of them at the Faculty of Philosophy and Literature. I'm enclosing the address of a professor friend of mine who'll help you to find one. Don't abandon him, at least until you reach Katmandu, and be sure to leave him with enough money for a return ticket. Carry on with your journey, and don't come back until tiredness or old age get the better of you. You'll return to find that everyone here has become petty-minded, mad or old. Those are the only three ways of surviving in a country which did not make the industrial revolution in time.'

He added Sergio Beser's address and a few words of warning about people from the Maestrazgo. Then he put it all in an envelope, wrote Yes's name and address on the front, and drenched the stamp in a sea of alcoholized saliva. He went into the street, clutching the envelope. He despatched it into the depths of a mailbox, which he stood watching as if it were halfway between an unidentifiable object and the tomb of a loved one. Mission accomplished, he said to himself. But something was still troubling him. He realized what it was only as he was passing a shop window which had formerly been the Jai Alai.

'The baker's wife!'

He looked at his diary and joined the evening bustle of streets already animated by awakening night flowers. Pension Piluca.

'Are you Señora Piluca?'

'Señora Piluca was my mother. She died three years ago.'

'I'm sorry. I'm looking for a Basque with a name like every other Basque. He's lodging here with a lady.'

'They've just gone out. They usually go to the bar on the corner.'

'These streets are full of corners and bars.'

'The Jou-Jou.'

It was a poky little bar, which practised what it preached by reducing electricity consumption to a bare minimum. This simple expedient prevented customers from seeing the layer of flies covering the 'assorted snacks' and 'hot dogs'. The Basque and the baker's wife were eating a sandwich at a corner table.

'May I?'

He sat down before they could react.

'I've been sent by ETA.'

The man and woman looked at each other. He was dark and powerfully built, with a blue stubble adorning a heavy jaw. She was a fair-skinned, plumpish woman, whose blonde curls failed to disguise the brown roots of her hair.

'We've heard that you're going round boasting of being a terrorist. We don't like that.'

'I beg your . . .'

'You're pretending to be a terrorist so that you can lay ladies. We found out, and we've put you on our list. Do you know what that means? For much less than that, there are people still running round the South Pole. You've got two hours to pack your bags. And watch out they don't explode in your face.'

Carvalho leant back in his chair, so that his jacket fell open to reveal a gun sticking out of his belt. The Basque rose to his feet, looked at the terror-stricken woman, and then at Carvalho.

'Two hours,' he repeated.

'Let's go.'

'You can go. But not her. Do you want to go with this fake terrorist?'

'I didn't know . . .'

'I wouldn't advise it. If he's a good boy, nothing will happen to him. But one of these days he'll get up to his old tricks, and I wouldn't like you to be next to him when we have to deal with him.'

The man drew away from the table.

'Pay for this revolting sandwich before you leave. You can forget about the woman's things. She'll go and collect them later.'

'I left home just with what I was wearing.'

'So much the better. OK, mister, you can go. Take what's left of your memories.'

Carvalho did not turn to watch him leave. The job was half done. Twenty-five thousand pesetas. Now for the rest. The woman was a picture of frozen panic, sitting at the grimy table.

'Don't worry: nothing is going to happen to you. We've been keeping a close watch on him. This is the third or fourth time he's played this trick on us. He's not a bad sort, but he's too randy for his own good.'

'I've been really stupid!'

'No. I think it's very good that you've taken a breather. It'll have had a good effect on your husband.'

'He won't take me back. And what about the girls! My little daughters!'

'He will take you back. Who else would do the accounts for

him? Who'll look after the kids? Who'll take care of the house? Who'll go to Saragossa to get flour for him? From now on, make the most of your trips to Saragossa – but next time, choose your boyfriends more carefully.'

'Never again.'

'Don't be too sure of that.'

'My husband's a very good man.'

'Husbands have to be good, particularly when that's all they are.'

'And very hardworking.'

'It sounds like he's got a lot to be said for him. Anyway, you should go to back to him. I know for a fact that he's waiting.'

'How do you know? How do you know so much about me?'

'Haven't you heard of our intelligence network? We know more than the government about anything you care to name. We caught onto this faker when he was still living in your block. We sent one of our people along to live there too.'

'There's been no one new. Except for some casual labourers. They're always coming and going.'

'There you are.'

'How do you know he'll take me back? Will you come with me?'

'Just give him a ring.'

While she was telephoning, Carvalho finished off the Basque's half-eaten sandwich. A sausage sandwich. Not even dog-meat. Probably rat-meat. Or lizard. And instead of paprika, they had used minium to stop it oxidizing. She returned with a radiant look and tears in her eyes.

'I can go back. I've got to hurry. He says we'll go and pick up the girls from school. Thank you. I'm really very grateful.'

'Tell your husband not to forget me.'

'We won't forget you – neither of us. How am I going to get home? I'm afraid to walk alone in this part of town.'

Carvalho walked with her to the Plaza del Arco del Teatro and put her into a taxi. Then he went into the public toilets and pissed out the first streams of alcohol filtered through a body heavy like it was full of sand.

*

'I've put it all down in writing. I must be getting old. In the old days, I never used to write my reports, I just told my clients what I'd found out, and they were normally satisfied.'

Stuart Pedrell's widow had the drawers of her desk open. Her eyes were open too, and in one hand she held a pencil with which she was pensively scratching her forehead. A half-length chestnut wig covered her black hair. As she relaxed in her director's chair, she had the air and dignity of a woman executive with a notion to enjoy one last fling. She leafed through the report without reading it.

'Too long.'

'I could give a verbal summary. But I might forget a few details.'

'I'll take the risk.'

'Your husband was killed by knife-gang kids on the streets of San Magín. It was a question of family honour. He had got the sister of one of them pregnant. He tried to redeem the whole family. The whole neighbourhood, in fact. This was a bit much, particularly since he was one of the main people responsible for building that hole in the first place. It's very likely that the girl in question is bearing Señor Stuart Pedrell's child. But you don't need to worry. She's not making any claims on you. She's a modern, left-wing working girl. You're lucky – you and your children.

'The story doesn't end there, though. Your husband was fatally wounded, and sought refuge in the house of a former lover: Señora or Señorita Adela Vilardell. She was in bed. With the lawyer Viladecans. You might say that he died in the arms of Viladecans.

The two lovers were extremely worried at having the corpse of your returned husband on their hands: they destroyed his papers, and left only the note "... no more will anyone carry me south" in the hope of throwing people off the track. They dumped his body on a patch of waste land in Holy Trinity. The fact that I have uncovered all this is due mainly to a hunch I had, based on the location of that piece of waste ground. But you can read all about that in the report. Are you crying?'

There was a barely concealed irony in Carvalho's question. The widow retorted angrily:

'You're one of those who think that rich people don't have feelings.'

'They do. Only they're less dramatic than other people's. When rich people suffer, it costs them less.'

She had regained her composure, and cast an eye over the report as if assessing its worth as a commodity.

'How much?'

'There's an itemized bill on the last page. The total comes to three hundred thousand pesetas. In return, you have the security that no one will touch a cent of your inheritance.'

'It's money well spent, particularly if the girl doesn't cite my husband as the child's father.'

'It's in her interest not to – unless you hand my report over to the police. Then they'd go looking for her brother, and in that case everything would come out.'

'In other words...'

'In other words, if you want a quiet life, with your honour and fortune intact, you'll have to let the crime go unpunished.'

'Even if this girl hadn't turned up, I wouldn't have lifted a finger to help the police find the killer.'

'You're no moralist, I gather.'

'I need a rest. I've been a businesswoman for more than a year now. I've been working very hard, and it's gone very well. But now I'm off on a holiday.'

'Where to?'

The answer came in a quizzical gleam which further dilated the widow's jet-black pupils.

'The South Seas.'

'A sentimental journey? Or making amends?'

'No. It's a voyage of personal fulfilment. I understand that you're on very intimate terms with my daughter. I expect she'll have told you that my eldest son is in Bali, frittering away all the money I send him. So I'll take the opportunity to visit him, and then continue on my way.'

'The route that your husband charted on the map in his study?'

'Yes. The one he organized with the travel agency. It was all very well planned. I've been able to have the booking transferred to my name, so that I don't have to pay an advance.'

'You did that in the weeks following your husband's reappearance?'

'Yes. I put in a claim, and the agency gave me full satisfaction.'

The widow stood up and went to a safe embedded in the wall behind a María Girona painting. She opened it, wrote out a cheque, tore it from its book and handed it to Carvalho.

'There's a fifty thousand bonus.'

Carvalho whistled in the manner of a private detective being paid in dollars by a capricious client on the Rambla de Santa Mónica.

'Don't forget that all this is just between you and me.'

'You'll have to broaden that to include Viladecans, Señorita or Señora Adela, the girl from San Magín, her family . . .'

'I hope you haven't said anything to my daughter.'

'No. And I'm not likely to be saying anything, because I won't be seeing her again.'

'I'm glad.'

'I thought you would be.'

'I'm not a possessive mother, but Yes is still traumatized by the business with her father. She's looking for a father figure.'

'I'm getting old, but I haven't yet reached the age where I indulge in paedophilia under the guise of a wish to be young again, or vice versa.'

Carvalho was on his feet and he raised a half-opened hand as a token of farewell.

'Wouldn't you like to come with me to the South Seas?'

The widow's question stopped Carvalho at the door.

'All expenses paid?'

'With that cheque, I think you could afford the trip. But money wouldn't be a problem.'

Across the room, she suddenly seemed smaller and frailer. For some time, Carvalho had been practising detecting in adults the facial expressions and gestures they must have had in childhood and adolescence. As a young girl, Stuart Pedrell's widow must have been full of *joie de vivre*. And her soft features called to mind the hope on the face of a young girl as yet unaware of the brevity of that illness that comes between birth and old age and death.

'I'm too old to be a gigolo.'

'Why do you see everything in such a sordid light: either paedophile or gigolo.'

'It's an occupational hazard. I'd gladly go with you. But I'm afraid.'

'Afraid? Of me?'

'No. Of the South Seas. I have obligations: a dog that's only a few months old, and two people who, at the moment, need me, or think they do.'

'It'll be a short trip.'

'Some time ago, I used to read books. And someone wrote in one of them: "I'd like to reach a place from which I wouldn't want to return." Everyone looks for that place. I'm looking too. Some have the vocabulary to express that need, and some have the money to satisfy it. But there are millions and millions of people who would like to go south.'

'Goodbye, Señor Carvalho.'

Carvalho raised his hand again, and left without turning to look back.

*

He lit the fire, sank his feet into slippers that were worn virtually threadbare, and went into the kitchen. He was already on the trail of an as yet undefined meal when he realized that Bleda had not run out to meet him. He warmed a little boiled rice with liver and vegetables, tipped it into the dog's dish, and took it into the garden. Bleda did not answer his call. At first he thought that she might have run out after the cleaning lady. Or jumped over the garden wall. Or been shut in a room. But a nagging and increasingly painful sense of anxiety drove him to look in every corner of the garden, until he found her. Lying like a floppy toy in a pool of her own blood. Her throat had been slit, and her head hung loose when Carvalho tried to lift it. The blood had dried on Bleda's fur, giving her the appearance of a cardboard dummy. Her almond eyes were still half open and her muzzle wrinkled in a puppyish attempt at ferocity. Her flesh was cardboard now, and her bark and howl would be for ever silent. The gash opened by the razor was long and deep, as if they had meant to sever her head from her body.

Carvalho saw the city glittering in the distance, but its lights were swimming before his eyes. He took a spade from the cellar and began digging a hole beside Bleda, with all the reverence of a man performing the last rites. He placed the little cardboard body in the dark, damp soil, and beside it he laid her plastic dish, her bottle of shampoo, her brush, and the disinfectant spray that could do nothing to save her now. He tossed earth into the hole, leaving Bleda's profiled head and the deep sparkle of her tiny, half-closed eye uncovered until the time came for the last spadefuls. He topped off the grave with a layer of gravel. Then he flung the spade away, sat on the wall, and gripped the edge of the brickwork to prevent his chest from bursting with sobs. His eyes were burning, but he felt a sudden clarity in his head and chest. Looking towards the illuminated city, he said:

'You bastards...! You dirty, filthy bastards!'

He drank a bottle of ice-cold orujo, and was awakened again at five in the morning by the combined pangs of hunger and thirst.

Also by Manuel Vázquez Montalbán and published by Serpent's Tail

Murder in the Central Committee

Translated by Patrick Camiller

'A sharp wit and a knowing eye' *Sunday Times*

'Montalbán is a writer who is caustic about the powerful and tender towards the oppressed' *TLS*

'I cannot wait for other Pepe Carvalho titles to be published here. Meanwhile, make the most of *Murder in the Central Committee*' *New Statesman*

'Montalbán writes with authority and compassion – a Le Carré-like sorrow' *Publishers Weekly*

'A thriller worthy of the name: a taut, intelligent tour de force set in the shadowy minefield of post-Franco Spanish politics' Julie Burchill

'Splendid flavour of life in Barcelona and Madrid, a memorable hero in Pepe and one of the most startling love scenes you'll ever come across' *Scotsman*

The lights go out during a meeting of the Central Committee of the Spanish Communist Party – Fernando Garrido, the general secretary, has been murdered.

Pepe Carvalho, who has worked for both the Party and the CIA, is well suited to track down Garrido's murderer. Unfortunately, the job requires a trip to Madrid – an inhospitable city where food and sex is heavier than in Pepe's beloved Barcelona.

Off Side

Translated by Ed Emery

'Magical detection' *The List*

'If you haven't yet made the acquaintance of Carvalho, now's the time. He's the most original detective to come along in an age and the mix of political intrigue, Barcelona style, and Catalan cooking tips, makes for a great read' *Venue*

'Because you use your centre forward to make yourselves feel like gods who can manage victories and defeats, from the comfortable throne of minor Caesars: the centre forward will be killed at dusk.'

To revive its sagging fortunes, Barcelona FC has bought the services of Jack Mortimer, European Footballer of the Year. No sooner has Mortimer taken possession of his company Porsche than death threats start arriving. Are they a hoax, the work of a loner or are they connected to the awesome real estate speculation that is tearing Barcelona apart?

In a period of turmoil where Catalan pimps and racketeers are being hustled off the streets by crime syndicates from the Middle East, Pepe Carvalho is thinking of retirement, but the need to save the soul of his beloved Barcelona forces him to take on a case that can only end in disaster.

An Olympic Death

Translated by Ed Emery

Montalbán's Barcelona has a truly great sense of place. Essential pre-Olympics reading' *Northern Echo*

As Barcelona prepares for the Olympics, the city is turned over to make way for new roads, new stadia and the giant prawns of Mariscal.

Pepe Carvalho who remembers the good old days when a hammer was always to be found with a sickle is forced to work for Olympic entrepreneurs whose only game plan is to make a fast buck.

As Carvalho tries to come to terms with the new values of the present, his life – gastronomic, amatory and professional – confronts the disillusion of middle age.

The Angst-Ridden Executive

Translated by Ed Emery

'More Montalbán please!' *City Limits*

Antonio Jauma, an old acquaintance, dies desperately wanting to get in touch with Pepe Carvalho. Jauma's widow has good reason to believe that her husband's death is not what it seems. And who better to investigate than Carvalho, a private eye with a CIA past and contacts with the Communist Party.

DEMONSTRATION
PROJECT REPORT

The Impact of Urban Renewal on Small Business

THE HYDE PARK-KENWOOD CASE

Brian J. L. Berry
Sandra J. Parsons
Rutherford H. Platt

Center for Urban Studies, The University of Chicago,
in cooperation with
The City of Chicago
and the
Department of Housing and Urban Development

1968. Center for Urban Studies, The
University of Chicago

Printed in the U.S.A. by Keogh Printing Co.

Library of Congress Catalog Card No. 68–9490

The Urban Renewal Demonstration Project and the publication of this report were made possible through an Urban Renewal Demonstration Grant awarded by the Department of Housing and Urban Development, under the provisions of Section 314 of the Housing Act of 1954, as amended, to the City of Chicago.